The story of a man's passion . . .

Jared faced the warm westerly this night, restless because he had not found solace with his wife.

"Clarissa," he had whispered. But she hadn't responded. Now he paced slowly, unaware of where he was. He breathed deeply, full of his dreams. In his mind, he was back at Maui with Naliki. . . .

A woman's love . . .

Clarissa began to shake, tears and laughter coming at the same time. Then with a rush she was in his arms as snow fell from his clothes all about her. Her head pressed against his huge chest. Her Jared! Home at last! His bearded face moved down upon hers. She felt the sharp bristles, the cold snow, his lips seeking hers. Now, at last, she was safe.

And of the island girl who came between them . . .

Before Jared, in the circle of the clearing, danced the girl with midnight black hair, swaying delicately, her eyes fixed demurely to the ground. The Captain longed to grasp that swaying body and hold her. The drums hammered at his ears. She came close to him. Her full young breasts brushed his hands, then her entire body began to quiver in anticipation. . . .

ISLAND PROMISE

W. Ware Lynch

Exclusive Distribution
by
PARADISE PRESS, INC.

Printed in the United States of America

To my Karen,
who suggested I
write this book

CHAPTER 1

An unfamiliar smell had awakened Perpetua. She lay in bed thinking as she stared up at the rough beams of the farmhouse roof. The spring of 1850 had come early to her island of Martha's Vineyard. She thought of the long hot summer to follow, her mind on the trips to the beach, to Gay Head. Her long blonde hair bunched at the nape of her neck, untidily held by a bright blue bow of homespun yarn. Her nightdress had worked its way up her slim legs, which now, instead of feeling the cool air of a spring morning, felt a strange heat.

Suddenly alert, she glanced at the oak door which led to the hall and saw a trail of grey mist seeping under it. Then she heard a loud rushing noise coming from below, drawing near. From behind the door she heard the ominous sound of crackling wood. Fire! The house was on fire!

She leapt from under the down cover, sending the pillows and her rag doll to the floor. A long curl of smoke spiraled from the floor and reached for the ceiling. Opening the door, she was met by a thick bank of hot, choking smoke. The warnings of her elders came in a confusion of terror as she attempted to clear her thirteen-year-old mind. Get down on the

1

floor! A whimper of terror escaped her as she fell to her hands and knees. The boards of the hallway were hot to the touch. But the air was clearer and she could see a few feet ahead. Like some scurrying animal, she lunged forward toward her mother's room.

Was her mother awake? Her room seemed miles away. Perpetua felt a rumbling throughout their three-story farmhouse as if a wagon were being driven wildly over cobblestones. In panic she stood for a moment, ready to cover the last ten feet in a run, took a deep breath, and started to suffocate. On her knees again, she cried out, though her voice was swallowed in the noise of the violence about her. Unable to take a breath, she reached with one last great effort for the door to her mother's room. She saw her mother's ankles, her ghostly nightdress. She grabbed frantically.

Clarissa bent down, took her child's hand and pulled her through the door, slamming it shut. Perpetua felt the comforting warmth of her mother's body close to hers and felt safer as her mother gave swift directions.

"We'll go through the window over the woodshed! It isn't far to the ground."

Perpetua felt herself being firmly propelled across the room to the small window facing the five acres of newly planted corn. It was a north-facing window, boarded shut against the winter wind. Now that small window barred their escape.

Through the reddening smoke, Perpetua saw her mother grapple desperately with the boards, prying at them with a boot heel until several gave way. The window was broken open and Perpetua felt her mother's hands pushing her toward the opening, yelling something in her ear. Pieces of glass cut her arms as she went out headfirst. Her hands sought a grip on the shingles. She drew a life-giving breath of fresh, clean air. Turning, she saw the figure of her mother silhouetted against the flames.

"Jump!" her mother screamed, but the child was frozen, cowering. She saw streaks of blood threading her mother's milk-white arms. A ball of red-hot fire seemed to explode from the window. The air was turned into a rushing mass of searing heat.

"Jump!" Clarissa shouted again, but Perpetua was already tumbling downward, her fingers scratching for a hold on the treacherous, shingled roof. She clung for a moment at the edge of the shed roof, then fell, screaming.

The lilacs broke her fall, bending with her weight, gently lowering her to the soft ground. Perpetua lay on her back, stunned and terrified. Above her she saw an angry ball of fire climbing into the darkness, accompanied by a tower of thick, grey smoke. The farm seemed to be illuminated in a demonic glare.

"Mother!" she cried. Someone's strong arms lifted her and Perpetua felt herself being carried. Wild with terror, her eyes opened wide at the sound of a great roar as the farmhouse atop the Chilmark hill was consumed in the fury of hot flame. Pieces of sparking, searing timber fell around the young girl. The arms carried her easily and she looked up.

She hardly recognized the face of Timothy Vincent, the neighbor boy. His eyes were pinpoints of black, his face flushed with fright and exertion as he carried her to the rise in the corn field and gently placed her on her feet. As soon as he put her on the ground, she was stricken with a terrible fear. What had become of her mother? Where was she?

Blindly, without thinking, Perpetua stumbled away, back toward the blazing fire. She had to reach her mother quickly, before the flames claimed her. She felt a strong hand clasping her arm, pulling her back, and she heard Timothy's voice calling out, "I've got Perpetua. Bring Mrs. West here!" Then her mother's face was before her; her voice gasped "Thank the Almighty, you're safe!" and her arms went about her. Perpetua felt the tender presence, the soft comfort of her mother's body against her own.

Through tears, they watched with Timothy and his father, Ashbiel, as a funeral pyre of the once great farm reached into the sky, lighting up the nearby meadows, reflecting against the early morning fog bank and sending a beacon of distress which could be seen from Gay Head to Chappaquiddick.

Ashbiel Vincent spoke first. "Ye can stand here 'n' watch while it burns for three days, Clarissa West. Or ye can come to our farm and bed down in the extry room."

The thought of their home burning for three whole days sent a shudder through Perpetua. She heard her mother murmur thanks, felt the squeeze of her consoling hand, though her mother's voice was tremulous with tears. Suddenly, the complete collapse of the burning house told Perpetua what she didn't want to know. There was no saving a stitch. The new red gingham dress she had just finished was in those flames. Her Grimm's *Fairy Tales*, books by Sir Walter Scott, and the ones about sheiks and princesses were all gone!

"Ye'll save nothin'!" allowed Ashbiel, known more for his common sense than his tactfulness. "Best not stand and watch."

"You go with them, child," Clarissa directed, eyes staring as her home crumbled and gave its last timber to the hungry flames. "I'll come later." Perpetua hung back, dragging her feet against the gentle pressure of the hands that urged her toward a warm house and safety; then she walked reluctantly the two long miles down the sandy road where the Vincent farm lay hidden in the scrub pine. Perpetua understood her mother and she knew Clarissa would be watching and praying, standing witness as her worldly possessions evaporated before her eyes. Clarissa would want to be at the funeral until all was consumed. Her mother was a Tottle, and the Tottles battled until they won or lost.

On the stoop of the rambling clapboard farmhouse, Mrs. Vincent took Perpetua in her arms and pressed her close to her ample breast, comforting her, "Ye poor child. Homeless, 'n' yer father away at sea. Come in now and lay down."

Lie down while her mother was out there watching everything they owned disappear? "I just couldn't, Mrs. Vincent, thank you," Perpetua answered. For a long time she stood in the doorway, looking back at the red sky. She pulled at her nightgown, conscious of the stares of her childhood playmate, the young man who had saved her life. Timothy, the best runner in the township, was tall for his age. He had told everyone he would go away to sea, first chance he got.

Mrs. Vincent brought a patchwork quilt and drew it about Perpetua's shoulders. "All right, lass. Stay here if ye must. But sit in that rocker. I'll bring ye coffee."

Timothy looked at the large woman as she puffed and went inside, letting the screen door bang. "She doesn't know how to act, Perpetua. She's used to boys. A girl is strange in this house. Ef'n it's milk ye wish, I'll fetch some." The question was unanswered because of the lump in Perpetua's throat. She sank low in the rocker, worried about her mother and their future. Where would they live? What would she wear? It seemed as though everything must begin again.

Timothy squatted on the floor beside her and began to talk in a low, quieting voice. The storyteller among his peers, he knew the strength of a good yarn and a confident sermon.

"Don't ye mind, Perpetua. It'll work out like always. Like the time ye slid tail over teakettle down the cliffs at Gay Head at the picnic."

She looked straight ahead, weeping a bit. Determined, he went on, " 'N' ye stuck yourself full of rose thorns? 'N' ye was so mad at yerself? Then, I remember how quick ye cheered up right after the picnic basket was opened and we spread blankets on the top there and down the Sound came a whole fleet of whaling vessels, proud as gulls in the upwind, soaring along the blue water, skimming and shivering in the moonlight. Remember? An' ye said to me, 'Timothy, they're like poems to me.' I asked why, 'n' ye said, 'They rhyme with a beautiful form like Shakespeare only I don't understand him, but I understand them.' We all laughed. That is, the others did. But not me. I know what ye meant, Perpetua. They with all sails set, as it were. 'N' they was before the wind. All headin' for home port, like mares been out in the field, 'n' oats waitin' at the stable. Like herrin' goin' hell-bent through Herrin' Crick down Crackatuxet Pond to Katama to spawn. I knew." His voice trailed off. She stared at the sky, hearing and yet not hearing, liking him for what he meant to do.

"Now ye leave the child be, Timothy," his mother said, the screen door adding to the command as it banged shut behind her. "There's milk and tea inside, 'n' fresh-made doughnuts, 'n' coffee, if ye've a mind, child." She took Perpetua's limp hand and brought her to her feet. Through the doorway, Perpetua saw her mother at last, reluctantly coming up the path behind Ashbiel Vincent, still looking over her shoulder through the pines which hid the remnants of her home. Then she came inside, and Perpetua felt almost overcome with relief.

Behind her, Perpetua heard Timothy cough, scrape his feet across the broad veranda and walk down the steps. Dashing back, seeing his slumped shoulders, she called out, "Thank you, Timothy. You saved my life. I will never forget it." He lifted one hand in an embarrassed acknowledgment of her thanks.

• • •

The next day was a nightmare. Every hour or so, Perpetua and her mother went back to where their home had stood. It still smoldered, though the beams had gone and the three brick chimneys stood like tombstones over the rubble.

"Don't go near," Vincent had warned. "Ye best wait a few days to see what ye can recover. See that sky; it's a weather breeder. We'll be gettin' rain tonight and the embers'll cool. Then I'll come back with ye and forage what might be useful. In the meanwhile, Clarissa, I had a thought we all might get together, me and the boys and them farmhands. We could mebbe fix up the big icehouse and add a room for ye 'n' Perpetua, 'til Captain Jared comes home."

At mention of her husband, Clarissa felt a sob gather in her throat. She fought the sob and looked directly at Ashbiel. The man was tall and spare, with skin like wrinkled leather. His cap, which was never known to be off his head, sat at an angle over his right eye and shaded his beak of a nose. They stood in the newly planted corn field, the one which would

have carried them all through the winter of 1850.
From this height they could see the smoking ruin, the
broad Vineyard Sound which separated the island
from the mainland of Massachusetts. Ashbiel now
looked helplessly at Clarissa, his torn breeches bag-
ging at the knees, boots caked with mud and dung,
hands thrust into the pockets of his pea jacket. He returned her look, then glanced away. The sadness was
too much. It was unbecoming in a New Englander.
But she was a woman. What could one expect? Her
husband had been gone since 1846, the year the hurricane tore roofs from sturdy farmhouses, the year he
and his sons had firmed up the underbeams in the
Wests' house. And now that very house was
destroyed.

Clarissa wore a shawl over her shoulders. The
skirts of her long, borrowed dress billowed in the
easterly breeze. She stood with feet wide apart, as if
to balance herself against the recent violence of fate.
The shoes Rose had given her were too large for her
tiny-boned feet, but she was grateful for them. Running a hand through her hair, which, like Perpetua's,
was golden and glistened in the sun, she smiled sadly
and said, "It'll be difficult for certain, but it sounds
like the best place for the two of us, friend Ashbiel,
'til Captain Jared comes home." She tried hard to be
courageous, but Ashbiel sensed what hardship the
confinement would be to someone of her gentle upbringing.

Relieved that the woman had agreed to the decision, Ashbiel turned to Perpetua. She had been looking at the remains of the house, tears blinding her.
Her home was forever lost, like a smashed doll. She
wore an old dress of Mrs. Vincent's, hastily cut down
and fashioned crudely to cover her.

The once bright, blue bow of homespun yarn had

been mended and now held her hair neatly behind her ears. Beneath her lowered eyes, Ashbiel saw the pout, the trembling lip. The scrawny child stood with feet spread, braced against the blow she had suffered. How much like her mother she looked, he thought. How like her father she acted. For all her slender childhood frame, she might be facing Cape Horn's worst, head high, facing straight into the easterly wind, fearless, yet cautious. She surely seemed the headstrong child his sons had said she was.

"The icehouse!" she burst out. "How can we fit in that?" Then Perpetua realized how ungrateful she must sound and suddenly grasped old Ashbiel about the waist. He patted her head and looked away, trying to conceal his acute embarrassment.

"Oh, Mr. Vincent. It's just awful, but I'll help. I swear I will." When she let go of him, Ashbiel looked down at the child and a smile spread across his lean face.

"I'll have ye at the helm of the plow when we break ground for the bedroom. I've already got it in mind, Perpetua. Do you recall when you held the tiller the day we went sailin' to Tarpaulin Cove over on Naushon Island there, lass? That's how ye'll break the ground for your own home."

Perpetua nodded. Of course she remembered. The two of them had gone together across the Sound in a choppy sea across Middle Ground Shoals in his fifteen-foot catboat, with its big white sail cupping the wind, the boom a dangerous piece of oak timber ready to crack against an unwary skull as it swung at each tack and jibe. That had been three years ago, right after the hurricane when the new beams had to be set in the roof.

Shaking herself from her reverie, Perpetua felt a

comforting hand upon her shoulder. She looked up and met her mother's warm gaze.

"Oh, Mother, what are we going to do? Can Mary still come and help you? You can't do it all by yourself—the washing, the sewing, the baking. And how about our horse? Will John still come to feed her?"

Asking these questions, Perpetua wore the helpless look of one who sees the absence of everything that means security. Instinctively, she reached out for her mother.

Clarissa took her daughter about the shoulders, so thin, yet with a straightness which bespoke gumption. She held her away, looking squarely into Perpetua's blue eyes, bright with tears.

"My dear daughter. You are no longer a little girl. So you must understand what this really means to you . . . to me and Father. From now on, until he comes home, it will be much harder on us. Up until now you have been able to play often with your friends, Tabitha and Charity. It has been better for you than for many girls."

Perpetua frowned, disliking the note of gloom in her mother's voice.

"I have not asked your help because I wanted you to enjoy the good things we have. And there was Mary to help with the heavy household work. We let you be, to enjoy the days you could never call back later. But now we have to start without a thing, with no help because there is no home but that small icehouse for us until your father comes home."

"You mean I'll never see Mary again?"

"There is no house for her to tend now. She'll have to find work somewhere else. But John will still be able to help with the heavy things and the horse and the fields." Something in her mother's tone made

Perpetua look up quickly. "Let me tell you one thing which you may not believe now," her mother continued. "Later in life, when you look back on this, you will have learned how to depend upon yourself, as do all the islanders. You'll know what a woman has to know."

Perpetua wiped away the tears which had started again. For the first time, it seemed, her mother was treating her as an adult. Yet, what she was saying couldn't really be all that true. Grownups exaggerated, at times, to make their point.

Watching her daughter's face, Clarissa noticed the change. "Now, my little one, who has so much to learn, that's enough for the time being. Why don't you run over to the chicken coop right now? Maybe you'll find some eggs."

"Right now? Can I?" Perpetua brightened. She ran off, hopping through the tall field grass, clearing an old tree stump like a deer. She ran as Clarissa had run at her age, her child's hair flying in the wind, and Clarissa stood watching her for a moment, feeling tears wet on her cheek. She looked once more at what had been their home, where life had once been so safe, so secure, and she wiped the tears away roughly as if to put them away forever. Shoulders back, head bowed, she folded her hands. The words came. "Good Lord, give us both the strength we need right now. Today, let us walk through this valley of the shadow. Let my little girl be safe, and, dear Lord, let her be happy. And one more prayer, Lord. Send my Jared home to us soon."

Then, as she walked quickly back to the Vincents', cries of joy came to her across the field. Perpetua came running, holding fresh, warm eggs in her hands.

That night, with her daughter sleeping next to

her in the spare bed, Clarissa thought about what the future would hold, and traced her life on the farm.

Moving to Chilmark after her father's death, she had settled with Jared in his old family home as best she could. The change from a rather free life under the care of a doting father to the chores and duties of a farm had been drastic, even though, like all island girls, Clarissa had known how to cook and do rudimentary housekeeping. Though protected, Clarissa had acquired all that knowledge, both educational and practical, which comes to those who live away from the comforts of the mainland. On the island, people made everything they used—clothing, homes, furniture, medicine, everything. For Clarissa, leaving Holmes Hole for "up-island" meant learning to run a big farmhouse with its surrounding crops and livestock, while also learning how to handle illnesses, the inevitable repairing of tools and utensils, and the eventual upbringing of a daughter.

On this island of seafarers, she accepted Jared's absences as she did the strong nor'easters and the lonely nights. And her new home had been a good one. The West homestead overlooked a spring-filled pond and the scrub pine woods nearby were alive with small game. Adjoining the woods was a field used for general planting. The house, a three-story edifice of strength and beauty, faced the Vineyard Sound. Clarissa had finally become used to the farm and the work which faced its mistress.

Yet she had few hours to herself. Even with the help of Mary, there was much to be done and little time for amusement. Upon occasion she and Perpetua would go farther up the island to Gay Head. There stood the multicolored clay cliffs, a landmark for ships passing up the Vineyard Sound from New York to Boston. Gay Head Indians lived there on the promontory, hundreds of feet above the sea. From there, southward, stretched the beach. A picnic on its sandy, seaweed-covered shore was a rare treat and it was always with great reluctance that they left the beautiful beach to face their chores at the end of the day.

Trips to Holmes Hole from the West farm had once been a monthly occurrence. Walking on the boardwalk, lifting their feet high to keep mud from spattering their shoes, Clarissa and Perpetua would go from shop to shop. Clarissa's golden hair, clear blue eyes and delicate features always attracted the attention of men. Beneath the heavy, full dresses the fashion required, her twenty-inch waist, the subtle curves, the gentle sweep of her lithe body could only be imagined by them.

Mother and daughter would arrive by horse cart, tie up at the stable and begin an always exciting tour of stores. Clarissa always found time for animated gossip about local affairs with her friends.

But now all that was gone—the house, clothing, all the comforts, gone. Those carefree days of shopping and visiting were over. She would have to make do within the confinement of the icehouse. No trips to town, no picnics to Gay Head or South Beach. No Mary to do the heavy work. No clothing, no dishes, no books, only the toils of a woman in need. Though there were funds in the bank, they had to last until Jared's return. But in her heart Clarissa knew herself capable of everything. Her heart jumped a beat as she thought of the day's date. One week from this day, on June twenty-third, her daughter would be thirteen years old! She began to plan her party. Certainly the Vincents would help. Perpetua's school friends would be invited. They would bake pies, and Perpetua would be given a new dress, at least. A party, a gift could be managed somehow. Clarissa knew she could handle the challenge ahead. What difference did it make if the space was smaller? The chores would be, too! And she might even find some leisure time.

Clarissa smiled to herself, overcome with exhaustion. It amazed her how planning always gave her joy when it involved planning for her Perpetua, too. And she fell asleep, thanking the Lord that she now had all the strength she needed.

• • •

It was not long before Clarissa and her daughter were able to move into the reconstructed icehouse. It had originally been a frame and shingled structure covering a foundation dug deep in the dark earth. Its one room was twelve by ten feet. To augment the size, Ashbiel Vincent added a small bedroom and porch. Previously, preserves and casks had been kept cold under eaves in back, where cakes of ice cut from the ponds on the island's south shore lay wrapped in straw. Ashbiel separated this storeroom from the new living quarters with two solid walls. He added a new door so that Clarissa could enter her arctic cupboard from inside or out.

For the bedroom, which faced the sunny side, Clarissa purchased a bed at old Jabez Smith's furniture store in Holmes Hole. She withdrew more money to buy sheets and to restock her kitchen. She began to make rugs and sew curtains.

Perpetua's three months of summer vacation from the up-island school would be over in July. Another three months of reading, writing and arithmetic, and Perpetua would then have another three months of leave. Thus, each child spent six months each year under the tutelage of the oldest graduate who had agreed to teach the youngest.

Perpetua usually spent a great deal of time alone during vacations, although she would sometimes have serious, grown-up talks with the field hands helping on the farm. When her bright blonde head was seen bobbing through the green fields, they would lay down their pitchforks and shovels to fill her hungry mind with tall tales of their past. She had a way with older men, who saw in her eyes some of their youthful hope and a reflection of their long-stilled desire to see strange places and hear of exotic customs.

Because the Vineyard was so isolated, Perpetua studied maps and wondered at the great land which made up America. And with her maps and globe she explored the seven seas upon which her father sought the whales. With her mother she would often talk about the possible whereabouts of Captain Jared's ship, *The Polar Star,* and she demanded to know when she could expect "the Captain" home and safe. It was a risky business being in the whaling fleet.

"I'm thirteen today," she announced to Clarissa on her birthday, "and where is he? Not even a letter." She knew perfectly well that letters might be on the way. Passed from ship to ship, those hand-scrawled missives arrived when they arrived. Yet it somehow seemed too terrible that Perpetua heard nothing from him. "He won't be here until after I'm married!" she said in tears after the little party on the porch was over and her friends and the Vincent boys had consumed the milk and freshly baked apple pies. "I've only seen him once that I can remember, and that was three and a half years ago!"

"He said without question he would be sailing four years. So it won't be long now," Clarissa replied, vainly attempting to comfort her daughter. But there was no conviction in her voice.

"Father'll never come back! He'll never come home. I hate whales. I hate ships. And those horrible men that kill the whales—I *hate* them! Look, Mother! Father left us stranded! Why should we wait for him?" Then, frightened by the vastness of her hatred and the consequences she now expected, Perpetua began to cry again. "Why did he have to be away when the fire took everything? Why?"

Clarissa stood quietly and placed an arm about her daughter's shoulders. "Darling, don't cry. He *will* come back. Let me tell you about yourself and why there is such a strong bond among you, me and the Captain."

Perpetua sobbed once and quieted.

"I'm listening." It was a challenge.

Her mother poured Perpetua a cup of coffee from the pot which constantly gurgled on the back of the coal stove, a drink not usually allowed young people, except on special occasions.

"We decided as soon as we met that we would get married. I had met your father at my graduation and he swept me off my feet. My, what a handsome lad he was! I had many beaux by then, of course. There was one in particular. But he . . . well, he stayed away so long and your father was so insistent and he was . . . well, right there. Do you understand?"

Perpetua nodded.

"He asked my hand from my father, the Colonel. There was a big wedding—you've heard me tell you about it a thousand times—and then off we went to New Bedford on our honeymoon. Afterwards we came back here, to his family's farm."

Perpetua had indeed heard this part of the story

many times, for the telling brought the Captain to life
and home again in some way.

"When we knew of your impending birth, it
seemed a joy that would round out our love. That is
why you were named 'Perpetua.' It was to remind us
that our love was embodied in our offspring." Clarissa
ran a hand through her daughter's hair. "Perpetua,
you are the only child I can ever bear. The doctor
told me so." She watched her daughter's sober little
face. How she knew her moods. So much like her father in many ways.

"What does that word 'Perpetua' mean?"

"It meant 'forever' to us. The moment you arrived, the Captain leaned over the bed while Mrs.
Claghorn wrapped you in a blanket. You were squall-
ing like a wet kitten. The Captain looked up at me.
'What shall we call this wee girl?' he asked. You know
that all ship's masters wish for a boy; so we had no
name picked for you. I said, 'Let's call her Perpetua,
for that is as long as our love will last.' Then, as he
nodded, his beard brushed my face and his strong
arms were about me." She stopped, thinking of the
moment, while Perpetua sat very still. 'I agree,' he
said in my ear. ' 'Tis the truth.' " Clarissa looked at
her daughter, smiling. "I shall always love your father
for that, no matter what happens."

Perpetua felt a twitch of her heart, sudden fear.
"What could happen? What are you saying?"

Clarissa shook her head and forced nonchalance.
"I meant nothing. It's just that some nights I feel that
the future of the three of us—together, I mean—is not
going to last forever. Perhaps it's the life of a whaler
that has become my life, too. It's like a never-ending
battle on the sea. No one knows who will return from
each voyage." Clarissa paused thoughtfully, lost in
her memories. Then she looked at Perpetua and at-

tempted a weak smile. "But he will come back this time. I feel it."

Perpetua went to her mother and kissed her moist brow. Then she went to the sink and cleaned the coffee pot, carefully washing away the grounds. She placed the spoons on the rack with the pewter forks and knives and thoroughly washed her hands in the pump's cold water. Returning, she found her mother asleep in her chair and Perpetua tenderly placed a rug over her knees. Then she went to the window and watched the fog come in over the Vineyard Sound, wondering if she would ever see her father's ship out there.

What her mother had just said about her name was a thought indeed. It had made a great impression.

The next morning, Clarissa tidied the small house, remembering the romantic nonsense she had felt impelled to confide in her daughter. Jared couldn't wait—Perpetua had arrived not long after the wedding. Such things did happen, but they were best not spoken of—even to a daughter. It might give young girls ideas. Her absorption in romantic novels was bad enough. Jared had been impetuous. Clarissa decided she would never bring it up again. Her face grew hot at the thought.

While crossing another long day off the calendar, she looked out at Vineyard Sound. Soon she could expect to see Jared's ship out there.

A noise broke the stillness.

She turned to look toward the land. She could barely make out someone on a horse. A figure, hunched low to avoid overhanging branches, broke through the woods, thundering down the road to her house.

Could it be he?

Her heart began to beat wildly. Then she realized if the Captain had reached home port, she would have been notified. His last letter had promised his return in four months. That had been just a few weeks ago.

Then she saw that it was only Timothy Vincent, riding down to the barn.

* * *

That evening, Perpetua, alone in the bedroom, was trying to fathom the wrestling match she and Timothy had had in the Vincents' small attic.

Up there to forage for clothing and to explore, she had strained to pull the top from a box. Timothy had gently moved her aside, saying, "Let me do that."

"Why?" she had demanded. "I'm as strong as you are."

"Oh, yes?" There was sarcasm in his answer. With one quick motion he easily removed the top which had given her so much difficulty. Extracting an old silk top hat and placing it on his head, Timothy had said, "Look at a man!"

Infuriated, she had knocked it off. The hat rolled along the floor and fell down the hole into the bedroom below.

Suddenly, Timothy had grabbed her arms, tossing her lightly to the wood floor. There he had straddled her, easily avoiding her kicks, ignoring her tears. He had looked down at her helpless efforts. "Ha, ha! Who's the strongest now?"

A strange and novel emotion had flooded her. With Timothy over her, making her feel so powerless, she had suddenly felt a great languor, a kind of lassitude she had never experienced before. His pressure upon her arms, his body so close to hers had actually been welcome!

Then, with a fury of rejection, she had rolled violently aside and lashed out with a knee. Timothy had cried out, holding his groin in pain as he rolled on the floor. Frightened, Perpetua had leaned over to soothe him, had been mortified to see him laughing up at her. She had dashed down the ladder.

Shouts of laughter had followed her as she raced home, crying.

Now, playing with her doll and thinking about it, she spoke, "Don't worry, little boy. I won't hurt you. Come to mother. She will take care of you."

The doll did not respond. Besides, it was a girl doll. She took it from the curve of her arm and threw it across the room. Why did she feel so ashamed? She lay down on her bed and stared up at the beams. Had she been evil in some way? When Timothy had leaned over her, had he been trying to make love? If so, then what she had felt in her body had been a sin. Her eyes closed.

Perpetua felt her mother tuck her in. She responded to the gentle kiss on her lips. "I love you, Mother. Father will be home soon. Everything will be all right, as you said." Then she fell asleep.

CHAPTER 2

Naliki slowly opened her almond-shaped eyes, awakened by the sound of footsteps approaching her palm hut. It was too early for any of her friends to appear. Some days, they would come crying that the surf was high by the command of Kane and that the god of all gods on their island of Maui demanded her presence. But she knew the sea was calm. The evening before, she and her two brothers had taken a last look at the harbor, Lahaina Roads. More than five hundred whaling vessels were lying at anchor there—so many that she lost count of them all. What an exotic and incredibly beautiful place she lived in, her missionary teacher had said. He was probably correct, thought Naliki, though she could not understand how this place was different from any other.

Naliki's long lashes cast a gentle shade that softened her dark brown eyes. The whites of her eyes, her father had told her, were so white that "the gleam of the noon sun can be seen in them," the brown "like live gems which glow when you are excited." When she was brooding, as now, he had told her "they are as dark as the inside of a cave into which no one can see." She suspected her father was overly praising her, for he was a trader who always made things seem more valuable than they were. A smile came to her lips.

No, the footsteps were heavy. It would be her father, Kaiko, not a friend, nor one of the lusting sailors who had come seeking a young girl, one not yet ready or trained to pleasure him.

The mat covering of her palm hut opened. There he stood, her wise and canny father who went to the Christian church to keep peace with the missionaries. Despite the Christians' fervent preaching against wanton living and old customs, her father still held to the traditions carried to their island from thousands of miles across the open sea. Their ancestors, he had explained to Naliki, arrived one thousand years before the birth of the church's Jesus Christ.

She rose in respect, saying nothing. The lowering of her eyes, as a sign of obedience, was customary. When she raised them, she noted that her strong, muscular father wore a necklace of shark's teeth, signifying an important occasion. No older than forty, he already bore many deep lines upon his forehead and about his full lips. He had deep black hair, slightly crooked legs and black eyes. A benign smile spread across his face, a certain sign to Naliki that her father had come about certain business because this was her thirteenth birthday . . . as the white men counted time.

Naliki's head was lowered in humility. She sensed he was about to address her on her coming of age, the time when she would have to prove her ability to bear children. Her long, glistening black hair fell about her bare shoulders. The *tapa* which had been tightly drawn about her body emphasized her lithe, full curves. A slight curl came to the corners of her pouting lips, as she placed her graceful hands against her mouth, cupping her fingers to part them, showing the white gleam of her teeth.

Kaiko motioned her to be seated and slowly squatted before her.

His first words were of other things. "Has my daughter seen the whales which sport within our harbor?"

She nodded. They had come, as all knew, from their Aleutian homes to sport in the warm waters of the Sandwich Islands. It was a sign of early spring. Then it came to her. He was gradually leading up to her birth date and the tradition it brought.

"Have you seen the many ships?"

"Yes, my father, I have. There are five hundred, I am told."

"For many years, Naliki, the men from other lands have come here in their ships. Never in all that time have so many gathered as this year. In all that time, never have I seen a woman on this island as beautiful as you, my daughter."

Her eyes became dark . . . obscure and impenetrable. She was alert, but didn't wish to show it. She cast a look over her left shoulder as if at something far away. What he had said was impossible for her to believe. She had seen her mother before she had died. How could Kaiko speak thus to her? His wife had been an *alii*, a noblewoman. She had been tall, while Naliki was of middle height; she had been statuesque, while Naliki was lissome, but shorter. Where was her father leading?

"In all the years that the missionaries have been here, they have professed to bring us Christ. Instead they have taken everything they could, my daughter. They shall not take you, whose ancestors fought in the great battle which made these islands a nation, for you are descended from King Kamehameha!"

Inside the dark shade of her palm hut, Naliki could see her father's eyes flashing with anger at the thought.

"Your ancestors, Naliki, were proud and handsome people from Tahiti who traveled across the open sea in their canoes. They brought with them women selected for their fecundity, beauty and nobility with which to start a new race. Of all these women you are the most beautiful—and now it is your time."

There! It had come out. Naliki had been an excellent student in the missionary school, proving her intellect as well as her nobility. Yet she had also been trained in the quiet, placid ways of high-born island women, never revealing her innermost feelings except by certain mannerisms. That exterior of unruffled calm had become her shield, a way to enter womanhood gracefully, guided by her only parent, for her mother had died many years ago.

Now her father, the wily trader who dealt with the great sea captains, was about to initiate her in the traditions of her race.

"If I were to look at you as another man would— if I were not your father," he began, rising to his feet, "I would have to use poetry to tell of what I see. Your abundance of black hair is like the silk cloth from France which has flecks of silver woven within it, the cloth that sparkles in the sunlight. Your eyebrows are like the arch of a warrior's bow which curls with grace at the end. Your face is shaped with the skill of a sculptor whose knife is as sharp as the razor the *haolekane* use to cut the hair from their face. Your nose flares with delicate curves to breathe fully when you run or make love with your man. Your neck is like that of the graceful bird which flies overhead. Your shoulders are the color of sand with the sheen of a well-rubbed stone and your breasts are proud and tipped with dark standing nipples which tell of your hidden passion."

Naliki felt a flush come to her face and spread across her chest. Kaiko was listing her assets as if she might be a slave for sale, or any of her older sisters who had been offered for money. She had hoped for better than this. She was his favorite and—as he had said—the most beautiful.

"I have seen you dance," went on the older man, his breathing heavy and his voice loud with excitement. "You were bare to your waist, Naliki. I was proud of the curve of your hips as they swung from side to side, for they were enticing to the men who watched, and moved their minds to lust for you. Your buttocks were like moons, yet were firm and pliant, enhancing your movements of the dance as no other. Yes, Naliki, I know what is in your heart, what depth there is to you as a woman. It is now your time."

Naliki withdrew her cupped hand from her lip. Her dark amber eyes dwelt for a long moment upon her father's, testing his sincerity, for his speech was indeed unnecessary. It was known that Naliki danced with more fervor than any other, that within her lay a great zest for her womanhood, and also, a certain amount of pride in what the men's feasting eyes told her about her appeal.

"There are preparations you must make, Naliki. Now you are of the age to prove you can bear a child. Then, when you have done so, you will marry an *alii*, a man of noble blood. He is already promised, should you not be barren."

Her eyes were the darkest amber, revealing hidden flecks of orange beneath the shadow of her brow. She dropped her head in submission, her heart beating wildly. It had come—the time of initiation! But not in the way she had expected.

Other girls her age had been urged to get their training the usual way. They would line the beach not far from the arriving vessels, on which swarmed the love-starved sailors, men who had been without women for as long as four years. Dropping their *tapas*, the girls would stand nude and dance, then swim to the ships, urged on by the shouts of the men who awaited them.

Those girls had not been chosen to marry an *alii*. Naliki had. She was familiar with the old tradition of "training" a mature girl by selecting a man to teach her. Should she be apprehensive or pleased?

"The great whaling fleet has arrived in our harbor." Kaiko broke the silence. "Again, the *haolekane* will have been long without women. Again our young *wahines* will undress in a way that is forbidden by the missionaries. For the missionaries are unthinking—they dwell not on life and its pleasures but on death and its terrors. These men lack 'love,' but after the first *aloha*, they only want more and more. Other girls will stand naked on our beaches, then swim to their ships for money and gifts. Then the older *wahines* ashore will take their money. Some men will desert their ships and be sought in the hills. Others will be jailed in the *Hale Paaho*. Rioting will take place. Strong drink will turn them into animals. What other *wahines* do is their business, though it is called 'an abomination' by the missionaries. But for you, it is different."

He looked at her again. "You are one about whom men will write songs. You will not give yourself to a common sailor. You will not do as the others. You have been promised in marriage to a man of your class. First you must become pregnant. You may give your body to only one man before you are married. This man has already been chosen to train you. His name is Hanalai. He will teach you how to please men, how to use your body for this purpose. When you have borne a child, the *alii* will come for you from Kauai, the island to the north, and you will leave with him and I will be rich. It is my prayer to our great god Kane that this will be so."

Kaiko left abruptly. Naliki knew his word was binding, and everything would be done as he said.

She took off her *tapa*. She reached for the roof of her palm hut, stretching her lithe body to relax it after so many words. There was much to think about. Her full, young breasts were lifted, tipped with ripe brown nipples, the curve of her arms gracefully descending to the line of her breast. Her black hair fell loosely about her shoulders. Arching her back to relax the tension her father's pronouncement had caused, she slowly lowered her arms and bent her knees as she squatted on the matted flooring of her palm hut.

The cries of friends outside broke her reverie. Hastily covering herself with her red *tapa*, she ran out, shouting, "Wait for me! It is Kane's command that I swim in the great surf with you today!"

That evening, her father came again. "This is the night during which you will receive your first training. When the drums stop, the man Hanalai will come. You will be obedient. This will bring you happiness, Naliki." Again he left abruptly, not wishing to be unseemly with a woman-child.

Naliki waited, her fear mixed with excitement. Her friends had whispered to her that her first *kane* would rip her apart, that the man would bring great pain, and they laughed, "You will be filled with joy at the moment of pain. You will feel what it is like to be a woman."

The door opened. A man stood there. He was well over six-feet tall. His head had been squared by molding in infancy. His face was darker than hers, his nose flatter. He bore himself as a man who knew his station.

She looked into his eyes. They were dark and hypnotic. His sensuous nostrils flared. She spoke first. "I am Naliki."

"I am Hanalai." His voice was melodious. She felt her tension ease.

He sat down. Then he began: "Many years ago a great god came to us from another race of people far from this island. He taught our men and women many things. I have been given the ability to carry on such knowledge. I will teach you."

Naliki was fascinated, intent. She stared into his eyes while Hanalai continued: "We are given five knowledges for love, '*No ke aloha.*' When we use these knowledges with our *ipo*, our *hale* is a happy home. The first knowledge is of touching. Secondly, we have the knowledge of seeing, and thirdly, hearing. We stir within as we hear what words suggest."

He waited for her response.

"I know what words can suggest."

"We have tongues for tasting. With the tongue we taste of honey and the sweetness which lies in another's body."

Again she responded. "I have tasted many pleasant things."

"With the sense of smell, we fill our thoughts. Is this too much for you to believe?"

"It is not. The winds bring smells of flowers, of fish frying—and then there are other scents which fill me with longings I do not understand."

"I will tell you how to understand these thoughts. When you do, you will enter into the mist over Haleakala in a continuous heaven. You will be with the gods."

She couldn't believe him. Obediently, she waited.

"I will tell you when to use your fingers. When they must linger on the skin of a man, when they must grasp or caress. You will feel the touch of his body on yours and you will learn when you must move against him. You will learn how to wrap your legs about his waist, when to turn your back to him, how to lift your breasts in the act of offering. You will learn how to use the movements of the *hula* with your palms upon your hips to draw attention and desire to what lies beneath them. You will learn from looking into his eyes and watching between his hips when it is time."

The thoughts which entered her mind made her nipples stand up. A warm feeling flowed through her body.

"I see what my words have brought to your mind. You will be proud when your words have done the same things to a *kane*." He stood up. He pointed to the other end of the room. "Walk from me to there. Then come back. I will show you what the sight of you can do to a *kane*."

She arose, walked slowly on the balls of her feet, performing the *hula* movement, first striking the toes, then the heels. Her buttocks rocked from side to side, her hips gyrated gracefully. Then she turned, nude and enticing. She came toward him, feeling the slight movement of her breasts as she thrust her hips forward.

There he stood, tall, breathing heavily.

"Look down! See what sight of you has done to a *kane!*"

His organ stood swollen and rigid, throbbing.

A strange, sudden feeling of power came over her. The heat began in her groin, sending languorous sensations throughout her lower body. She had never

dreamed that the sight of her own body could create
such an instantaneous effect on a man. There he
stood, waiting and ready.

Hanalai sank to the floor. "Come. You must know
about feeling a *kane*. Your fingers are like ten Nalikis,
each taking part. The *kane* must feel them on his buttocks, on his organ and about his groin. There is the
center of a man's feeling. The fingers must enfold his
organ in their coils while you pronounce wonder at its
size. You must touch gently, as if it was the stem of a
flower, then firmly as if afraid to lose it. You must offer your lips, your breasts, for they bring memory of
peace and safety while he begins to know you as a
separate thing—a *wahini* who is about to be his."

Naliki breathed heavily, unconscious of the sound
of her sighs. A flush came to her chest, spread across
her upthrust breasts.

Hanalai leaned forward, spread her knees and
placed his hand upon her at exactly the right place.
He gently kneaded with his fingers, moving his palm
against the full mound of hair and the smooth bone
behind it. He rubbed gently, with great artistry, as if
feeling a jewel.

She moaned. A rippling sensation tore through
her. She felt herself thrusting against his touch,
wanting him never to stop. She had done this to herself before. But never had it been like this. She cried
out at the first spasm. He held her until she was
through.

She felt like a bird in space—alone, yet with her
kane.

"The gift of smelling the body's musk, tasting the
sweet salt taste of the skin, and the exotic hot wind of
both breathing together is now given to you."

He stood up. Again he was a god without the
feelings of a man. He walked to the door. "I will

come back. Then you will learn what it is to be a *wahini* with her man."

* * *

For two days, Naliki thought of what Hanalai had said, speaking about it to no one. The night of the second day, he returned as suddenly as he had appeared before.

"I have told you of your five feelings. Now I will become part of you and you will use them. You are my *ipo*, my sweetheart. Together we will go to heaven, to the *lani*."

He lifted her with his hands upon her hips, let them run across her stomach, downward, while holding her closely. The press of his hardness, erect against her, sent flutterings through her body, sensations such as she had never known.

She felt him move against her. Then they were upon the mat. She felt the strength of his muscles, the tightness of his buttocks, the bulge of his arms, the heavy chest upon her soft breasts. His organ grew within her ten fingers and she wondered at its size. She became afraid of the hurting to come. He spoke softly, gently. Her fear was stilled. She became pliant as he moved over her, moved her legs apart. The thrust tore into her. He moved slowly. She felt the hot blood within. Anticipation mingled with pain. He did not move.

Her legs spread to accommodate him as he penetrated slowly. A thrill began, driving her wild with desire. She started to move against him, giving way to his thrusts, responding with the surge of her own body. Her excitement mounted. Soon she was at the fringe of eternity, over the volcano Haleakala. The spasms began, explosions followed. His body within her swelled, impaled her. He was so imbedded that his organ seemed a heated part of her. Her legs clasped him tighter and her hands flayed at his back, moved to his hard buttocks, locked him there inside her. He answered with violent thrusts. He swelled to an enormous size, then, together they reached the highest peak.

The elation was so high it carried her beyond the earth they lay upon. As her mind was consumed with the awareness of her shaken body, Naliki cried out.

In his house not far away, Kaiko heard her and smiled. If all went well, in the time of nine months, Naliki would bear a child. Then she would be married unless another, better offer for her came to him. Valued above all things which he traded was his daughter. He expected great rewards.

* * *

It had been the middle of winter, four months earlier, when the great whaling ship *The Polar Star* stood off the Straits of LeMaire near Cape Horn at the southern tip of South America. Under the masterful hands of her Captain, Jared West, she was about to make the most hazardous passage known to men of the sea, the rounding of the Horn. If the passage was successful, the ship would pass northward to the Juan Fernandez Islands to rest, then make its way to the Sandwich Islands. Captain West planned to seek whales in the Archer and Off-Shore Grounds to the north and west, and then put in to Maui.

Standing some three inches taller than any of his seamen, black-bearded Jared West was known to have bent an iron rod over his knee. Rumor had it that he once hurled a two-hundred-pound man overboard to sober him and then leapt among the sharks to save him. Each night at supper, the Captain read aloud from his Bible before allowing his chief, second and third mates to appease their appetites. The men knew that Captain Jared West was master of two things, his Bible and his ship. It was not known to them that his piety also served to keep his secret passions bridled. He knew himself to be an unusually virile man of lusty appetites, but somehow his passion for religion helped to quell those other lusts, so much deeper and more sinful.

He was not alone in his secret thoughts. His men thought only of whales and women, and spoke only of women and whales. They were a motley crew. Some were Indians from Gay Head, that westerly promontory of Martha's Vineyard, and some hailed from the islands of the Azores, where whaling vessels on their outward-bound voyages often augmented their crews. Some came from Africa, some from the islands of the Pacific. Such men were willing to endure many years at sea for the sake of shares of the ship on which they sailed. On *The Polar Star*, as on all whalers, the white man commanded. But whalers all, commander and his crew lived together aboard one ship, their prey their common bond, the sea controlling them all.

Jared knew on that day of their passage—as did all the others—that their ship was in danger. The Cape weather had "come to meet them." The first sign had been a dismally cold fog rising where the warm waters of the Atlantic met the icy waves of the Antarctic. Captain West immediately ordered all hatchways covered. Bedding and material below deck were beginning to mold. The bunks had been soaked by the seas, which had swept through the fo'c's'le like an unleashed pack of wild dogs. With the hatches closed, no air carried into the foul-smelling depths of the ship's hold. Men began to grumble. Their knees and elbows were chafed and bleeding from being so roughly buffeted.

At this point Jared commanded his helmsman to take a more southerly course. There were rocks and promontories to be avoided at all costs.

Standing aft, near the helmsman, he thought of the hard passage which surely lay ahead, and of the soft flesh of his wife, Clarissa, whom he had left behind. His groin ached with the need her memory brought, but he had little time for reverie. He had done as others in the Azores, committing acts which his Bible would not forgive. Many of the New England men had begun colonies of their own, far away in the North Atlantic, unknown to families left behind. Even at his last stop, Captain West had seen small half-castes bearing Yankee names—children who ran, jumped and shouted as did their half-brothers and sisters on the islands off Cape Cod—all oblivious to that distant kinship. West did not consider himself a hypocrite when he called upon the Lord to keep his ship, his men and himself safe though he knew they all had broken the commandment he spoke aloud at supper. Nor did he believe he was any different for having seized the plump, young woman who willingly gave herself to him.

With a prayer for safety, and all thought of sin dislodged from his mind, Jared West watched as a vast curtain of Pacific snow and sleet swept upon them, lifting *The Polar Star* high, then causing her to broach so violently that cold sea water inundated the decks.

His men had made themselves fast to standing rigging, lashing themselves to the stays and shrouds. There they clung with all their strength, boots filled with icy water.

As the ship recovered, wallowing in the swells,

the crewmen looked at each other with fear in their eyes. And the Folger lad from Nantucket, stationed at the wheel, cried out to his captain, "Shall we turn about and run for the Cape of Good Hope?"

"I shall never be spoken of as a man who could not double Cape Horn!" shouted his master. "Blast ye, keep her firm and on the point!"

"I fear we shall founder, sir!" the lad cried back.

"Then let it be so!" Now the Captain seized the wheel alongside the boy, his beard encrusted with ice, his deep blue eyes fixed on the plunging bow and the taut canvas sails, stretched to the breaking point.

"We can't take on more sea," yelled the lad.

"The rocks, Captain West!" howled Old Talbot, a bent old mariner who was the master's closest friend on board. "We still have to mind the rocks!"

Captain West raised his head, his beard like glistening diamonds. The ice had made it fast to his chin, shaping it like a dagger. A symbol of ferocity, his bejeweled beard shone like a reminder of the man's intense purpose, threatening those who would run from the enemy.

"We will make the Horn. It is destiny!" His words were hurled into a swirl of snow.

The ship fought desperately for purchase in the sea, digging her keel and hull at every advantage. Often on her beam, lying helpless in the huge troughs, she dug deep for leverage in the icy spume. West shoved the frightened lad aside and took the helm alone. Into his mind came the words he had said. Destiny? What destiny lay ahead?

"Clear the 'top!" he cried, seeing that the lines above him had jammed in a pulley. The topsail had been set to backwind the fierce tempest and hold his ship to the wheel. The men were still lashed to the standing gear. At his order, three cut themselves loose and scrambled up like wild monkeys, reaching the block aloft where the tip of the vessel's mast whipped back and forth in great arcs.

A sudden clearing allowed West to see the crew where they hung aloft. One lost his footing and fell screaming to his death, passing the horrified men on deck like a lead weight before plummeting into the churning, icy sea.

The two other seamen, murmuring prayers they alone heard, worked frantically along the topsail spar. After ten minutes of frantic struggle, they had finally made the line run free. Once on deck, they were taken shivering below to soggy bunks, their clothing made of ice. Next to them sat a man reading his Bible, firmly believing he would soon meet his Maker.

Captain West felt the wind on his frozen face. It came from dead ahead. He smiled. A steady headwind could be handled.

One terrible hour after another passed as the ship plunged and fought for survival. They passed without a change in the light about them or in the strength of the wind. West persisted on his course as the ship drove its way through massive seas. Ahead, they faced the most turbulent portion of the passage round the Horn, where the Pacific lashed at the ship until every beam shuddered. Captain West shouted, "If we can but hold to this tack, we will clear. Steady, men, steady!"

He seemed to grow even taller. His eyes assumed an unaccustomed brilliance. There was no fear in his voice, only exhilaration as he yelled, "Ease her two points!"

He is mad, his mate thought. There is no turning back. Words from Psalms came to the man: "Though the waters roar and be troubled, the Lord of Hosts is with us. He is our refuge, and ever present help in trouble."

Jared had always been a man of few words, as had been his taciturn Yankee ancestors. Yet, at this moment, amidst vast and mountainous seas, he had a sudden urge for speech to ease the minds of his men who clung to life so tenaciously. He knew that death on the sea often came to the mighty flotilla of ships which plied the deep in search of the leviathans. When face to face with what seemed inevitable disaster, the whaling trade needed a word, a sign— and he meant to give it.

"We'll make it, men! I see the clearing ahead!" The radiant smile on his face gave them hope, the strength of the man at the helm gave them heart, and the words of confidence moved them to action. All hands bent to their work. As if a sign had been given, the heavy mist of the Pacific cleared about them and before their eyes a great deep trough of quiet sea opened in the heart of the tempest. It was through this opening that West skillfully guided his ship.

They had doubled the Cape.

In his log that night, Jared West reported *The Polar Star*'s location, her condition, the bearings and the nature of the weather. Nothing other than what affected the silent, wooden hull entered the book. Deep in his heart, though, Jared had other thoughts, but none that he shared with this log or with the men under him.

Brought up to respect women and to make life comfortable for them, he had been known as a wholesome, God-fearing man who cared for his elders and loved his woman.

Until he had married, Jared had often dallied with native girls on the islands of the West Indies, at stopping places off the coast of South America, and in

Tahiti. As master of a whaler, he had kept such affairs quiet. After his marriage to Clarissa, however, he had tried hard to remain "pure in body and mind," as he put it to himself.

As for his crew, however, their behavior ashore was always in keeping with what one might expect from men jammed into close quarters with others of their own sex. At the first sight of Lahaina in Maui, all hands thought of only one thing.

And the same thought lay floating in the shallows of Jared's mind, though he tried to get rid of it. His abstinence on this particularly hazardous voyage made him long for the comforting hands of a woman, a longing which ached in his groin.

As his ship made anchor in Lahaina in late spring, he stood on the afterdeck and watched as the young island girls lined the shore, dropped their *tapas* and began their swim to his ship. A canoe approached, making its way ahead of the giggling, naked young girls. In the canoe sat a man whom Jared recalled at first glance, a trader of goods—animal, vegetable or mineral.

With a wave of his hand, Kaiko drew alongside beneath the imposing figure of the Captain.

It had been two months since the commencement of Naliki's training. Though the trainer had been sent away, the needs his work had aroused were fully instilled in Naliki.

Now she must wait, docile and unrewarded; though the fires had been kindled, they now were banked. Knowing his daughter, as he knew all women, Kaiko understood that a discreet meeting with another man would help contain her ardor while she continued with what he hoped was her pregnancy, and made ready for her marriage.

Kaiko was sure that Captain West would be the answer for his Naliki. He was rich, and a discreet man. As for Naliki, she would do Kaiko's will. It would take little urging, for her body commanded her now.

Of these plans, Naliki knew nothing. When she arrived on the beach that morning, she was eager to walk into the cooling sea, to ride her surfboard. She hoped that swimming in the cool water would ease the ache within her.

Dropping the *tapa* from her body, the young girl pushed out. Paddling toward the great curl of a wave, she saw a man from the newly arrived ship board her father's canoe. He was a tall man with a beard, surely the most handsome *haloekane* she had ever seen. He looked stronger than any island warrior and bore himself like he owned the world, imperiously looking about his domain—the sea, the island, and the girls frolicking with his men—as if all that was beneath him. Yet, even from a distance Naliki sensed his manhood, and her heart responded with a surge of desire.

Kaiko's canoe came rapidly towards Naliki as she skimmed smoothly over the waves. Then, standing naked, her feet spread for balance, she took the curl on her surfboard and let it carry her near her father's canoe, for she meant to have a closer look.

Her father made a gesture indicating that he and his daughter should beach together. She skillfully guided her board so that it landed simultaneously with the canoe. The *haloekane* was wearing a blue jacket with gold buttons, and his brilliant blue eyes bored into her, almost as if he were touching every inch of bare skin. She felt a sudden thrill, a tingling in every nerve. Her father and the man approached and now she saw that the noble-looking, tall man had heavy black brows, a quick, wide smile and a chest as big as an oil cask. What a mighty man was he!

Naliki ran a hand down her long hair, letting her fingers brush against her nipples. Then she stood, eyes downcast, her lovely body wet with the sea, glistening and tempting.

"This is my friend Captain West," said her father.

"I am Naliki." Her eyes met those of the big man. Again the shock. His eyes were dynamic, filled with intense passion. She knew the look.

"He wishes to go with you."

Kaiko said the words as naturally as if he had offered the man some fruit. Naliki's eyes again lowered and she recalled her father's previous lecture about waiting for her *alii*. Then she knew that her father must understand her better than she suspected. Perhaps it was something in their blood. Needs had to be answered. When hungry, eat. When tired, sleep. When aroused, respond. He knew. Naliki could see it in the smile that creased her father's lined face, in the way he stood before her, and in his eyes, which said, "Yes."

The three waited, motionless for a moment. The man, West, was not embarrassed, yet he stared at her as if measuring her worth. Apparently a great sum had been suggested. With a nod, West turned to Kaiko, his voice deep, saying, "Let us go. It is done."

She led him to the place of the dance in the dark hills.

At Jared's first sight of the incredibly beautiful young girl, standing with legs spread, head held proud and high as the great curl carried her to him, it seemed as if he must have her immediately. Impetuously, he had asked Kaiko the girl's price. The trader had replied that she was his prized daughter, promised for a great sum to another. But a deal was made, as Jared had known it would be.

As she reached the beach and bent over, Jared had followed her every motion—her grace in lifting the board, the sight of her breasts, her lovely face, her sweeping thighs and hips were unbearably tempting. After seeing her, all his actions and words seemed inevitable. Yet, as they walked to the place where the dance would begin, Jared began making excuses to himself. No one would know. He had been away so long. The need was so great. His men were doing it. Everyone was expected to enjoy the island and its loveliness. Lovely? She was unbelievably beautiful! But she would be forgotten tomorrow, he was certain. In the first flush of his desire, he was unconscious of how much he underestimated her and overestimated himself.

The beat began in the guileless fashion of the Tahitians, fast and sensuous. Before Jared, in the circle of the clearing, danced the girl with midnight black hair, swaying delicately, her eyes fixed demurely to the ground. He longed to grasp that swaying body and hold her knees apart, taking one tantalizing position after another. The drums hammered at his ears. She came close to him. Her full young breasts brushed his hands, then her entire body began to quiver wildly. She seemed overcome by a sudden ardor so fierce that she was uncontrolled. She signaled for a faster beat. The rhythm mounted. Her body shone with glistening perspiration as she took one frenzied posture after another, each more suggestive, ending with her knees close to the ground, legs apart as if he lay between her thighs and she were ready for the act of love. Her buttocks began to jerk spasmodically as she reached a climax. Jared could stand it no longer. He must be a part of this.

The drums and the girl neared the finale. The couple met, her gyrations slowed. The drums stopped. He and she were alone in the clearing. Naliki took his hand and with undulating hips led him swiftly to her palm hut.

There she demonstrated what she knew. He felt her many fingers on him, the clasping and stroking of the inner caress. He knew her silken body, warming to her smooth flesh. He smelled her dainty perfume, she his musk. They met in a climactic ending, her cries carrying them both over the hills of Maui. Then Jared fell into a drug-like sleep.

Some days later, bound for the whaling grounds off Japan, Jared kept seeing an image of Naliki in the billowing sails. He shook his head, but the image persisted. His experience with her had been so bewitching, he would never be the same.

CHAPTER 3

That December night, Perpetua had begged to be allowed to read in bed, for she had dearly wished to finish her new book by Elizabeth Barrett Browning, *Sonnets from the Portuguese*. Her mother had objected, for she felt the child should get her sleep after spending an active day with Timothy. And Clarissa worried that the book might give her daughter ideas beyond her years.

"You are not yet a grownup, Perpetua, though you will be soon enough."

With that, the girl had obediently dog-eared her page, snuggled down on her pallet and permitted her mother to kiss her good night.

When the oil lamp was doused, a heavy odor filled the small room as the smoke from the dying wick wafted through the air. Clarissa moved into the kitchen where she began to make entries in her journal. The infinite boredom that befell the wife of a whaling master at sea was broken by these comforting daily entries—a recitation of that boredom for the dear Lord to see and understand. In a way, the keeping of a journal was her prayer that times would be less monotonous.

Time had become a vacuum. Jared's ship was

overdue. Once more Clarissa wrote of her sense of loneliness, cramped within the house with a growing child, burdened by chores and with a rising fear that she would never see or hear of her husband again.

As she returned her pen to the inkstand and read the first few lines, she was vaguely conscious of the distant neighing of a horse, then the creaking of harness—the sounds of a cart approaching along the mud-rutted roadway. Startled, Clarissa dropped her journal. She stood up, straightening her nightgown, and reached for a shawl. She felt her hair and the ribbon which held it.

She listened, wondering if it wasn't just another dream she wished would come true. She heard the neighing and stomping of hoofs upon the roadway that led travelers from the pine forest to the door. Then she heard the loud voice, unmistakably Jared's!

"Thanks, Nehemiah!" he was shouting. "Thanks!"

She ran for the door, letting her shawl drop behind her. But before she could touch the handle, the door opened. And there he stood, bigger than any man alive, taller than she had remembered—and, at second glance—older in a way which made her sad.

He stood there without saying a word.

She began to shake, tears and laughter coming at the same time. Then with a rush she was in his arms as snow fell from his clothes all about her. Her head pressed against his huge chest. Her Jared! Home at last!

His bearded face moved down upon hers. She felt the sharp bristles, the cold snow, his lips seeking hers. A sudden chill went through her. She was acting shamelessly! But she let him hold her, eased against him as he ran his hands along her back. How strange and foreign he felt! But now, at last, she was safe.

He stepped away, glancing quickly at the way

the wet nightgown now outlined her breasts. The cold had made her nipples rise. He admired her openly. A flush came to her face. She lowered her eyes, feeling his response as he appraised her.

His black beard appeared encrusted with snow diamonds. His deep-set dark blue eyes seemed to be tearing her gown away. Aye, Jared was home . . . she must control herself.

"Clarissa," he said in a way she remembered. It told her he had used the word to himself many times. "How I have missed you!"

"Jared," she breathed. His strength surprised her. His arms seemed to crush her body. She had forgotten how it felt to have a man hold her. A flush came to her chest.

He let her go, looked about the tiny room.

"Where is Perpetua?" He looked back at her appraisingly while he spoke, almost as though he were evaluating her. She felt uncomfortable for a moment, then straightened her back and looked up at him.

"Perpetua is asleep. Let me help you, my husband!"

She helped him off with his coat, brushing away the snow, shaking it.

Then, stiffly, he said to her, "When I heard in the village the farmhouse burned down, I feared for you terribly. But I see that all is well."

His words helped even though the attempt at conversation sounded awkward. The sound of his voice, loud and strong, filled the emptiness of the room. He seemed so huge. Clarissa felt she must make him feel at home. There were so many things to say. So many years had gone by. Then she saw Perpetua standing in the doorway. Forlorn-looking, bewildered by the man who had just hugged her mother, Perpetua was shivering.

With one lunge her father crossed the room and swept her up in his arms, pressing the wriggling, squealing child to his scratchy beard. "My baby!" he cried, kissing her forehead. Finally, through sleep-dimmed eyes, she understood who he was.

It was nearly dawn before they stopped talking. The fire was doused by Jared, who was afraid they would all doze off and let a log roll into the room. Clarissa saw that Perpetua had fallen asleep. Her eyelids fluttered in a dream.

"Here, let me take her. She's used to my arms."

Clarissa half-carried Perpetua back to her pallet in the other room, struggling to make her walk straight, for she was no longer the thin stalk of a child she had been last summer. In bed, the comforter pulled up, Perpetua looked at her mother, then smiled with such sweetness that tears came to Clarissa's eyes.

"He *is* really here, isn't he?"

Then, before her mother could answer, Perpetua fell into a deep sleep.

The Captain and his wife talked for two more hours. The snow had stopped. The sun was breaking through the overcast. Finally, Jared stretched, put down his coffee and said he must sleep. He looked around the small room.

"I am very tired," he said, looking at the bed. "I have been traveling for twenty hours."

"Leave your clothes on the hooks there," Clarissa replied, indicating the back of the door. "Take your time. But, tomorrow, I must look over your things." Clarissa slipped into bed and lay on her back, staring at the low ceiling. When she heard Jared approach, she moved as close to the wall as possible, pulling her nightgown to her toes.

She shuddered slightly as she felt his heavy body on the thin springs, his warmth next to her. She knew a wife's duty, but she felt that at this particular moment, she could not appease Jared. It had been a long denial for him, that she knew, and yet she hoped he would not touch her. Perhaps he really was very tired, would go right to sleep. As she waited, her heart thumping, her body cringing, cold and stiff, she finally heard what she had prayed for, his first deep breath and the beginning of his snore.

But it was not to last.

She was just beginning to doze when she felt his hand start to move, to touch her belly as she lay face to the wall. Then she heard his snort, felt his building desire as he pulled her fiercely to his body.

Oh, if he could only be tender this first time! Four and a half years of abstinence had stilled her blood. She prayed, as he turned her to face him, that he would be understanding of her reluctance, more sensitive than he had ever been. The past came rolling back to her. She recalled their first years together when she had been full of life, supple and not houseworn. He had been slow and patient, had realized that as a young woman she didn't have the need he always had. Or had she? Now, he was handling her body as though on some rough exploration. His large palm exposed her breast and held it. She remembered how his warm, tender touch had once stirred her, how she had sighed and clung to him afterwards. Now, it seemed as though some strange, huge animal had begun to paw her. She tried to pull away.

"Clarissa," he spoke. It was a reprimand.

Was she only to be a receptacle, then? Would the two of them never recapture the pleasure of those first tender years? Her body was as unprepared as her thoughts. His two hands were upon her buttocks, but she could not respond.

"They are so soft," he murmured to himself.

Then he was upon her, his body pulsing and jerking insistently. She relaxed as best she could, closed her eyes and tried to imagine that they were meeting again a long time ago at the dance, he the lover, she the beloved.

A violent toss, and she was on her back. Jared buried his head between her breasts, then ran his rough, bearded face over her soft, sensitive skin, kissing her body and murmuring, "How smooth you are. How soft."

Clarissa cried from deep in her throat, digging her nails into his muscular broad back. She felt the comforter fall to the floor, felt him take her about the waist and literally stand her on her feet in the room.

She felt violated in the light of the morning sun. She clung to him, rather than be seen as she was, for her nightgown had fallen to the floor.

He was more aroused than she had ever seen him before.

Again he said, "You are so white, like cream." He touched her skin and let his hand run down her back, then move around to rest upon her mount of Venus, pressing against the golden triangle.

"Like some plump, succulent tropical plum!" he whispered hoarsely. "I want to see you as you are."

He stepped back. She was horrified at the man's strength and the thought of being impaled by him—wounded by that eager and mighty part of his body which rose before her. She began to shiver.

"You are cold."

For an unendurable moment, she waited, hoping he would simply let her return to bed and rest. Without preamble, he lifted her quickly, as if she might struggle, and placed her upon the bed. Her legs were spread to catch her fall. He stood over her at first, looking down, eyes darker than she had ever seen them, his mouth a straight, grim line. Then he quickly moved over her and plunged his erection into her unyielding body.

She screamed in pain . . . then thought of Perpetua and put her fist in her mouth, praying their daughter would not wake up. His movements were violent. Distress became a kind of relief as she was ravished. She felt him move into his final throes, thrusting without consideration for her as he reached his climax. While he spent himself, he grasped her buttocks, forcing himself deeper. At that moment, she felt the first stirring of her own desire. But it was over as quickly as it had begun.

Jared lay heavily upon her, asleep.

She couldn't breathe. Gently, but with all her strength, she finally rolled him from her and stretched full length hugging near the wall as though to find protection.

"How white, how smooth you are," he had said.

"Weren't all women that color, that soft? She wondered why he had said that. Then she began to wonder what her future would be, now that Jared was home. In lovemaking it had always been he who had made the moves. Women obeyed their men in such matters. It was the unwritten law, the custom. Only loose and sinful women led men on. Oh, yes, there were certain, subtle ways of making this happen. But men were the masters of their wives as they were of their ships. "Up sail! Down sail! Up emotions! Down! Obey and do for me. Devil take your feelings!"

There he lay, slowly breathing in deep slumber. But Clarissa could not force herself to sleep. She lay beside him, wide awake, hot and raw from his attack. She had just begun to feel the first hot move of blood, the need. Then, finished. Body tingling and punished before it began!

His snoring angered her. A flailing arm struck her. She began to sob. As she heard Perpetua move about in the other room, she closed her eyes, praying that the child had not listened through the wall.

* * *

After only a few days of living in the old ice-house, Jared began to exhibit his usual restlessness. Having checked and rechecked the stores, mended the roof and caulked the ill-sealed walls, he stood spraddle-legged at the door and faced his wife and Perpetua.

"You've done well, Clarissa. And you, Perpetua— you are a daughter a man can be proud of. But I have to go down-village."

Clarissa knew the signs, had been watching the way Jared constantly peered out the window, search-ing the waves of Vineyard Sound. It was almost noon and soon the men would be gathering at the general store on Main Street in Holmes Hole. Jared had a right to see old friends, compare voyages and share his stories of success and failure. Such talk would set his feet on familiar ground again. With the fire, all his ancestral roots had gone up in the flames—the faded oil painting of his grandfather, the first Captain Jared West; the silver cup from which he had been fed by his beloved mother, Heather Vincent West; the many logs, journals and hastily-scratched maps of harbors in Asia, Africa and the North Sea off Germany. All these items, like living memories, meant more to him than he could express.

"There are things I mean to do at the bank."

Clarissa smiled, stood up and kissed him, for he

seemed so like a child begging his mother for time to go out and play.

At the door, fully dressed for the winter air, he turned. "Perpetua, get your duds on! You're going with me."

With a shriek of pleasure, Perpetua started up at once. She pulled her warmest clothes about her thin figure, then wrapped a bright, red wool scarf about her neck and knotted it with a jerk.

"Now do as the Captain says," Clarissa cautioned, kissing her daughter and placing a red cap upon her blonde hair. With another scarf, Clarissa tied on the cap, making a knot beneath Perpetua's chin.

"Ye Gods, woman, she can hardly breathe," Jared objected, picking Perpetua up as though he were lifting a five-year-old rather than a growing young lady. He carried her out through the snow, put her atop old Lucy and mounted the horse himself.

Perpetua resolved to speak to her father about something he would perhaps understand. Hugging him as closely and tightly as she could, she yelled out, "Father, are boys better than girls?"

She heard him laugh. "It all depends on whether you are a girl or boy, Perpetua. Why do you ask?"

"Well, it's Timothy. You know, the boy who lives next door."

Her father didn't answer right away and Perpetua could feel him stiffen at the mention of Timothy.

"What have you been doing with him!" It wasn't a question but a statement. It made her feel very strange, as though she and Timothy. . . . She could not blurt out how she had felt that time when Timothy had pressed down over her and made her feel so odd and weak inside.

"Never mind, Father. Just never mind. It's nothing."

They had reached the main road now. The snow had been cleared a bit. Jared leapt off old Lucy and helped Perpetua down, lifting her by her arms.

"Now just what have you and Timothy been doing?" He was so big, so fierce. What should she say? How could she explain anything to him?

"Nothing, Father. Please, you're pinching me."

He looked at her for a long moment, then released her.

"I want you to be careful with young men. I don't want anyone . . . well, Perpetua, you are a child. Do you understand? And if I know anything about your young boy friend, he isn't. That fellow must be two years older than you. Fifteen, isn't he?"

She shrugged. She wished she could just disappear into thin air, like angels and witches in storybooks. She knew what she had felt. And it bothered and mystified her. Maybe such a feeling was sinful.

"Now you just let me boost you up again, child. You should play with your dolls. Leave young Timothy alone. Hear?"

The rest of the trip was more pleasant. Her question remained unanswered. Maybe she wasn't supposed to care about anyone, not even her father. But, riding along behind him, she felt very proud.

* * *

Waiting for her husband and daughter, Clarissa wondered why Jared had as yet said nothing about rebuilding the West farm. For her, it symbolized security, the past, ancestry. Instinct kept her from bringing up the subject. He must have other things on his mind.

When Jared returned with Perpetua, they spoke of the "voyage," as Jared called it. She was first with news. "The Peases have a little girl. Her father is in the Pacific. Can you imagine, by the time she sees him, she will be three years old!"

"I met my ship's agent," Jared told her. "My share of the voyage on *The Polar Star* should last us comfortably for a full year." This meant to Clarissa that nothing now stood in the way of rebuilding the farm. Then Perpetua began pleading to go to a spelling-bee. "The winners get to be on the two teams at the next tug-of-war in Cottage City."

Clarissa reveled in the chatter, the noise of a man about her house, the sudden happy lilt in her daughter's voice.

The next morning, Jared departed alone.

The snow had stopped. Perpetua went outside to explore. "I'll be right back. I just want to see the snow shapes."

"What do you mean?"

"You know. When the snow covers everything, it makes new shapes. The whole world is gone. There's nothing but snow!"

Clarissa smiled and nodded her head. When Perpetua had gone out, slamming the door behind her, Clarissa returned to her housework.

Later, with Jared still absent, mother and daughter started their noontime meal. Perpetua was silent, poking at her ham and sipping the cider.

"At least eat your greens, child," Clarissa warned.

Perpetua shoved the plate away, drank the cider in one gulp and sulked. Clarissa stood up and started to clean away the plates. Later, when Jared came home, she'd make sure he gave Perpetua a talking-to. At least some of the burden of discipline should be on his shoulders.

"Come now, child, help me bake the pie." Clarissa spoke sharply.

"Father seems strange."

Clarissa looked quickly at Perpetua, but her daughter averted her eyes.

"What's strange about him?" The flour was dry . . . the apples needed paring. "Here, Perpetua, get to work and don't cut yourself. Cut them into thin pieces and save the skins."

Perpetua didn't respond. First her father had rebuffed her attempt to bring up the subject of Timothy, and now her mother was shutting her off. Her father's homecoming had been the most important event in four years, surely, but there were things bothering her, too. Her pout grew; she wasn't satisfied.

Clarissa meant to find out what her daughter was holding back.

"Of course, he is strange. He is strange even to me. You haven't seen him since you were eight. Can you even remember that far back?"

Perpetua looked straight into her mother's eyes. "I don't mean how he looks. It's how he acts. I expected him at least to pay more attention to me."

"He's just home, child." Clarissa was busying herself with the pots. She didn't look at her daughter.

"Long enough at home to be hugging and kissing you. Don't you think I don't know. How about me?"

Clarissa put down the pot. A sudden chill ran up her spine, made her flush. Had Perpetua heard them that first night? And what about the other times since then? The child's face didn't show resentment, but she certainly stood tall and defiant before her mother, as though she shared something that existed only between women. Was there something else on her mind?

"What ails you, Perpetua?" Clarissa's voice was as kind as she could make it.

"Well, I feel like I can't talk to anyone, now he's home. First him and now you." Perpetua was glad that she had put up a barrier. She would never tell her mother—or her father—about her strange feelings for Timothy. Never!

"I'm here to talk to you whenever you wish. What is it? Are you sick?"

"Sick?" Perpetua paused, then looked out of the window, away from her mother. Her own mother—this stiff, uncomprehending woman! The mating sounds Perpetua heard between her mother and her father, her timidity about speaking of Timothy, made her feel ashamed of herself.

"Sick?" she repeated. "Yes, I'm sick. Sick and tired of being stranded out here when I could be in Edgartown with other girls . . . and boys. Are we doomed to this ice hole forever? I hate this whole mess. I hate being alone . . . with only Timothy for company."

There. She had finally said it, mentioned his name. Would her mother notice? Would she understand? But no. Clarissa only frowned, burdened with other concerns.

"Your father doesn't know what he wants to do. He's gone to scout the village, to see his agent's representative on-island. He has to write letters. He has lots of things he must do now. You just wait, Perpetua. Everything will work out."

"I have things I want to do, too."

"You've been reading too many books, Perpetua." Clarissa looked sternly at her daughter. "It's a good thing he's home. I hadn't realized how willful you've become. Now, if you'll just get on with the apples, we'll have his apple pie ready by dusk."

"Mother?"

"Yes?"

"I hate whales."

"You hate whales? Perhaps I can understand that. What do you love?"

"I hate ships and whales."

"And you love . . . ?" Clarissa put her hand on her rebellious child's hand. Perpetua stopped peeling. Finally, she looked up.

"You."

"And that's all?"

"Should I love Father? I don't even know him. I told you he has no time for me. Well, *I* have no time for him."

Clarissa thought she understood her daughter. She, too, had known loneliness, an eternity of loneliness. Obviously there came a time when a girl needed a father. No one else could substitute. And her child had been lonely, away from other children, made to share in her mother's every mood, becoming part of a dull, dreary existence. No wonder Perpetua had felt disappointed at not being included in the homecoming. They had shut the door on her.

"Tonight, we'll stay up as late as we can," she said. "All three of us. And we'll talk and talk, and you'll be part of it. I promise you. Would that make you happier?"

"He's my father. He should act like one."

"And how does a father act?"

Perpetua frowned, picked up her knife and the half-pared apple and fretted, "I think he's been away so long he won't listen any more. He only knows what he wants. He doesn't know what *we* want. You wait and see."

It was Clarissa's turn to remain silent. She realized there was truth in what her daughter said.

"Let's give him time, Perpetua. Time will tell. It

may not happen fast. Remember, he's been with men doing a man's job. It isn't easy."

"Was he sweet with you last night . . . when you were here alone?"

Clarissa didn't answer that one, but explained urgently, "Your parents are together again. We love one another. We'll make a home for you, all safe and sound. Don't worry. I promise."

"It always ends that way in books. But does it ever happen in real life?"

Suddenly, unable to control her tears any longer, Perpetua threw down the knife.

"Oh—it's always so cold here! I'm so miserable! Why did he have to come back?"

She buried her face in her hands.

"Perpetua, darling—" Her mother came to her quickly, sat down beside her. "Perpetua, look, you've cut your hand."

* * *

But by evening Perpetua's mood had changed, and when Jared returned to the house, his daughter seemed cheerful and talkative. She was scampering about the house like an overgrown puppy. How old was she? Jared tried to remember. She must be thirteen. A young girl's face came to his mind, the eyes dark, the black hair shimmering: Naliki. Perhaps she was a year or so older than his daughter. But so mature, aware of herself and sensual. And what was Perpetua? He hardly knew. Yet she seemed, by comparison, self-conscious, a tall filly, still awkward in her movements, thin in body and immature. Would another man see her as he saw Naliki? Try as he might, Jared could not imagine it. Try as he might . . . what was he thinking? Shaking his head, Jared tried to shut out the memory. And yet she came to him, Naliki, in his arms, atop him, screaming out what she wanted, accepting his manhood with such wanton abandon, and yet a mere girl, a girl like Perpetua.

What was he? How could he endure himself, living with such ever-present memories?

Looking at his daughter, as Clarissa stood by Perpetua in the small cot, tucked her in and knelt to hear her simple prayers, he felt a sense of guilt, watching with Naliki in mind. He remembered, shame mixed with pleasure, how Naliki had felt in his arms, full and womanly, silken and hot to the touch, responsive to his fingers, his body. He envisioned her writhing, grasping him. But it was Perpetua, his own daughter, who lay before him on her stomach, head buried, her body hardly making a wrinkle in the comforter. Clarissa stood up, smoothed her apron, and looked at his strangely agonized face.

"What is it, Captain?"

He brushed his forehead and reached for his pipe, as he always did when he was at a loss for words. "Just thinking, wife. Just thinking."

Clarissa knew he was concerned about where they would live, that he still felt strange at home, almost like a visitor. He must be wondering what Perpetua's life held in store if he didn't resume his position as head of the house. Surely, he felt responsible for his daughter's future on the island. And he must be worrying about her isolation here.

"I know what you are thinking about."

His hand shook, the pipe jerked in his mouth. He looked at his wife quickly. Then, forcing himself to remain calm, he returned to the ritual of breaking in his new corncob. Of course she couldn't know. It was unthinkable that a father should have thoughts of this kind about his daughter. Yet, he hadn't been thinking about Perpetua. Or had he?

He remembered Perpetua the way she had looked ten minutes before, her breasts just budding, her flanks flat, her buttocks tiny, high mounds.

He smiled. No, he hadn't been thinking sinful thoughts about his daughter. She could never become another Naliki. Never.

He blew a fierce cloud of white smoke into the room.

• • •

Some days later, returning from town, Jared announced that he had decided to move to a more central location, closer to Edgartown. The farm, it seemed, was good for only one thing, its land value. Besides, he told his wife, he wanted her near other folks, not up-island with a growing daughter. With great anticipation, Clarissa went house hunting with the Captain. They found an ideal one on South Water Street, but the owner, Mrs. Emma Look, wanted to "stay put" until summer. "A body can't just sell all she's accustomed to and move into a boarding house in the cold of winter."

Thus they bought a parcel of land. But a house would have to be built. One day when they were walking from Main Street northward to the lighthouse, they saw the house they wanted to copy: the old Sullivan house. It stood four stories high, a fine white clapboard with green shutters to close out the winter winds. The windows were made of diamond-shaped glass, sixteen pieces carefully set in place. The doorway was a beauty, enhanced by a classic scrollwork carving. The house faced the street, but was angled to catch the southern air and morning sun. Behind it stood a well-kept garden and a large barn.

"That is the home we'll have," Jared announced. "I know the man who built her. I'll pay him a call."

Clarissa was ecstatic. She had to stop herself from clapping her hands at her husband's words. A new home meant a new life. It was almost like being given her freedom after years of imprisonment.

When Perpetua was taken to see the new house, she tagged along behind her parents with a pout, sullen and unyielding. Wasn't she happy about moving to town? her mother asked. Perpetua didn't answer, just shrugged.

She knew she was supposed to be happy. Why wasn't she?

When the moment came to say good-bye to the old icehouse, to the fields and barn, to Timothy—only then did she realize why she felt so crushed.

Timothy stood in front of his stoop; over his shoulder he carried a huge lobsterpot. He pretended to be indifferent, but Perpetua knew he was not.

Jared and Clarissa were packing things into the cart. Perpetua tried to help. But when she saw Timothy, she had to go to him.

"Good-bye," she whispered.

"You movin', eh?" Timothy wouldn't look at her.

She didn't answer at first. He knew well they were moving. Then why did he feign ignorance?

"Well, Timothy, take my hand. It's proper."

"You are very proper, Perpetua. Everything you do is as your mother and father wish. Don't you ever feel like we did that time on Naushon?"

She stood there and suddenly, to her own surprise, she began to cry. It was so embarrassing! How could she tell him how she would miss him, his roughness, his kindness? The lump in her throat almost choked her. Then, with a half-smile at her own display of emotions and a wave of her hand, she ran off. Like a child! she thought to herself angrily. Just like a stupid child!

Their house would not be finished for a whole year. In the meanwhile, they would move into a boarding house. The parcel of land they had purchased stood near the lighthouse at the far end of North Water Street . . .

Then it happened. All evening Clarissa had felt a sense of impending tragedy, almost as if the wonderful life they had planned was too good to be true. Jared was sitting quietly at the boarding house table. He stirred his fish chowder nervously, gazing blankly into the bowl. His feet kept hitting the heavy table legs.

Leaving ahead of the rest, he walked into the parlor and began studying the *Gazette*, the local newspaper which contained news of shipping. Absorbed in his reading, he did not see Clarissa walk up to him. Her heart skipped a beat when she saw what he was reading. There was only one reason why he would study the comings and goings of ships to and from the island. Somewhere among those arrivals and departures, she was sure, was the name of another ship that would carry her husband. Clarissa's hand trembled.

Perpetua broke the silence, announcing that she wanted to go upstairs to her room and read. Jared nodded his consent. After his daughter had gone, Jared looked up at his wife, then motioned Clarissa to follow him. She saw that his steps were carefully measured as she ascended the stairs. He acted as though what he wanted to say had not yet formed in his mind. His face was set, grim and uncertain.

"What is it, Captain?" she asked, as they entered their bedroom.

He was abrupt. "I leave in two months. A new command. It's *The Horatio*, being outfitted in New Bedford. My ship's agent and I have had meetings. It will pay us well." He stared out of the window, finished with his news, waiting for the shock to wear off.

"Merciful God!" was all she could manage. "I thought you would be home at least a year, that we'd be in our new house . . ."

"If I miss this chance . . ."

"Chance! Is that what our life is going to be? Never planned, like a weather vane moving with whatever new wind blows our way? Jared . . ." She couldn't go on. Her hands were at her throat. She stood up and started walking about the small room. He stood behind her and held her, then leaned down to whisper, "Clarissa, you know I must go. It's my life."

She turned angrily. "Our life, Captain! Ours! Yours and mine . . . and Perpetua's. Had you forgotten her, too?"

"I mean to make this a 'greasy ship,' to bring home enough money to keep us four years at least. After this voyage . . ."

"How long will this *Horatio* be gone? Where will she go?"

He looked away, moved to the window again, feeling the flush which his new guilt had brought him. Out there, far away on the Sandwich Islands, he had betrayed himself . . . and her and . . . "Four years," he whispered. "Only four years more."

He heard her quick sob, went to her and lifted her close to him. Then, seated on the bed, he buried his head between her breasts, shuddering, feeling both a chill and a sudden warmth as he crushed her starched blouse with his bearded face. Her hand touched his hair, then left quickly as if he were a child, too old for a mother's comfort.

A religious man of the sea, where forebodings of disaster and "signs" were seriously taken as warnings from the Lord, Jared felt that somehow her touch upon him might be a message from God, that through her his "sin" had been washed away. Yet, in his heart he knew that the form of Naliki was in that room, would always be with him, her lithe body mocking him, enticing him. There was no other reason for his leaving his wife now, after promising her so many times that he would stay home. Clarissa was crying bitterly, overcome with the news. He struggled to control his voice, to tell her convincingly why he had to go, calm her so that he could feel better inside. Suddenly she stopped crying, wiped her eyes and stared at him. Her eyes seemed to be looking far away, visualizing something. Abruptly, she glanced at the portrait of her late father, the Colonel, as if for advice.

"I'm going with you this time, Captain!" It was a command made by the daughter of a colonel.

"Impossible," he started. "Unthinkable . . . You will not leave this island and our daughter. A whaling ship is no place for a lady, for a woman."

"Captain! I am coming. So is Perpetua! That is all there is to it. I will not stay here alone." She stood directly before him, her face drawn, her eyes seeking his.

Jared knew of the wives who had gone with their men to sea. Though their letters home described the voyages as an adventure, a lark, there was an unspoken undertone in their reports. The dank confinement, the weather, the life aboard a small ship crowded with uncouth men—none of these things was pleasurable. Each voyage was an eternity of solitude.

"Aye, Captain," she replied sharply when he voiced these doubts, "and an eternity at home if I don't go with you. I am with you this time and our child must come, too."

Clarissa listened to her voice and couldn't believe what she was saying. She had looked forward to living a different life without the constant trial of farm work, or the responsibilities of living up-island, far from town. She had seen herself in the great new "Captain's house" on North Water Street, with a servant, a carriage and money in the bank—and, most of all, with Captain Jared West at her side at last. No more loneliness. No more emptiness. Their family together. Now, here she was actually demanding that it all be put off for four more years! Four years? It seemed endless. She would be well past the age of thirty by the time they returned. That meant middle-age! But she'd rather go to the ends of the earth with him than slip into the life of a sea widow again. Wives from the island had gone with their men before. Why not she? Some had even borne children while on board. All women faced such a trial when they chose to be with their loved ones. She could visualize herself in four years if she chose to remain on the island. Here, alone, she would join the small army of aging women without their men who slowly lost whatever grace or refinement they had as the years hardened them.

Jared West was stunned at what she said to him. Her plea was totally uncalled for, completely unexpected. He had money to build their home! It would be ready for her and Perpetua in one year. Just a little while longer in the boarding house, and then they would be settled forever. He would see to the plans for the house before he left the island. He would pay for all the help needed. Clarissa's outburst and sudden turnabout had shocked him. As he studied her serious and strangely set mouth, her eyes glistening with tears, it came to him that perhaps the good Lord was trying to tell him something. Maybe, he thought, with Clarissa beside me and with Perpetua, too, I can forget my great longing for Naliki. So tightly has she wound herself about me that I am truly enslaved. If I were alone, I could never find release or be free of her.

Jared shook himself from his reverie. He was being selfish. He must continue to tell Clarissa what to expect. For the trip would be dangerous. Such a voyage could mean the death of them all. Only if Clarissa insisted, despite all warnings, would he take it as a sign.

"*The Horatio* is bound for the Pacific. After the Horn, we hunt the whaling grounds off South America. Then we stop over at the Sandwich Islands and proceed up to the Arctic. I will be a busy man with no time for you, Clarissa. I am a different man afloat than ashore. There is but a small cabin, wet most of the time, with barely enough room for one man. If you imagine yourself having all the comforts of a home in Edgartown, you will be vastly disappointed. As for Perpetua . . ." He paused, took a deep breath. "Is it fair for a girl her age? She should learn the ways of a young lady here. Clarissa, you are asking too much of all of us."

Clarissa realized she had not thought of her daughter. Jared was correct. Yet, to Clarissa, the child had always seemed like one of those brave crocuses which thrust its tender blooms through the snow, braving the treacherous frosts of spring. Perpetua would be better off with her mother and father the next four years. She could not be left behind.

"We have faced great difficulties together these last months," Clarissa responded. "I know her better than you, Jared. I don't care what argument you use. I will not stay on this island like some cast-off trollop. I am coming with you this time. Both Perpetua and I will be better for it. I have made up my mind."

"Trollop?" he repeated. "You?" The word disturbed him. Naliki, if anyone, was the trollop. He had treated her as one! She had been left on an island, cast off, used, and his conscience now suffered for his treatment of her, although the ache of longing never left him. In his sleep, he still reached for her. As he lay with Clarissa he still saw Naliki in his fantasies.

"The house will wait, Captain. It will have to." Clarissa seemed to be reading his mind. "Where you go, I go," she added.

She was insisting, he realized. She was speaking the word of God. Maybe, through his closeness to her, he could expiate his terrible sin.

He closed his eyes. She stood a foot from him, looking up, watching his mouth above the black beard as words seemed to form. She believed he was in silent prayer.

"I must put off things of the body and return in spirit to the Lord." The words remained unspoken, but his hands shook with strong emotion.

He thought of his original plan for the voyage of *The Horatio*. Yes, he had intended to see Naliki. He admitted it then and there. Now what would he do? Perhaps by the time months went by—with his wife and daughter near him—the thought of Naliki would slowly disappear, as a ship vanishes into a fog bank. But, in agony, Jared realized he would always know Naliki was there. To shut her out of his mind forever, to do it all in one brave and final act, he must see her just once more. One more time with Naliki and then, he believed, he might at last be at peace with himself.

* * *

When Perpetua learned that her next four years would be spend aboard a whaling ship, she felt such a wild mixture of gladness and sorrow that she could not, herself, say whether she was more pleased or disappointed. She had not lost touch with Timothy, for he had been making many trips to Edgartown to get medicine for his ailing mother. She would miss seeing him, for he always seemed to be able to cheer her up, rattling on about his own future and the vast sums of money he would make at sea. Such tales always reminded Perpetua of the fairy tales she had read once, but now put aside for more adult novels. How sure he always was! And how strong he seemed. It was too bad his mother was ill, that his father was now confined to a chair. She would miss him terribly. But when she told him of her family's plans, he became very excited for her.

"Oh, Perpetua, you'll be doing what I want! Imagine looking out every day and night at the ocean! No land, just water. And beneath that water those great, huge whales. I envy you." It hurt her somehow that he didn't feel the impending loss as much as she did. Maybe she was still just a child and didn't understand men yet. She had sighed, as if destiny itself was parting them, then laughed as He painted that ridiculous picture as he saw it, of her running up and down masts, spearing one of those giants and living like an abandoned native on some faraway island. How romantic he was!

Later that day, as she listened to her mother discussing the prospect of the long voyage with her father, Perpetua felt herself caught up in the thrill of being a "voyager," someone who might never come home. Perhaps she would wander about the globe aboard a giant ship and do all the things Timothy had pictured her doing.

She rushed over to Jared, interrupting him in mid-sentence.

"Oh, Father, I'll never get in your way. I'll be like a mouse. I won't ever say a word, or . . ."

"Perpetua!" her mother exclaimed, laughing at her daughter's enthusiasm. "But, darling, I thought you hated whales!"

The look her daughter gave her told her she had meant that secret to be between the two of them. Now that it was out, she added, "I hated ships, too. Whales and ships kept Father away. Isn't that so, Captain?"

"Captain? So I am no longer your dear father, but 'Captain'?" Jared kissed his daughter's forehead. These two women were precious to him: This scrawny, growing child, now becoming an adult, how dear she was to him! And his beautiful, soft wife, so blonde, so spirited. Perpetua reached for him and he felt her slim arms about his neck. What strength she had! Maybe, through their love and trust, he could forget his past, bury his memories so deep they could never be resurrected.

Perpetua began to sob with a mixture of relief and fear. Four long years! Jared calmed his daughter, suddenly feeling tender and understanding. Yet, in his journal that night, he wrote as follows:

"Today we decided not to build the house here until we return from our voyage on *The Horatio,* for I have determined that both my dear wife and sweet child shall come with me. I am elated at the prospect.

Though I do fear that they may suffer from the natural dangers of the voyage, I fear not for their strength and purpose in the disposition of sea life. I have already begun making plans for their comfort aboard. Before I lie down to sleep tonight, I mean to pray for a safe voyage with the three of us together, bound in the holy bonds of the Lord, safe within the sides of a great ship 'til we return to my island." He paused in the writing and then added his customary observations. "The wind blew northerly today. Clear sky. The gusts blew to ten miles-per-hour. I have placed the sum needed in the bank so that when I return, we may enjoy the bounty the Lord has seen fit to give us."

• • •

That night, Clarissa made up her mind to seek out her friend Mathilda and ask her what a wife might expect aboard her husband's ship.

Her friend's words were not reassuring.

"If you can relinquish everything—all the comforts you cherish—your home, friends, sociable companions, the comfort of knowing where you are and what your schedule will be, then go! If you don't care whether you live or die, whether your child receives an education, whether you turn into a dried-up pea pod, then go! If you can live with sweating men, the eternal stink of oil and the touch of grease, the bilge water, the blood and the cold icy sea, then go. If you can uproot yourself and forfeit your comforts just to be with Captain Jared, go with him. But remember, you may never come back—and if you do return, you'll be someone else."

Mathilda paused in her lecture and looked

directly at Clarissa, seeking her eyes with a deep,
searching look that made Clarissa feel uneasy.

"Do you love him?"

Yes, she loved him. It wasn't just because he was
handsome, it was . . .

"Well," Mathilda interrupted her thoughts.
"You're going to have to love him more than your life,
because there will be days and weeks when you'll
hate him for what he did to you. I know. It happened
to me." Mathilda drew in her breath. She was no
longer looking at Clarissa. Her eyes were moist. "He's
promised you what mine did me, before I came home
alone after two years . . . after he died. We would
have a brand-new house, he promised. Look where I
live! We'd have great parties, would go to Boston and
New York. If I wanted to, I could take the steamer
home any time I wanted. I was not to remain aboard
a single day longer than I desired. His promises were
those of a gentleman. How was I to know he could
never keep his word?"

"He died, Mathilda," Clarissa pointed out gently.
"You cannot blame him."

Mathilda's eyes flashed when she answered.

"He was alive aboard ship! He was alive in port! I
learned what men do when they're away from home
and no women are about. Things I never wished to
know—*I learned!*"

"Not Jared. He wouldn't!"

"Why not? Why not Jared? Isn't he a man?"

Clarissa didn't answer. She didn't even want Mathilda to know how Jared had begun to treat her, as
though she were a kind of servant during the day and
a concubine to take at night.

"Yes, he's a man," she answered defiantly. "But
he wants Perpetua and me to be with him."

"Did he ask you? I thought you asked him."

At that moment, the first trace of doubt entered Clarissa's mind. The doubt would come back again, day and night. But she could little guess how this first suggestion of wrongdoing, the first question, would some day gnaw at her soul.

* * *

When the West family took the packet for New Bedford, Mathilda and a host of friends saw them off. As the packet rounded East Chop headed toward the Cape, Perpetua watched the last of the little white houses turn to the same grey-green of the land and soon become absorbed with the rest of their island on the horizon. She could not contain her excitement. Gone were the ever-present scrub oaks, the tall pines of Huzzleton's Head, the wharves decked with huge rusting anchors. Ahead were the spars of the great whaling fleet of New Bedford.

Stepping off, Perpetua and her mother entered a strange world. There were broad, open wharves, supporting ships in various stages of being refitted—some still discharging their cargoes.

The noise of many men shouting and running caused Perpetua's mind to whirl. She looked high above at the tall masts where men aloft were bending sails. She felt a breeze from the nearby Acushnet River, and with it came unfamiliar smells: seaweed drying upon caskets of oil on the hot wharf, tar being applied to the decks, ropes and rigging carrying the salt hot smells of their making. Cords of wood, caskets of water, unfamiliar whaling gear and many anchors seemed to surround her.

Her father pointed out *The Horatio.* The ship seemed large among the others.

"She's a sperm whaler," Jared said, as if that ex-

plained it. "My command," he added proudly, though
she certainly knew that. "Come, I must see the agent."

At that moment, as they started down the broad
wharf, the breeze picked up. It seemed to circle about
her mother's head, lifting her bonnet and whirling it
away toward the water. Luckily the bonnet landed at
the feet of a sailor who was just coming aboard with
his sea chest perched on his right shoulder. With unusual grace, he lowered the chest, retrieved the bonnet and dusted it off. Then he approached and
handed it with great deference to Captain West.

"Here you are, sir. Your fine lady's bonnet."

The lean man smiled, bowed to Clarissa and
walked off.

"What a nice man," Perpetua remarked to her
mother. Clarissa was busily tying the ribbon securely
under her chin. Her face was strangely flushed. The
man was walking toward one of the office buildings
that stood alongside the wharf. Abruptly, he stopped,
turned back and cast a quick but devouring look at
Perpetua before entering the shingled shack. The old
building bore the weathered sign "Tobias & Smith,
Agents."

"He's signing on a ship . . . ," allowed Jared,
carefully watching the man as he shut the door behind him. "I could use a decent sort like that. They
don't often come with manners, I tell ye!"

Clarissa didn't speak. She held more tightly to
her duffel bag and clutched Perpetua's hand as if she
had suffered a shock of some kind. Clarissa's eyes
were downcast, her face still red.

The moment she stepped inside the office, Perpetua felt overwhelmed by the crowd of men, the smell
of their bodies, the murky air. The desk before them
seemed everyone's target. Her father elbowed his way
through and stood before a man with a long beard,

squinting eyes and a pen in hand. "Ah!" he spoke, looking up. "It's you, Jared! Now let's get underway here." Jared motioned his family outside. Perpetua looked about and saw the man who had rescued the bonnet standing off to one side—another seaman looking for a berth.

Outside again in the clean air, Perpetua and her mother sat on a bench. The wharf was a madhouse of men, horse-drawn vehicles and casks. Her mother spoke quietly, as if trying to take her mind off something that bothered her.

"You see how well your father is received? He's like a king, they say. A ship's master is in full charge once he steps aboard. He has power of life or death over all."

"Not over *me*," disagreed Perpetua. "He's just my father."

"You'll do what he says on deck, and fast, you silly goose. I want you to remember, and remember well, that every man aboard snaps to it for him. You mind your manners and obey as they do."

"Does he flog his men?"

"Not in these days. But he's been known to tie a man to the mast."

As Perpetua watched Jared approach, a logbook and other papers bulging from his greatcoat pockets, she tried to imagine him lashing a seaman to the mast. Look how tall he was, how fierce with that black beard, his cap aslant and that hawk of a nose! Beneath his shaggy, overhanging brows, his eyes defied any response. There was a faraway look in them.

Without a word, he waited for Perpetua and her mother to gather their things. Then he stalked before them toward the ship which would be their home for four years.

CHAPTER 4

Once aboard *The Horatio*, Perpetua was introduced to her quarters, a cabin so small she could cross it in three long strides. Though the ship, with its tall masts and rigging, had appeared enormous from the wharf, her heart sank as she thought of it being her home for four years. The road to riches apparently was confined to a twelve-foot cell.

While her mother fussed about, making noises of disappointment, Perpetua went to look through the small, narrow portholes. Instead of the vistas she had been accustomed to on the Vineyard—lilac bushes, meadows, rambling stone walls—she saw nothing. The salt encrustation from the sea had made the windows opaque.

"Perhaps the horsehair sofa will fit at the end here, lengthwise," her mother speculated. "But I'll never find a place for the hand organ!" Clarissa had changed her clothes, leaving her best dress on the bunk. She now wore a plain dress of blue which brought out the color of her eyes. "Take off your coat, Perpetua. We must unpack." Clarissa tried to force a smile. "This is our home now." Then, thinking of something to get their minds off their disappointing cabin, she suggested, "Let's take a look around. Let's explore this . . . ship."

So they began where they were. The aft cabin—the Captain's—was a lean room lit by a skylight. Looking up through the skylight, Perpetua and Clarissa could see the ship's wheel. Across the stern end of the cabin were cubbyholes. Forward was a writing desk for the Captain, fixed to a partition. Leaving the Captain's cabin, they followed a narrow corridor to the officers' mess. A few steps more and they met the housing for the mizzenmast. Nearby was a table equipped with "fiddles," little rails which prevented the plates from rolling off when the ship was underway. Farther along the corridor, they opened a few doors and peeked into small cabins with upper and lower berths jammed with the men's gear.

"There's nothing homey, I'd say," murmured Clarissa. "It's so . . . unyielding. Nothing where a woman can make improvements!"

Her hand went unconsciously to her daughter's shoulder. Perpetua held her mother close. For the first time in her life, Perpetua felt she could give support when her mother needed it. It was so like her mother to try to pretty things up.

Perpetua spoke soothingly. "We're as good as those whaling men, Mother. We'll make it. You'll see!"

Later, as evening drew on, Perpetua asked permission to stop unpacking long enough to get a breath of air. Feeling freedom approach with every step, she climbed the ladder to the deck.

The Horatio had settled in for the night. Dusk had brought quiet to the wharves and shops. One man stood alone on deck looking out to the river. Perpetua recognized him as the man who had rescued her mother's hat.

His head turned as she approached. She saw that he held a book in his hands. To her own surprise, Perpetua spoke spontaneously.

"Hello! My name is Perpetua West and this is my father's ship. What's your name?"

"Everett Norton," he replied pleasantly, with a bow, "at your service."

"Thank you for helping my mother. If your name is Norton and you come from the Vineyard, I must know about a hundred of your relatives."

"That you must, Miss Perpetua." He smiled and added, "Or at least half a dozen!"

He was very tall, almost as tall as her father, but he was lean and his open blue shirt exposed flat chest muscles. A blue, polka dot kerchief was wrapped about his neck. He casually took a pipe from his pea jacket pocket and filled it with pungent tobacco. "Isn't it a great time of the day, child?" he went on in a singsong kind of voice, strong but gentle in tone. He must have been about twenty-eight. Perpetua thought his clean-shaven face, strong square jaw and bright black eyes made him look very handsome. He was almost too good-looking for a rough sailor. Puffing at his pipe, he gazed across the water to the red sun dipping into the horizon.

"That's not an ordinary sun this evening," he observed in his calming voice, his brows together. She waited for him to explain.

"When she is red like that, it indicates fair weather. Red sun at night, sailor's delight. Red sun in the morning, sailors take warning."

"Did you really come from the Vineyard, sir?" she asked, wondering at his accent. "You don't sound like a Yankee, nor look like one."

"I have lived in France for many years. I shipped out on a six-masted freighter from Boston, ending up

in Lyons, France. There I accumulated a lot of fine
lace and brought it home to the Vineyard. I made a
small fortune. This would have allowed me to . . ."
He looked away. She thought his face seemed drawn
for a moment. Or was it the sideways light which appeared to sharpen the hollows beneath his
cheekbones? He stood in sharp silhouette at the ship's
side, his back to the rail. Then he turned his back on
her. Impulsively, she reached out for his arm as she
might reach out to comfort a playmate her own age,
but when he turned toward her again, she was reminded that he was a man and a stranger. His face
composed again, he went on, "I left for France to
make my fortune. Behind, I left a girl. I always knew
she would be waiting for me. She was almost as
pretty as you, Perpetua," his voice lowered. "But
when I came back, I found she had already married.
That was a long time ago. More than ten years ago,
in fact. I was not yet twenty then. Do I look so old to
you?"

She shook her head, loosening her hair. How she
wished she could let him know she understood. His
sad story was as tragic as a novel. But before she
could respond to his romantic tale, he cleared his
throat and said, "You'd better go below. Mrs. West
will be worrying about you." With that, he turned
and walked toward his station at the gangway.

There he stood, beneath the hanging lamp, his
face unreadable.

During this time, Clarissa had been below deck
in deep thought about the same man. What was he
doing aboard her husband's ship? She had reason to
concern herself about his being so near, so much in
evidence. She made up her mind to avoid him as
much as possible. Though the whaler was small, Clarissa and her daughter were supposed to stay within

certain boundaries aboard ship. Most wives aboard
their husband's commands had free movement only
about the afterdeck and cabin, and the rules that applied for Clarissa would hold for Perpetua, too. At
meals, Clarissa knew, she and her daughter would eat
ahead of the officers. Their table, always supplied
with the very best food aboard, would be shared only
by the Captain. Perhaps there was little chance of
running headlong into the man after all.

Clarissa breathed a sigh of relief. And wondered,
at the same instant, why her relief was so strangely
mixed with a feeling of disappointment.

* * *

Everett Norton was a man whose deepest
feelings lay beneath the surface. He rarely saw himself as a major influence affecting the affairs about
him; yet he knew exactly where he was going. Returning to the Vineyard after his exploits in France,
he had discovered that his beloved Clarissa was "up-
island"—"sout' in Chilmawk," as the islanders called
it—and married to Jared West. Not only was Norton
unable to accept the fact, he was unable to communicate with her. His only recourse was to get drunk and
stay drunk. Or so it had seemed to him.

In thinking back, he knew that he had created a
shell about his feelings. He had courted Clarissa, certainly. But he had not actually proposed, nor spoken
to her father, nor slipped the expected ring upon her
finger. At eighteen, Clarissa had been kissed soundly
by him, with all the fervor a man could summon. He
had interpreted that wordless, passionate embrace as
a complete commitment of body and soul. He remembered her young body against his own as if she meant
it to stay there.

But more was required, much more than one heated, silent embrace. And in trying to make that next commitment, something had failed him. Sudden impulse was not his nature. In school, in business and even aboard ship, he found himself waiting for others to act, so that he could counteract, intercede, play the politician to smooth opposing sides. He would have made a good attorney. He had left the island, bent on making his fortune, setting himself a private task that would make him worthy. He had looked into Clarissa's beautiful blue eyes as if to remember them that way forever. He had announced his desire to come back for her, "soon." And had seen her only once more.

Having scanned the foreign newspapers, and after talking to dry-goods merchants in New Bedford and Boston, Everett Norton became convinced that French lace—from certain areas in that romantic country—would be in great demand, were it to be offered at the right price. Norton determined to proceed to France, where he would arrange for supplies of fine lace to be shipped to merchants in Eastern cities. He took all his money from the bank. And before his departure, he spoke to Clarissa about his trip and their future. They were at the wharf.

"I'm heading for the South of France. Clarissa, I will come back to you a rich man. I must. I have nothing now to offer you except my love. I couldn't take you from the grand house in Edgartown unless I could offer you at least some comforts, and the promise of a future. The Colonel would never approve of the wedding. You are young. Can you wait?"

"Just bring me a lace handkerchief," she had replied, her voice concealing laughter, amusement at his seriousness and dedication. Such promises had never been offered her before. "And when you hand it to

me, all tied up neatly, and there's a look in your eyes
that tells me what I now want to know, I'm yours."

And after that? For years he had not written a
word to her. He had returned at last, but by then
there was another man, a man named Jared, and a
young child with the strange name, Perpetua.

What faced them both was his doing. Certainly
he had made a small fortune in lace. It was almost assuredly banked in Boston. But without her, he had
wandered without a future. Finally he had heard of
Captain West's voyage, that she would go with him.
Such information was easy to hear about if one lingered around the docks. What would happen, Norton
wondered, if he shipped out on *The Horatio*?

True to his nature, he made the decision to go
along on the voyage without any clear understanding
of his own intentions. At least he would see her, be
near her. And who knows? He had read enough philosophy to know that while man supposes, God dis-
poses. It was worth the risk. The pleasures of being
aboard *The Horatio* four years would at least give
him the opportunity to find out what was the matter
with him. Above all, he couldn't stand being rebuffed
without knowing why. And there would be an end to
the torture of his imagination. For he still imagined
her as the girl she had been, tall, leggy, and with the
most beautiful eyes and hair of any young woman he
had ever met. And there had been something else
about her, he thought, standing on that night
watching the gulls and the tiny fish astern.

The girl he'd courted had a dedication to life, a
verve which made everything seem worth trying.
With her, he knew he could have gone to the top in
anything he wished, for she would have supplied the
energy and the reason for his ambition.

● ● ●

In three months aboard ship, Everett's friendship with Perpetua began to grow almost as though their closeness was foreordained. He saw so much of the young Clarissa in her daughter. Like many a man who dares not face things head on but prefers to await for events to lead him, he had not approached Clarissa. God knows she hadn't changed. Only now every talent, every blessing had been enriched. And her body had matured, become more beautiful. It was obvious that she and West were no longer Romeo and Juliet, and also apparent that Jared and Clarissa's years apart had not been happy ones for her. He felt that though West might dominate Clarissa, the stern Captain could not reach the soul of the woman—nor would he, ever. Living in such close quarters, who could help but know that their cabin contained a man who constantly forced himself upon an unwilling woman.

One thing was certain to Everett Norton, as it would be to any man who had observed women. He knew Clarissa had been faithful to her marriage vow during her forced celibacy of four and a half years. This faithfulness might have turned off her natural desires and left her as cold and frigid as a widow.

Could this be the reason the Captain had to force himself upon her? In any case, Norton knew that his own courtship might take a long while, if he should ever succeed at all.

That night he spoke to Perpetua about Shakespeare's works, which she had found him reading.

She spoke enthusiastically, "You always make things sound so interesting. Like tales from a fairyland." As she looked at Norton, she wondered who in the world wouldn't want such a handsome husband. Who wouldn't have waited a century for him. Who on Martha's Vineyard—holding the memory of this tall, vibrant man—could have allowed another to win her heart away? Though Norton never spoke of himself or related the name of the heroine in his own lost romance, Perpetua knew that he was a sad, lonely man.

"Do you love your mother?" he asked suddenly.

"Of course I do. Why do you ask?"

It was a sudden change of subject.

"Because mothers are always close to their daughters for a while, that is, until they grow up and become young women. Then the day comes when a grown woman finds it's her father whom she loves the most."

"I'll never be close to the Captain."

Everett looked at her, a squint in his eyes as if he were trying to peer into her soul. "I've heard you call him 'the Captain' and not 'Father' or 'Papa' like other youngsters. Isn't that a bit formal between daughter and father?"

Perpetua didn't answer. She had been sketching the sea birds and there was an open pad in her hand. Now, aimlessly, she began drawing concentric circles with her pencil.

"Pull in that lip, Perpetua. It makes you look stubborn."

"I am stubborn," she replied and stuck her lip out farther. She hoped her father would die! Sometimes, when he went up the mast, she imagined him falling, ending up dead on the deck. Should such a thing happen, she knew she would feel sorry for being so vicious and mean. Her backbone was stiff. She felt stifled by Norton's penetrating look.

"Why do you call him 'Captain'?" he asked gently.

"He is. Isn't he?" There was harsh anger in Perpetua's voice. She blushed, but her eyes blazed. He deserved the rebuke—this man, with all his questions! Did she detect a smile on his lips?

Everett turned away and sniffed heavily of the freshening wind. He pulled a pair of glasses from the case that hung around his neck, scanned the west for a moment, then with a sigh lowered the glasses.

"That he is, Perpetua," he went on, "and for months you have been staying as far away from him as you can. It's bound to hurt your mother. That's why I ask."

"I always stay as far away from him as I can. And I've never been near him, either. Not ever. He was never home all my life. If I hurt my mother, I don't mean to." Perpetua thought about it for a moment. She knew she was hurting her mother. But why did her mother allow the Captain to do those horrible things to her? Perpetua shuddered. She didn't want to think about it. Her mother hadn't asked her why she never addressed her father. Of course, everyone on board was afraid of the Captain and maybe her mother thought it was contagious.

Everett was talking. "So . . . I know if you love your mother, you won't hurt her feelings. After all, it's trying enough for a wife to sail with her husband. Anyone with half an eye can tell that you're breaking your mother's heart."

"You must be pretty able, Mr. Norton, to know when someone's heart is broken. Are you a surgeon, sir?" She hoped her little laugh would soften the sarcasm. How did Everett Norton know how her mother felt? Putting on paper what she could not speak aloud, her penciled circles became interwined hearts. He looked at her as if trying to penetrate what lay behind her lowered eyes. His frown became a smile. White teeth gleamed in the sun. His tanned face was so lean and handsome.

"It's in her face, child, and in her manner when you ignore the pleading in the Captain's eyes. She's begging that you'll be more kind."

"You watch them very carefully, Mr. Norton, I do say." Perpetua did not wish to look at him, half fearing that he could read the thoughts forming in her mind. "They are only together when below . . . unless you spy on them when they walk the deck together at sunset. Or do you ever see my mother alone? I mean . . ." She stopped at the idea which struck her. Breathlessly, she looked up at him to see if his face betrayed a sign. But he was staring out to sea. She felt cold, then hot. The pencil in her hand moved blindly, drawing two hearts in a row, putting initials inside those hearts. A thousand things became clear. Why of course! Everett had started to call her mother "Clarissa" that first night, then changed his words to "Mrs. West." Could it be? Was it really her mother who had broken his heart? This man who knew so much about broken hearts and who knew so much about how her mother felt. The hearts, like valentines, were finished, a pair of initials carefully placed in each.

That would explain Everett's deep interest in her mother's feelings. It would explain why her mother had seemed to flustered when Everett had retrieved Clarissa's bonnet on the wharf in New Bedford. And—of course!—Her father didn't know! How could he? The Captain had swept her mother off her feet. In all the retellings of that episode in Clarissa's life, never had her mother mentioned Everett Norton's name.

Suddenly, her mother's past took on a new aspect. So shy, so prim, and all the time she had concealed a love affair with someone else before her father! How *could* she? She, who often said how much she loved the Captain! Shocked at what she was thinking, Perpetua turned to gaze in the face of the man who stood behind her. "Judge not lest ye be judged," her mother had always told her when she became critical. Good heavens, what a hypocrite! And this man Perpetua had begun to care for, was he going to upset her family, ruin her life?

"What are you doing?" asked Everett Norton, who had silently moved behind her, looking over her shoulder.

She looked over her shoulder at him. His eyes took in the initials "C.W." and "E.N." Her heart began to race, for she knew he saw that his secret was known to her.

Everett didn't move. A voice rang out from the masthead.

"Blows! To the starboard!"

Everett still didn't move. He just stood still, as if he had not even heard the lookout's cry. And these were the words they had all been praying for during the long, dreary months!

Suddenly, Everett turned and grasped the rail so tightly that Perpetua thought he might wrench it from the deck. She went to him. "Am I right, dear Everett?" she asked, for that is what she called him to herself.

"Where away?" came a shout from her father, aft of them. The men scurried to their places on deck.

"Child, there's the cry! Let me be!" And Everett hurried along the deck to his station.

Perpetua watched the crew as the men busily lowered two of the three port whaleboats, each forty-feet long. One remained, tied up on the starboard, and there were two spares stored below.

There were loud cries, dashing about and general confusion, yet Perpetua was too upset by her own thoughts to become excited about the sighting of a whale. The hunt had begun. There was no way to end the feelings that tormented her now. This was the only way her father's fortune was to be made. When the ship was filled with the whale's oil, they could go home. But not until then, unless . . . for the first time, Perpetua realized that Everett could be dangerous. And compassion for her father crept over her even as she watched him order the men about, bellowing his commands.

One boat was already underway, heading towards the whale. One small spout, about three feet high, could be seen rising in a proud fountain over its head. She felt sorry for the poor thing, destined to be killed by all those men.

Perpetua watched as the boat drew close. She heard the cheer of the men, then saw the head boatsman let go the harpoon he held aloft, plunging into the flank of the whale with mighty force. Shouts from the whaleboat rang out, then a command, "Stern all!"

"They're in for a 'Nantucket Sleighride,' I fear," said a voice near her. She turned to see the old, bent man with a wooden leg, the sailor called "Old Talbot." Though they all respected him for his age and experience, the leg kept him from the whaleboats. "Y'see, Miss Perpetua," he grunted, "that thar sperm is about to tow that boat to kingdom come, the way the line's a-runnin' out. Then the next boat'll take the line and add its weight, so's the sperm is haulin' two boats . . . Watch 'em go!"

She saw Everett, in the second boat, grab the line from the stern of the first whaleboat and make it fast to his bow.

"Thar they go, by Godfrey!" yelped Old Talbot, stamping his wooden peg upon the deck.

"Is he . . . I mean, are the men in danger, sir?"

Perpetua asked. Yet she was thinking of only one man as she asked it.

"Not as yet, lass. They yank on the line when the sperm slows, and haul it in 'til they get as close to the critter as they kin. Then the mate in command will get nigh him and lance the sperm." Even as Talbot spoke, Perpetua saw a tall, heavy-set man stand, raise a lance and drive it deep into the body of the surfaced whale.

She screamed in fright as the huge beast turned on its tormentors, passed under the boat, heaving it on its side for a terrible moment. As the whale sounded, finding a new direction, the men, waiting, backwatered their whaleboats and let them swing about. They hugged the gunwales, squatting low. Then, suddenly, the whale rose to the surface. It ceased struggling. Blood colored the white spume of the sea. It turned toward the direction of the wind and Perpetua saw its fluke raised as if signaling its distress. The whale eased on its side and floated quite still.

"She's a goner. Sure sign, when that happens," explained Old Talbot, now moving upwind, sending Perpetua the stink of his body.

"Matters 'bout whales are a particular interest to me, lass. Eyein' from this distance, I kin tell her length and tonnage and the oil she'll most likely bring. It's a good deal like the measurements of a woman, you might say. Everyone knows a thirty-six-inch bust makes a proper armful, 'n' I know full well that this here sperm is a big one, too."

With the boats lying alongside, the thing looked larger than an elephant. The harpooners raised a signal flag, known as the "dead whale" sign.

"She'll bring 'bout a hunnerd barrels of oil," Old Talbot allowed. "Now they'll lower the cuttin' stage yonder, 'longside the ship. See, they got her over the whale now."

Perpetua watched them. It seemed inconceivable that so few men on such a small boat could bring such a mighty beast to its death. Some of the men cut a large hole in the blubber behind the whale's head and slipped a heavy hook in the hole.

"They'll cut the head off 'n' haul her aft," Old Talbot continued, delighted to be informing his Captain's daughter, and pleased at scaring her with his gory details.

"Them men with longboots standin' on the cuttin' stage are a-scorin' the blubber first with five big swathes."

They were using what Perpetua saw were long, sharp spades, easily carving into the dead hulk. Then the tackle begin raising the hook and peeling the blubber from the whale like birchbark from a tree. Perpetua thought she was going to be sick. Old Talbot's smell added to the general stench. She walked away to fresher air, then looked aloft. Strips of blubber were being raised to the maintop.

"Up thar they'll use a razor-sharp boardin' knife and slash that thar blubber into 'blanket' pieces, thin as yer own flesh." He grinned.

She watched, horrified at the speed with which the once proud mammoth had begun to disappear. The main hatch was opened to receive the thinner pieces below deck.

"Jes' so ye'll know, once 'n' fer all, down thar the blubber's carved agin' into small or what we call 'horse' pieces, then up on deck they come fer mincin'. Mind how ye carve a slice of bacon? Well that's about the size of it. Then these minced pieces are ready to be forked into the try pots where they're boiled."

She watched Everett approach. His left arm was bound up with a band of white cloth. Old Talbot moved off. "You're hurt!" cried Perpetua, rushing to Everett's side. "What happened?"

He held up his good arm. "Nothing serious, little one. I seem to have been struck by something when the whale turned on us. Might have been a lantern keg."

She took his arm gently and looked to see whether the winding cloth was secure. "Where does it hurt?"

He shrugged his shoulder and grinned. His smile made Perpetua relax and forget about the smell beginning to rise from the trying pots below.

"I see Old Talbot's been telling you all about it!" Everett changed the subject. "Right now they're cutting into the head. They'll get about thirty barrels of the purest oil from the case, which is on top. Beneath it is what we call 'junk'—oily, with ligaments about a foot thick, called 'white horse.'"

He saw her pale face, how she clutched the stay, and he swiftly changed the subject.

"You know, Perpetua, your mother is a lot like the California grey whale or devil-fish, 'cause she will stand by her calf when it's in danger. If you injure the calf of a devil-fish, the mother will fly into a rage that is awful to behold. She'll tackle the boats and smash them or drive them ashore. Though she's liable to kill her own calf in doing it, she'll flap her flukes and fins and try to destroy her enemy."

"How does she know the enemy?" Perpetua asked. And suddenly she herself felt the danger . . . so close.

Everett shrugged.

"Who can say?" His smile cut Perpetua as deeply

as if he had patted her on the head. So condescending!

"Does she know?" Perpetua heard her own voice go shrill, felt the tears coming. "*Does* she . . . ?" She couldn't go on. He bent closer, trying to understand, and suddenly, there it was again, that feeling of imminent peril. She flung around. "Oh, go away!"

Everett stared at her a moment, opened his mouth, closed it again, bowed to her and went below.

Why was this man preaching to her? He had nothing but sinful intentions towards her mother! Perpetua knew one thing very clearly. She disapproved of them all—her father, mother and Everett. And none of them really cared what happened to her.

Recklessly, Perpetua walked to the shrouds and grasped the first knot. Then, trying her strength, she pulled herself up hand over hand until she was dangerously high, her long legs wrapped about the stay, her heart beating, hands raw. Then she looked down. The ship looked like a toy beneath her, the tiny men entirely unaware of the girl who swung above them in the shrouds.

No one seemed to care. Aloft or below, she went unnoticed. Why shouldn't she think of leaping outward, away, into the rich, green sea?

She began her downward trip, hand over hand, as she had seen the men do. She became one of them. Gone was the child. Perpetua, able and fearless, descended the ratlines fearlessly. On the deck, unnoticed after her daring exploit, she hid the bloodied palms of her hands, tried to forget the tear in her dress and walked with great dignity to the cabin.

CHAPTER 5

Perpetua felt she was the only one on board who wasn't involved in killing whales and cutting them to pieces. The voyage had been successful, her father told her after they had been at sea for seven months. "It won't be long before we get into the thick of them." What a ghastly, inhuman way to make a living! Perpetua determined she'd never marry a whaling man, nor anyone who killed anything, for that matter.

Everett Norton came to mind constantly. He was a whaling man, yet he seemed so different from the other sailors.

Her friend. Or was he? She couldn't make up her mind. He had always been gentle with her, so different from her father's way with her mother, so different from the Captain's stern, foreboding authority that he wielded over his men. Maybe, just maybe, Perpetua could continue being close to Everett. At least he would talk to her, tell her details of the whaling industry. No one else ever seemed to have time for her!

One day, when he was standing on the foredeck, she could not hang back any longer. She had to speak with him, find out what he was thinking. She came to the rail beside him, put her hands on the halyards and looked out to sea.

"A fine day," Everett remarked casually, as naturally as if they had just parted yesterday. Yet it had been many long days. Was he mocking her? Perpetua's hands shook with repressed anger and she spoke quickly, cold and unfriendly in her response.

"I was wondering what 'gamming meant. I mean, why do whale ships speak with only one another and not others?" She was really curious about the habit of passing ships, some of whom drew near enough to speak with one another, others to share captains and mates. The custom was for a mate to stay aboard and host the mate from the sister whaler. On the other ship, the captains met to compare their successes.

"A ship at sea is an island," explained Everett, "each with her own secrets. In each line of shipping, it's a different manner of greeting. A man-o-war goes through a series of ensign-duckings and flag-raisings, bowings and scrapings, like a dandy on a city street, and meanwhile each is criticizing the other's rig like merchantmen do. As for whalers, they sing out 'How many barrels?' which is the nut of it all. Now look at us honest and hospitable whalers! In any decent weather we 'gam' upon sighting. It truly means a meeting between whaling ships. Sometimes we meet a weary crew, out for four years. Our men at the masthead pass so near to theirs you could jump from one to the other."

As Everett spoke, shouts came from three mastheads at once.

"Blows! To the lee! It's a sperm and she goes under!"

Everett turned away, his companion forgotten, and made for the boat.

Hours later, Perpetua, in her cabin, heard the cries. "She's fluked and spouts thick blood! Stern all!"

She held her pillow to her nose, sniffing deeply of her mother's violet eau-de-cologne. The odor of whale oil and blubber was so heavy, cloying. There was no escape from it, nor from the knowledge she was a part of the nauseating experience. This bloody slaughter, this awful stench, was not the great adventure she had imagined.

* * *

On past sailing trips, Jared had reserved his cabin to himself. Now, with his wife and child aboard, there seemed no end to the ducking and weaving, the "pardon me's" and "may I come in's?" So he often took to the deck. There the wind would wash the sweat away. The night world enclosed him with the privacy he needed to think and to dream. With his day filled with action, the inner man had little time to examine his thoughts. The deck of his ship offered him this solace, wrapped in the night, with others asleep or standing a quiet watch.

Jared faced the warm westerly this night, restless because he had not found solace with his woman.

"Clarissa," he had whispered, but she hadn't responded. Now he paced slowly, unaware of where he was. He breathed deeply, full of his dreams. In his mind, he was back at Maui with Naliki.

He envisioned her against the moon rays which shivered across the waters: The soft, jutting breasts, the brown-tipped nipples, the slender, silken legs entwining themselves about his body. In the gentle night, Jared's mind was entranced with the memory of their clasp; he could almost feel her, reaching and twisting under him, sucking him into her eager, hungry body.

He wondered if she remembered him. His last visit had been long ago, at least as the girls on Maui thought of time.

Time. There was a factor in his life! So much of it spent alone, so few hours with people. Ashore, fighting the natural urges within him, he became frustrated from trying to obey The Ten Commandments. And on ship there was no one to confide in. Later, writing in the ship's log, he would give the whaler's position. He would note the wind direction and write of the day's catch. No other word. No word denoting emotion or passion. Above all, no mention of a girl named Naliki.

"Ah, passion," he philosophized to himself. He knew that passion was elastic, that it came suddenly, then was gone like the sun on the sea's horizon, leaving him wondering over its great strength, its sudden disappearance. He always thought of Naliki and of how she had enchanted him with her frenzy, her widespread thighs, her dark, almond eyes. No other woman was like her.

Clarissa? Her needs were not at all like Naliki's. She was his wife. She was a good woman.

Jared West walked slowly across the deck. He felt cheated. He had had Naliki. He didn't have her now. In a way he hated Clarissa for the morality of marriage bonds and Perpetua for her dependence. Only these two kept him from Naliki. He didn't consider himself hypocritical or unjust. Fate had been terribly unkind, baiting him beyond endurance. If Naliki hadn't been forced upon him in all her violent beauty, Jared would have found another Polynesian, as pleasant and utterly forgettable as those who had come before. They didn't count. Naliki did! Others were born and brought up to drain the strength of men whose desires overflowed after so many years. It had happened to every captain, every pioneer of every South Sea island. And the New England women waited as did the wives of Crusaders, with iron girdles locked about their loins. The Bible, the toil, the gossip of the other, waiting wives were the lock and key. No wonder these waiting women sometimes looked like men, Jared thought. Most of them became like nuns, with devotion only for the spiritual man. For them the unseen guiding hand of Christ took the place of the rough handling and the coaxing of mortal man.

Jared realized that Clarissa had remained beautiful and desirable. He recalled the day after his return home, finding her there in her nightgown, her body so tempting beneath it, an unfamiliar female there for the taking, morally correct, obedient, seemingly willing. He hadn't quite understood his own violent attack. But it was his right! Even though he thought of Naliki when touching Clarissa's body, when entering her in one thrust, penetrating the ungiving body, he had enjoyed his right. She had cried out, always did, could not know of the inner caress, the wild pleasure, the flailing and moaning of man against woman, each taking equal pleasure in ecstasy. How could she know? She was the daughter of that austere man, Colonel Jeremy Tottle. Imagine drawing sperm from a man such as he! Why, Jared realized, Clarissa barely abided him! But it wasn't his fault.

No wonder he had fallen in love with Naliki, body, soul and mind.

There was a glow on the eastern horizon. Jared realized he had walked the dogwatch away. It was time for his morning ritual. Each morning at five his men would gather while Jared, stripped naked,

awaited a dousing. Cold sea water was thrown over
him in bucketsful. The watching men laughed. They
thought him daft. This kind of cleanliness seemed ex-
treme to them. They did not know that the water was
needed to cool the fever of a tortured mind while it
cleansed the grime from Jared's skin.

*   *   *

It was a few weeks later when Perpetua finally
spoke alone to her father. The two had not been together except when he came below to eat or change,
and on these occasions, her mother was ever present.

Jared was a man, and there were things Perpetua
needed to know from him. She would find the Captain on deck just before dawn, she knew.

Jared stood aft, watching the stars as the ship
scudded along, the man near him holding fast to the
wheel, intent on the course he had to follow. The tiller touched his waist as the ship yawed in the waves,
then the man pushed it from him to keep the ship on
course. Jared seemed hypnotized by the helmsman's
movement. To Perpetua, this seemed a good time to
speak out.

"Father," she called from three steps away.

"Aye, Perpetua. Come close. I can't hear you."

She stepped nearer, took hold of the rough
material of his sleeve. "Can I speak with you?"

"What is it, lass? Out with it quickly."

"Oh, it's nothing, just . . ."

Jared walked slowly away from the stern, guiding
Perpetua to a secluded spot near the mainmast.

She looked up at him, remembering how she had
tried, once before, to speak with him about things
that were close to her heart. Now it was too late to

change her mind. She started out with a simple question.

"We've been gone from the Vineyard for eight months, Mother tells me. Do you think I've grown much since then?"

"Daughter, it'll be two years before we reach Maui. And by then, Perpetua, you'll be filled out more. Yes, you'll be a big girl then, well-nigh a woman and, I shouldn't doubt, as when I met your dear mother."

"I thought she was eighteen."

"Aye, she was, Perpetua. But you've grown faster than she; perhaps you've had to. Being sixteen will put you on the edge of maturity, child. You'll have to be speaking with your mother on these matters." He looked away, as if thinking of something in the past.

"We have spoken . . . in a way," replied Perpetua, lowering her eyes. "But there are things I would ask of you, Father." Did she only imagine that his back stiffened at these words?

"For example?"

"When I am courted—what shall I do?"

There, she had said it. She could not bear to look at her father. It seemed ages before he replied.

"I can tell you that when the times comes, when you have feelings about a young man, you'd better come to me and to your mother, Perpetua. Young men ashore will be hardened seamen, used to the trollops they meet in ports and on the islands. The kind of man meant for you is still at home. On the Vineyard, there are many good men whose families have set them up in business, solid men with a future, not seamen, or the rough types who've settled on the mainland. The island men will be seeking a good wife by the time we get home. By then, you'll have a fine dowry settled on you, too. Now, mind that bell? It's time for me to wash down. You'd best go below."

He turned, his duty done for the moment. He would have to talk to Perpetua again . . . and to Clarissa. What ailed Clarissa, he wondered, that she couldn't see how her daughter had grown? Look at the strides Perpetua took going forward to the hatchway! How fine and strong her legs and hips!

But Perpetua didn't go below. She found another spot where she could stand, could think private thoughts. As she watched the way the dolphins danced about *The Horatio*, she pondered the dull-sounding future her father had painted. Then she saw him aft, while his men climbed the rigging over him. His clothes were at his feet. He stood naked, in position under the men aloft.

He was a giant, knowing it, proud of his body. Unseen by the men, Perpetua stared at the white flesh exposed, at the triangle of black at his groin.

The men shouted from aloft. "Will ye take another bucketful, master?"

His nod brought down a shower of cold water, spilling from a skin bucket above him. Willing hands dragged up more salt water and poured it over him in a flood that glistened upon his bare skin, then dripped from his loins to the deck.

Old Talbot stood near, as did the others. The rite demanded all hands, for it offered them all a chance to make ribald comment or subtle, caustic remarks about men and their most precious parts. More than that, now the Captain could be the target for their good humor. His curt tongue was silenced, and not a single man aboard need fear the lash.

"Look at what the cold water has done. Aye, the Captain's hook has shriveled to a worm! He'd catch no fish with that! 'Tis the size of my great-great-grandchild's at birth!"

"The happy warrior sleeps—from his tent the maiden creeps," rhymed Jethro, the seaman-poet.

"No charge of rape could ever be placed against Captain Jared West," attested Jeremy, a would-be "sea lawyer," "for in court it would be testified by us all that he couldn't enter a chicken. And there's the evidence before us!" He pointed gleefully, his remarks drowned in a chorus of laughter.

Another bucket of water came from above. This time it splashed about the Captain's shoulders in such a way as to strike the heads of the men who mocked his condition.

West turned on Old Talbot, who laughed raucously at each remark, repeating the taunts as if to remember them forever. "You, old man, call me what you will. Your days with women have long gone. Hold your tongue. And mind the fillies we tumbled with when we were young, old man. I treated mine to ten and a half inches of hardened flesh! Yours had to settle for a penny's worth of soft candy."

Suddenly, as though aware that someone beyond his laughing crew might hear him, the Captain looked quickly about. But he saw no one, least of all his daughter, cringing behind the longboat.

She was shocked at what her father had said. Was there no man as decent as Everett? Perpetua was sure he was a true gentleman. As soon as the bath had begun, Everett had disappeared quietly, as though not wishing to be a part of the ribald ritual.

"When we reach Maui, Captain West, you'll have to keep that weapon sheathed," Old Talbot commented meaningfully as the shower ended. But his voice was now lowered and, it seemed to Perpetua, serious with warning.

The men dispersed, leaving West to wipe himself dry. He donned his heavy linen pants and shoved his feet into his boots. Perpetua took the opportunity to scurry below. Her father unfaithful! A twinge of fear, a tug at the heart, so vague she couldn't truly identify it, lingered when she recalled Old Talbot's statement that her father would "have to keep that weapon sheathed."

Dazed and confused by what she had heard, and by the exciting male flesh she had seen, she sought the safety of her bunk.

* * *

Clarissa was writing in her journal:

"Aboard *The Horatio*: We are nearing the Cape. Perpetua is on deck and I am alone with my thoughts as the men above enjoy Jared's bath with him. Though he be clean of body, I know now about his mind, for he cries out in his sleep. I dreamed last night of Everett, though I could feel the warmth of Jared. Everett had my hand and we strode along the beach. Perhaps the waves lapping against the sides of the ship made this come to me. He told me how much he loved me. He spoke of the bayberry, the scrub oak, the pine woods and the sandy promontory above us where we once stood together. It made me sad when the dream ended, and I awoke."

As Perpetua came in, her mother closed her journal. "What is happening on deck, child?" she asked, knowing full well.

"I saw Father." It was a confession, too meaningful to escape her mother's notice.

Clarissa looked at her daughter, a child among men who were half-naked—rough, uncouth and lonely men thinking only of women. Perpetua had already filled out. Her interest in her own body had increased, and she did not have enough modesty about her. Clarissa was shocked, distressed—and worried.

"Keep away when the Captain bathes! How could you, Perpetua!"

"Mother—they said things about him!"

"What things?" asked Clarissa, afraid of the answer.

"What the cold buckets of water did to his . . ."

Clarissa sighed with relief and put away her journal. With a look over her shoulder, she drew closer to Perpetua.

"Each man aboard has either a sweetheart, a wife, or some such womenfolk waiting for him. You are the daughter of the Captain—and his wife is aboard. I doubt whether they'd have spoken thus if you had been seen. Where were you?"

"I was hiding."

"From now on, you must make certain you are heard and seen when you are abovedeck about this ship. Then no harm can come to you. If anyone approaches you, scream for help. Do you understand?"

Perpetua didn't quite know what her mother meant. Men approach her? For what? Who was her mother to give her proper directions about men when she and Everett . . . ? There were things going on that Perpetua didn't understand! Somehow, she felt betrayed. And once again Clarissa changed the subject. It angered Perpetua, but she felt helpless.

"The men are not only restless for land but for good food. The very meat is moldy!" Clarissa stated, as though suddenly vastly interested in their wellbeing. It brought a grimace of impatience from her daughter. "Aye, they must subsist on salt beef, salt pork. No wonder they've lost most of their teeth. Leave them be, child."

"I have done nothing to interfere," Perpetua replied petulantly.

* * *

Below decks, while mother and daughter talked, the men lingered over their morning ration. After a year at sea, their discontent was growing.

"I have consulted the books aboard this ship. Having found more worms than potato last supper, I checked the book to see their nutritious value." It was Jeremy, the sea lawyer, who spoke. "And I'm sorry to tell you, men, that a worm has nothing at all in it to sustain a man." His pronouncement was greeted with laughter. Jeremy winked. "But there are other delicacies aboard, which the master has served before him whenever he wishes to indulge."

"Aye," agreed one man. "I could stand the food, if'n I had his diet abed. She's a pretty one, ain't she?"

"But she's been much too long ashore, to my mind," offered another. "Not a woman on the island but doesn't suffer from going without a man. Though 'tis none of my business, for sure!"

" 'Tis the right of a man to have food aboard his ship, but not women. They bring back luck," reminded Jeremy.

No one spoke for a moment, and it was apparent all were thinking of the two, unavailable sweet women aboard, and comparing them to those wantons they expected to find in Maui.

"Ye'll have a boatload when we reach the Sandwich Islands, mates." It was Everett who sought to turn the conversation. "There's no law among men says you can't have all you can handle."

"Aye," interrupted Old Talbot. "They'll line the beach, as fine a bevy of young, fresh bodies as ye've fancied in yer wildest dreams. The missionaries will try to hold them back, but they'll leave the shore, yearning from head to toe for what ye've so proudly kept for them. Mind me, we're sure to be greeted by the warmest, most saucy lot of heathens the world has seen. Missionaries be damned! They rut like pigs with their own frozen, hatchet-faced wives, leaving small specimens of their seed within the scrawny-legged, wrinkled women who walk behind them!"

"I've been there—as have many of us, Old Talbot, and what you say is true," responded a dour voice from the corner. "The native girls have been taught to give man pleasure when young—younger than Perpetua—and they might well drive men wild with the magic of their hulas. What can a good Christian do but cross himself, pray that he'll match their skill and drive on between those writhing legs which are heating both man and saint?"

The man who spoke was Frank Jernegan from Gay Head, whose wife had passed away before he'd shipped out. At home he had left behind grown and married children.

He continued. "I was there before, many's the time. That was ten, twenty years ago when first I came, and I was a married man. I loved my wife and by rights I should have been celibate, out of respect to her as well as to my religious beliefs. This time, though I am well over fifty, it will be different." He stopped and looked toward the sky as if his wife might be listening from Heaven. "She will know and understand. Her name was Charity."

Everett spoke, as if half-asleep. "Once a woman has given you her heart, men, you can never rid yourself of the rest of her!"

"I know the part I want!" shouted one. "It's a part of her that doesn't speak with words, and that's certain. The pleasure of the New England women is to talk. Now, in Maui, I'll find women deaf and dumb to everything except what I have to take o' them! You'll not find any like them in Edgartown."

"There seems to be one," hinted Old Talbot.

"If you mean Mistress West, you'll be right from what I observe," said Jeremy. Then, with a look at Everett, he continued, "Nonetheless, when we near Maui, you'll see the Captain with our complaint as clear as the beard on his chin. As he did before, he'll meet old Kaiko, whom he knows there and has spoken about. Right, Old Talbot?"

Talbot nodded wisely.

"Then they'll go off together, while we near kill ourselves with lovin', our backs bowed and knees bent . . . He'll come back with a wise smile on his face—as if only he knew how a woman can satisfy a man!"

Perpetua had heard every word. With the skill of a squirrel, she had found a hiding place outside the galley. There she stayed, fascinated by the talk.

Now she raced away, heedless of whether they heard her or not.

As she reached the hatchway, a hand touched her shoulder. It was Everett and his face was grim.

"Men boast when together. That's men's talk. You shouldn't have listened."

"Is what they said about father . . . ?" she began. Then she saw the men breaking up, several coming her way. Everett's finger was at his lips. "Go below. Forget what you heard. Their talk is idle and filled with lies."

* * *

That night, Perpetua watched her parents sleeping together, her father's arm flung across her mother's breasts. His palm rested upon one breast that was bare, exposed to the heavy night air. Perpetua was frightened. She couldn't identify why. Slipping into her bunk, she put her head down on the pillow.

Then she remembered half-sentences she had heard between seamen, jibes about what they would do when ashore, how much they would enjoy the "offerings of the islands' women," how this man or that one had fared before, making fun of what seemed so sinful. They took it all so casually! What kind of women were these? And were all men like the crew, like her father? She remembered her father's statement that they were rough, uncouth, not for her, that only back home, ashore, would she find a suitable man to marry. Perhaps the young women, whose beauty they spoke of, were like the men themselves—bold, sinful and uncaring. They must be as wanton as the men described them. She tried to piece together an image from books about island natives in the South Pacific. It was frightening, yet strangely exciting.

That night she dreamed of a ship docked in some tropical harbor's wharf. Men swarmed all over the ship, each with his own "dusky native," doing what she could not imagine. The young girls were her age, silken and dark of skin, and they laughed as the men pawed them!

The thoughts of the night before stayed with Perpetua the next day. She moved about, gravely eyeing each man, imagining his postures, trying to fit him into the picture left by her dream. Then she saw Everett. Somehow, he didn't fit in. Though he had come between her father and her mother, he still seemed a decent man. Maybe she only felt this way now that her father's sinful ways had been revealed by the words of his crew. Just what had gone on between

Everett and her mother? Would she ever know? Her
romantic nature pined with curiosity.

It wasn't long before she found out. That evening, the ship lay hove-to after a "trying out" and
stowing of oil. The Captain, exhausted, went below
early, leaving her mother on deck. Perpetua had
found her own place by the bulwark where she
curled, unnoticed and unseen, trying to find a restful
position. The longboat guarded her from the breeze.
She had been lying there a long time, listening to the
sails snap in the wind, seeing the fluorescence in the
water. She had almost gone to sleep, lulled by the
constant roll, when she was startled into full wakeful-
ness by voices. She saw a man walk slowly toward
her mother, framed by the riding light for a second,
then buried in total darkness. From the sound, she
judged they were speaking together. Perpetua heard
her mother's low cry first. "Is it you, Everett Norton?"

Everett did not answer at first.

"Why are you on my husband's ship?"

Perpetua held her breath, waiting for an answer.
His reply came at last, in that mellow voice so familiar
to Perpetua.

"You must know, Clarissa—to be near you."

"You mustn't speak this way. I . . . it is too late
and you know it."

"You are a fickle woman, Clarissa. You gave me
your promise."

Perpetua heard her mother's gasp as Everett
came nearer.

"Don't!" her mother's whispered plea cautioned.
"Leave me be." Then there was a long silence.

"I never will, dear Clarissa. Never."

Then Perpetua saw him move away. Her mother
stood watching, sighing heavily. Then, seeming to

gather herself, she walked past her daughter, looking neither left nor right.

This mother was a stranger to Perpetua. This wasn't the woman of Chilmark, the Captain's wife so sedate and prim; this was a woman another man desired. Yet, even now, Perpetua could not picture her mother as a provocative woman.

Going toward the gangway which led below, she saw Everett watching the white spume as it shot away from the bow. Her father never spoke to him. He rarely spoke to anyone, except to command. The hierarchy aboard a New England whaler was close to that of a British man-of-war. The master spoke in conversation only to his officers. Everett was a "hand." Perpetua doubted whether her father knew what she knew about Everett. Though Clarissa was his wife, she was unknown to him. Perpetua knew—yes, she knew all. But what was the good of such knowledge? There was no one in whom she could confide. And the truth was almost too much to bear.

A sigh escaped her, and it seemed to come from the very depths of her being. Turning from the empty stillness of the night, she stepped to the gangway and went below.

CHAPTER 6

It occurred to Everett that no matter how shipshape they made the whaler, everything above deck could be stored below except the stink. There was no way in which a shipful of men aboard a whaler, butchering their reeking catch almost daily, could wash away the cloying, penetrating smell of the dead whale. Between the cracks of the deckboards, behind cleats and around the inner coils of rope, evidence lay in bits of skin, drops of oily grease and slivers of blubber. Heated by the sun, the vapors rose like a ghostly cloud that polluted the fresh sea air. After a thorough holystoning of the wood planks and tarred cracks, the ship still smelled, would smell until the men and two women aboard got so used to it that the odor disappeared.

A different, more human odor struck Everett's nostrils. Turning from the leeward rail where he had been keeping watch, Everett found Old Talbot two feet from him, about to speak.

"When we reach Maui, Everett Norton, that's when it will all come to fester."

The man's body odor was bad enough, his attitude worse, and his breath stank of rum. But this man was tolerated by his shipmates, for he held some sort of charmed place aboard ship, maintaining a special relationship with Captain West which he never let the others forget.

Talbot spat a stream of dark brown tobacco juice over the rail into the white spume below. The trajectory of the foul stuff was no more than three inches from Everett's nose. He calculated that the man, even though drunk, must have figured the wind to a high degree in order to miss Everett's face. If the old man's accuracy had failed, Everett's response would have been to land a right hook on the point of the son of a seawitch's jaw. In order to quiet his rising blood, Everett gripped the rail harder and kept his back to the smelly old rascal.

"So ye're goin' to be one of the silent ones, eh, Mister Norton? Well they say silence is golden, but in this case ye'll not gain by it. It were better ye speak to me, Mister. For ye are involved ... in a way."

Everett turned quickly, as if just noticing him.

The turn was made with such speed and natural grace that it did exactly what Everett meant it to do. The older man stepped away and his wooden leg caught in a knothole filled with warm tar. Down he went, landing full length on the deck.

Everett quickly offered the old man a hand. Aboard ship the oldest was never aided, for only as an able seaman would he keep his berth and share. This seemingly unconscious reaction, thoroughly planned in advance, was the insult he meant it to be.

"No y' don't, Mister Norton! I'm an able man!" cried Old Talbot, who got to his feet with a quick glance about to see whether the incident had been seen by his shipmates.

"Next time I'll shoot off a cannon to warn ye I'm ready to board. Now don't ye swing on me again, sir. Save yer strength for the girls we'll be meetin' and to

fight off the husbands ye cuckold." Then, as if in
added thought, while he adjusted his wooden leg, he
said, "And from the way things seem aboard this ship,
ye'll be needin' all of it."

Husbands? Was this a warning? Had he been
seen staring at Clarissa? He must have been. Decid-
ing subtlety rather than force was required under the
circumstances, Everett placed an arm about the
greasy jacket of the other man and said, "What was it
you wished to tell me, Brother Talbot?"

"When we reach Maui, Mister Norton," Talbot
replied, his proximity causing Everett to wince, "we'll
be where I first became a man." Though the man's
eyes were watery-grey and his hook of a nose took a
starboard slant, he straightened up proudly.

"There are two excitements in whaling. One is to
enter a strange port. The other is to enter a strange
woman. For ten years afloat, I remained aboard ship
due to my youth. I was a shiphand and never met
strange women. I sailed from port to port, from the
Mediterranean Sea to the Isles of Japan, and never set
foot ashore all that time. I listened to the tales of others 'til my organs hurt and I had no release for them.
I wanted no man, as some did under such unnatural
conditions—but a woman!"

"Why do you tell me this?"

"It has to do with ye. It has to do with the Captain and his wife, and the ways of the world. So listen
sharp and learn."

Everett lit his pipe, carefully eyeing the old
man.

"A lad joined me when we reached Maui," began
Old Talbot. "He was about fourteen. I chose to take
him with me, for we were both inexperienced and I
had no wish to be laughed at should I be found

wanting in the eyes of the other men. So we went to 'The Street of Strange Desires.' "

Talbot warmed to his tale, his slurred voice growing louder. Everett felt he was being held in the grasp of the Ancient Mariner.

"The street was near Iwilei. It stank of piss and garbage, and the air was so still the flies had trouble movin' about. There were many silent men walking with me, passing others on their return. Their business, Mister Norton, was as mine . . . very private. Though I'm certain they knew one another, they never spoke.

"At the door of a small shack, a man stopped me. He was Chinese. He noticed the two of us and spotted us as innocents. 'Come in,' he said in a singsong voice, and promised us such enticements that I fair went blind with the visions he presented. The lad went in with me. That lad was more sturdy than most, near as high as he is today, and he went forward with firm footsteps like one who meant to prove his manhood. Inside it was dark. And what girls awaited us! I still can see the tall, black-haired Italian *bella* from Florence. And the breasts, all pink and white, of the lass from Scotland. There was a pair of Javanese, so sly and slow to move. But the other, ah—she was a girl from Chile, who had shipped from Macao. And she it was who began to dance before us. Ye wonder how I made a choice?"

"And how did you, Brother Talbot?"

"I said, 'Blast 'em all! There's not a woman here who comes up to my dreams. I've been waitin' too long to begin the rites with anything as scrawny as this lot! Give me a woman who'll teach me things I'll never forget! I intend to continue the practice for many years to come!' Oh, I figured that Chinaman was holdin' out his best, for I was a shrewd one even then. Soon enough he got the idea and then that Chinaman sent them packin', all sad-faced and cursin' me. Then he came back with two Chinese. One was tall, all smooth-skinned like satin with two full moons for buttocks and breasts big as ripe melons."

Everett stopped him. "Now what does this all have to do with me?"

"I'll get to that. Ye see, my friend, this lad who was with me, the young one?"

"Aye, the young lad."

"Years later that one saved my life, returning kindness with generosity, in a manner o' speakin', as I had started his life, proper, in that brothel."

"I was wondering what he had to do with you."

"It was ten years or so later. By then he was in his twenties and a good hand aboard ship. He was from Martha's Vineyard, that one. We were stuck in the ice pack in the Arctic on the old *Emily E* from Edgartown. I was one of the volunteers asked to go look for food, out where the seals abounded. The ice was there as far as my eyes could see. No break-up in sight. Mist all about us. I went off and never come back whole."

"That was when your leg. . . ?"

"Aye! After two days, this lad came lookin' fer me. I had been caught between crushing floes of ice, and they were grindin' one against the other. My left leg, the one gone, was caught between the ice floes as they rose, carrying me twenty feet high. I was scissored so's I couldn't bear the cold 'n pain. I lay danglin', head down, my leg near cut in two, unable to move. The lad found me. He took me back. He read a surgeon's book and cut it off. Then he sewed me up."

"He read a book and did that?"

"Aye, there's one aboard our own ship, though few know how to read it. When I got home to the island he promised me a berth aboard any ship he would command, wooden leg or no."

"And this lad, was it. . . ?"

"Jared West, the same."

"The same lad who went with you to 'The Street of Strange Desires'?"

"Aye, and what a man he was that night! He has put his learnin' to practice ever since. And never a one seized his mind—until it came to Naliki."

"Naliki? Who is that?"

Old Talbot looked at him slyly. "I can't tell you that. I'm faithful to the man who saved my life."

"Ah well," sighed Everett. "And so you must be."

But Old Talbot was in his cups. "Naliki. Well, she's the most beautiful creature on God's earth. Aye. And she's taken the heart of a fine Captain, sure as that ice floe grabbed onto my leg." The old man clenched his fist and held it closed, knuckles trembling.

"Where is Naliki?" asked Everett gently.

The old man shuffled from one foot to the other, then looked up. "No. No, ye don't trick me like that."

Old Talbot smiled, showing a few rotten teeth. "I'll tell ye some day. She waits for him on this voyage. That's all I'll say, for the time."

Everett gripped the old man by the shoulder. "The whereabouts of this Naliki. They all want to know. I hear the men talking. They all know there is something on their Captain's mind other than Clarissa. Other than whaling. He talks aloud, you know. He talks without knowing it. The men have sensitive ears. Now, old man, you have already talked too much! You must say no more!"

Old Talbot's mouth opened like a half-wit's, as he watched Everett leave. He had lost his audience, drat it! He spat ferociously.

In the shadows, unknown to the two, Jeremy, the sea lawyer, and Frank Jernegan were watching and listening and concocting a deal.

Several minutes later they came out of their shadowy retreat and approached Old Talbot, who was hanging soddenly onto the halyards.

"We're here to offer you a great prize," began Jeremy.

"A prize, ye say?" He brightened up and his eyes glistened greedily.

"Aye, a great thing which you will win, if you answer the one question which bothers us all—you might say the entire crew in fact."

"And what is this great prize?"

"A root. It's called ginseng. It comes from the Orient and is much sought after by older men or those young ones who have need of it."

"And what does it do?"

Frank Jernegan let his eyes roll and threw his head back in laughter. The old man's wits must be very dulled by the rum. "If ye eat it, yer peter will stand up of his own, whether ye are wantin' it to or not—at the mere thought of a woman! Ye'll be the envy of every man, and the sight of ye in that condition of rock hardness which cannot be downed no matter how ye make use of it time and again will drive the maidens mad. Have ye a mind to accept our request? If so, and ye answer our question, the prize is yours."

A huge wink from the smiling one kept his friend's mouth shut.

"So ask away. . . ," responded Talbot, licking his lips greedily. "We're near enough Lahaini to make my old cod move about and tremble from thoughts of it."

"Well, it's this way," began Jeremy, taking command as he usually did in any judiciary matter. "We are here talking and we figure you could solve a riddle. The two of us have been in contention . . ."

"What?" asked Talbot, looking about him. "In what?"

"Contention. In law, that means . . . er, well it means we've had an argument. Simple as that, in a manner of speakin'."

"Then why in blazes didn't ye say so? Get on! I can hardly keep my mind on ye two what with your promises of just what this thing I eat can do . . . all day and night, did ye say?"

"Ahhh!" said Jernegan, "And the next day and night, too. Ye'll have a hardness you've never known. Ye won't know what to do."

"Well if that means I got it up and can't get it down for two days and nights, I'll know what to do!"

"The question is," continued Jeremy, "who is the young woman named Naliki and where, in a manner of speakin', does she live?"

"Naliki?" The old man's face clouded over.

"Aye, that's it. The nub of it. Plain and simple."

"In truth, all ye want to know is about her? And for the answer, which I know well, ye'll give me a mighty root which will . . . do all that?"

"Youth rediscovered." Jernegan winked.

"The secret of the Orient," added Jeremy. "Makes a man hunger at the thought—don't it, Talbot? Why ye can eat half and split yer days and nights into two equal parts. Find ye two women or ten, in a manner of speaking."

"For the answer?"

"Get on with it, will ye? Do ye know, or don't ye?" demanded Jernegan, who had taken an arm-folded position before his witness.

"And where is this . . . what you call it?" asked Talbot, squinting. "This ginseng?"

"I'm aholdin' it in my pocket. And it's yours, though I'll miss a few tawny maidens for givin' it to ye," replied Jeremy, placing one hand over the great pocket on his pea jacket. "It's in here, safe and sound and ready to do its work, for it'll need the strength of a Goliath to do what it has to do with ye, Old Talbot."

"Well, men," Talbot began, " . . . she's on an island. Now give it to me." He reached out for it.

"Hold on!" Jernegan cried. "On an island! Why ye know perfectly well there are thousands of islands. And for that sly answer ye expect to go for days and nights standin' so strong that a whole island of women will swoon! Come on, Old Talbot, under such conditions ye'll be made a king."

"Aye, a king, he said," echoed Jeremy.

The two men watched the old seaman intently. They had heard rumors about the pleasures of Naliki. Now the secret was almost theirs. They licked their dry lips as they waited for him to reply.

"Tell us which island, or ye'll never get your prize. That's the truth!" urged Jernegan.

"That's the whole story. We sighted same on our last voyage, mind ye. And we didn't find it on no map. That is to say, not marked as an *island*. Which it seemed to be, 'cause we circled the land afterwards."

"And she lives there?" Jeremy asked.

"He speaks of her to himself. We hear him. How does she look, Old Talbot?" demanded Jernegan.

"Not part of the bargain, though she'd be a delight in any of your beds, that's a fact. No, I said I'd tell you where she was. Not knowing exactly, I can't name an island. But it was near Maui."

"Ah! Near Maui!" they both chimed in.

"We heard drums ashore."

"Drums, say ye? And what would they be for, Old Talbot?"

"They play them, as full well ye know, while dancin' the nuptial dance and arousin' their men and women to fornicate."

"Longitude and latitude, man?" demanded Jernegan. "Just where in tarnation is this Naliki?"

"Give me my . . ." Old Talbot's gnarled hand snaked out.

"No, ye don't. We are offended. Ye lead us on tellin' tales of a dusky native and our Captain and then ye fail us. We all have our fancy girls here 'n' there, that ye know full well, be it on this island or that." Jernegan spoke what was on all their minds.

"Go ahead and let him have his prize," ordered Everett, who had quietly appeared from the gangway. "He did what you asked of him. It seems he's told us something which we must keep to ourselves, too. For love of Mrs. West, if nothing else."

The three other men looked at him curiously, then Jeremy spoke. "Love, ye say? Well, that's a mighty powerful way of sayin' it. But I prefer the more legal terminology. It is, in fact, what lawyers call 'privileged information.' Which we cannot speak of to others. So under those circumstances, and with respect for Mrs. West, we will keep our mouths shut about this—right?"

"Right!" affirmed Jernegan loudly.

"Right!" rejoined Old Talbot, his hand out.

"Right!" Everett's voice was so soft as to almost be inaudible.

Jeremy reached into his pocket and pulled out an envelope made of oilskin. From it he extracted a knot-like root which had been wrapped in another oilskin inside of the first. It was about three inches long and tapered like a root, though the whole object had the appearance of a man's parts, with hairlike rootlets about its thicker end.

He gave it to Old Talbot, who held it aloft, and examined it greedily before taking a considerable chomp from it.

"So that's about the size of it," Everett concluded. "And we are sworn to secrecy."

The men shrugged, looked at him in silence and walked away. Everett knew, watching them walk away, there would be considerable talk in the fo'castle that night.

CHAPTER 7

Standing there under the tarpaulin, Everett seemed to Clarissa the man she had known fourteen years ago. His slim figure, sharp profile and clean-shaven face were untouched by the passage of time.

What went on beneath the high brow? What secret brought such a soft smile to his lips? What strange power preserved his youthful grace, gave him such inner strength and allowed him to have great patience with the violent, often bitter men about him?

Clarissa stood aft, deserted by Jared, who had returned to his cabin to bring his log up to date. The sun beat down on the roof of the galley. *The Horatio* was in the doldrums, bobbing on the heavy, long waves that looped in from the west like the mild backwash from some distant storm.

Unaware of the woman watching him, Everett lit his pipe with a match from his oilskin pouch. Slowly sucking in his cheeks, he exhaled with a sensuous pursing of his lips, looked about, then cast the match to the spume of the leeward waves. He wore a thin shirt which could not hide his chest muscles. The shirt tapered to his waist where it was caught loosely by his broad black belt. His worn breeches bagged at the knees. The cuffs were buried in heavy boots, now set

wide apart as Everett took a stance against the rolling
of the sea.

He was, to Clarissa, every inch the Everett she
had known—strong, yet gentle; knowing, yet curious;
unchained from an island which had never lived up
to its promise. Surely his trip abroad must have spent
some of his dreams. He must have met and wooed
many a girl. Remorse at her impetuous marriage to
Jared, the man who was master of this ship, touched
Clarissa for a moment—then, like a gull sweeping
through the air, her remorse was gone. She pushed
away from her mind this evil regret which could only
lead to unhappiness. Everett, as he stood there being
examined by the unseen woman, had surely not
achieved such self-control, such peace of mind, without having had the love of a woman far more responsive to his romantic nature than she had been.
No—she could never have waited for him to come
back. She knew herself better than that. Participating
in country games like "I spy," she had always been
the impatient one, the daredevil who kept running after the count of ten, hoping to find a hiding place before being tagged. She had never been ready to wait
for anything placed on the table before her. She'd always been eager to demonstrate that she was the
best, the fastest, deserving reward before all others.
Catching the island's best, Jared, had been her goal,
whether she called it, romantically, being "swept off
her feet" or not. Clarissa knew that she told her feet
just where to go. Now, as the wife of the Captain, she
had position, she had a daughter—though it hurt her
bitterly that no son would be born to them—and Jared
had promised to reward her with a great home.

Ever since her first encounter with Everett
aboard, when he had explained why he was there, she
had tried her best to repulse him by staring away

when he looked at her, by moving quickly. Yet, for the past nine months, he seemed to be everywhere she looked!

Never, though, had she indulged herself in the pleasure of his presence as now. The thought of her child, the daughter she had borne for Jared, brought to mind Perpetua's relationship with Everett. He had seemingly won her over completely, yet there was a certain reticence there. As she watched Everett, she realized what a romantic figure he might be to an impressionable, growing girl. As Everett turned and began to walk her way, she meant this time to hold her ground and speak to him. She stepped from the shadows.

"You avoid me," he said simply. "This is the longest voyage on record for me, Clarissa! I had hoped we might speak more often."

"You know why, Everett. No matter what we meant to one another before Jared came into my life, he is all I have now, except for the daughter you have charmed. Do you really like her, or is she just a way to my heart?"

"You know better than that. She is herself, a young lady with her own mind, her own ways. She will make someone very happy some day . . . if he can handle her!" He put his hand on her shoulder.

Clarissa swung around at the touch, a lock of hair escaping from her black ribbon. "Though we are alone, Everett, it is not seemly for you to touch me. Time has taken us far apart, in distance, aboard this ship and in our hearts. Yes, though you may not believe so, I still have a heart. But I dare not let it tell me how to feel."

"I know. But I also know you have deeper emotions and fires than you think. If you could ever be free of the Yankee imprint, then you would cease to hold yourself back. I know what you are going through. I feel it and I see it. You are close neither to your daughter nor to your husband. You may have been, when you were alone with Perpetua, and you may have thought yourself in love with a dashing sea captain when he was away, but these things have changed."

She wouldn't let him reach her. She mustn't! Yet, how dark his eyes, how noble his forehead, how boyish and endearing his long hair covering his ears, the blue stocking cap set so jauntily on his head. The years had left little lines etched at the corners of his eyes, deepened the strong lines at the corners of his sensitive lips. Yet, unlike all the men about her, there hung about him no smell of sweat, no breath of anything but tobacco.

"What a speech to make to me," she started lamely. "Don't you know we have no time for philosophical conversations?" She hoped he would go away, yet she also hoped he wouldn't. He stared at her, then smiled, and with the pipe stem held like a baton in his hand, he looked around the silent, swaying deck.

"The entire ship is at rest, Clarissa, my dear. No whales for days. No wind to bring them to us, nor us to them. There's naught to do but dream in this intolerable heat. I saw you spying on me—the cat and mouse. I moved near that you might put the bell upon me, should you wish."

"You are a stalking cat, Everett." Clarissa felt her anger growing, a blind resentment which had no foundation in reason. "You play with me with your questions which have no answers. I shouldn't be talking with you. Not at all. I should spend every free moment with Perpetua. She needs a mother now. She has grown by leaps and bounds during the past nine months."

"She should have been left ashore, not taken aboard this shipful of men, Clarissa," replied Everett. "You should have left her on the Vineyard. There are girls her age on the island. Aunts or uncles would surely care for her."

"We have no family but the three of us—Jared, Perpetua and me!" cried Clarissa, stung by the rebuke. "Besides, I wouldn't allow her to grow up there during the early years as I had—as all others do. She has a chance, now, to see something beyond the shores of our island."

"Men grow up there. Look at Jared."

"You don't know the life of women from our island. We are brought up with hard winters and hot summers to face. The winds from the cliffs and the sea have to keep us company until we are of an age to be married. When the ribbons and the dolls are gone, we are made to choose our men. To us, they seem hardly men. They are the same lads who pushed us off the clay cliffs at Gay Head, who stole from our fish lines, who hit us from behind in class, who mocked us for being girls. All along we are treated as a lesser breed, until we are of age for making children. We are put out like chum to attract a bluefish; dressed overnight in strange, tight-fitting corsets. We are given brief lessons in keeping clean, in smiling (though it pains us to be patient with the vulgar, foul-smelling boys who take to us) and then, if we are passed by in this hurricane of courtship, we end up old maids, virgins for life, never knowing what it is to be truly desired, never knowing anything but frustration and loneliness, while the men roam the world—as you did! Do you wonder I married when Jared asked me? Do you wonder I am with him now, whether the four years were to be a hell on earth or not? So be it, Everett. I made my choice."

He stood silent awhile, as though he had to absorb what she said. "It is your moral sense speaking, Clarissa," said Everett at last. "You know so well what is correct and incorrect. But I believe you must envy men—even their lack of morals."

"Do you mean to lecture me, Everett? You who must have dallied with many a lass in your travels?"

"If I were ever to lie to you, I would say now that I remained celibate. But I can't and I need not. Men, as you so rightly say, hear morals taught from their mothers and from the Bible. Life has pulls upon their poor, weak natures which women and the Bible could not know. A man often feels an irrefutable urge, which women do not.

"You took this voyage and brought your dear girl because your only other choice was to remain an old maid. Had you never thought of the ten thousand dollars your man will certainly bring home from such a voyage? Is there no greed in your behavior? Do you find whaling improves the mind and spirit? No. I know better. You have gone with your man so that he remains yours."

The blunt truthfulness of his words left Clarissa aghast. And yet, she knew then what appealed to her so much about this tall man whose nearness caused her such consternation. He inspired her to look about herself, to take stock of what she was doing and why. He was finally forcing her to analyze herself—and for the first time in a great while. She liked the feeling of freedom and mastery it gave her.

"Have you ever asked yourself . . . would you tell me now why you are really on this ship?" Clarissa stole a glance at him, hoping she had caught him off guard.

At first he didn't answer her, but then he began to speak in a low monotone, as if addressing himself. "Some women do not know what drives a man or how sincere his feelings can be for them. Some women are carried away in sudden passion, then relent, but it is too late. Promises fade, faces are forgotten, time has eased the parting. All this being true, still, I had a world ready for the woman I loved!"

She noticed the quick clenching of his jaws. A sudden feeling of compassion made her reach for his hand on the rail. "For whom, dear Everett? For whom did you have the world? Where is this treasure? Aboard this ship? At home on our island in a great house?"

He laughed bitterly, his voice rising. "Great houses on our island? They are but farmer's cottages with white paint. They are nothing compared to the baronial homes I saw in England and France. Suffer this trip to build that! Above us the bleak and cloudless sky, the stink of oil and tar all about us, the creaking of old timber as we wallow here. This a way to find one's treasure? And yet . . ."

She faced his back as he looked to sea. She couldn't speak. He still loved her. What could she say? What did she feel for him that was so powerful she felt like taking him gently to her bosom, not to comfort his hurt but to tell him he should have none? Dare she feel so strongly?

He turned to face her, surprised at the look of compassion on her face. "And as for you, Clarissa, no woman who spent years aboard a whaler ever got over it, ever returned the same. Nor did she forget, years later, when she reread her journal full of her lies or her master's logbook, filled with his!

"No woman ever truly got over it. What woman can erase the memory of the confinement of a moving jail, with forty lusting men only a few feet from her. Her journal might contain pretty words about the dainty curtains she'd stitched, her daughter's great progress in her lessons, the little things members of the crew did for her. But all that is false to the memory of a voyage. Empty talk!"

Clarissa bowed her head. Everett knew her suffering then. And yet, even so, he knew only half of it. The other half could never be spoken of, and not to Everett in any case. Clarissa thought of Jared, the way he had moved hard against her last night, grasping her about the waist, pulling her nightgown high, his pressure fierce and demanding. And—as she turned her back to him—how he had pushed angrily out of bed at her sleepy rejection to pace the deck above until the early watch; how he had returned to take her, almost in exasperation, without thought of Perpetua so near. He cared no longer how one-sided it was or how she felt.

"Blows!" a cry rang out from the masthead. "Off to starboard!"

The ship was suddenly mad with action. Everett ran to his station. Jared appeared among the shouting sailors, blinked his eyes against the sun, looked right through Clarissa as though she didn't exist. This was no place for her. She moved as quickly as possible through the melee to the gangway.

She tried to concentrate on what Everett had been saying. What was her destiny? What part was Everett to play in it?

• • •

That dawn, Perpetua had lain awake listening to the two near her, listening to her own mother and father. They rutted like animals! Though Perpetua felt somehow very guilty listening, she could not have done otherwise. First the moaning, then the outcry and the heaving upon the nearby bed. Didn't her mother know Perpetua could hear? How could her mother just let it happen?

The Captain was writing in his log. Perpetua watched his bent figure. Such a bulk! She wondered how a fragile woman like her mother could bear his weight. What must it feel like, having a man's naked body against your own? How did men feel? Their skin was rough, their hands calloused, their beards scratchy. Did a wondrous feeling come over a woman when a man handled her, touched her, made her feel as Perpetua's books had told her? Would she experience great desire? Just thinking about it made her squirm in her bunk. She pressed her legs together as though denying some naked man entry. She felt immediate shame. Surely this was a sinful thought!

Her father moved, breaking her thoughts. He stood up, stretched and bent his head to avoid hitting the beams. Perpetua had looked upon her father with fear and discomfort since the exhibition of his naked body on deck. Now, for the first time, she saw him as a virile man, someone who might lure a woman to his bed, who might viciously attack this woman whether she liked it or not. To avoid his eyes, to hide her sudden sense of guilt for thinking such thoughts, Perpetua buried her head in the pillow, feeling the sudden sense of desire recede.

Clarissa, heading for her cabin, bumped against a man hurrying along toward the taffrail. Her hand flew to her nostrils to block out the sudden odor that almost overwhelmed her.

"Pardon, Miz West," Old Talbot grunted, "but men have their own business to tend to."

Without replying, Clarissa turned and went be-

low, shocked at his sneering manner, his complete
lack of respect. He unnerved her, made her itchy and
uncomfortable. What was there in his manner that
suggested he knew a big joke at her expense? She entered Jared's portion of the cabin space and passed
his journal. He had left it open.

The lamp swayed over it. Jared's agonized scrawl
was almost illegible. "Lahaina Roads not far away.
The water, the smells, the birds. May the Lord send
us strong steady winds. I cannot contain myself much
longer for lack and want of her . . ."

The ship suddenly tipped; Clarissa caught herself. Two longboats had been lifted from the port
side. The motion added to her own panic at the
words she had read. She held on tightly with both
hands, gripping the Captain's desk to steady herself.
Feeling as if she stood on the fringes of eternity, she
remembered something from Psalms: "Let not mine
enemies triumph over me. I trust in Thee."

She heard the cries of men. They seemed a million miles away as they went out to kill. Then a blur-
ring light entered her mind and Clarissa felt a
different kind of fear. The fear was not for herself,
nor for the future, but for Jared. It was a selfless
concern. She knew now that he was going through a
trial beyond his control. The realization that he had
never confided in her brought her true physical pain.
Then a voice within her said quietly, "I will not be
afraid of what man can do to me. I will listen for Thy
guidance, for the idea which will free us all from fear,
disaster and hopelessness."

The ship steadied and Perpetua came in. Clarissa
looked at her. Perpetua's face was bright.

"I came below to write in my journal, Mother."

"Journal?"

"My own journal. No one shall ever read it but

me. Maybe later in life I will take it out and remember how I felt today." Her head went down, then up. "Mother, I'll hide this. Don't look for it. I won't leave it around like Father does his."

Perpetua knew her mother was staring at her, but it was an effort to meet her mother's gaze. Maybe her mother knew about the Sandwich Islands. Most women from the Vineyard did. They had heard about them enough. They were told that the islands were settings for bacchanalian scenes, for orgies. But a few women closed their ears to the gossip and wild tales. They thought only of a warm, tropical paradise, where life was gentle and easy.

"Mother," she began, "what can we expect when we reach the Sandwich Islands? What kind of life will we have there?"

Clarissa cleared her throat. "Well, I have heard and read about the islands. I doubt whether we will actually stay there long—just while the ship is being refitted for the north. But you should be warned, child, few women would approve of the way the natives dress. They wear but few clothes, or none at all. I am told the men cover themselves with a small loincloth; the women are bare from the waist up. The children run naked." Clarissa's eyes clouded, as if with some fear she could not repress. "I want you to stay close to me when we first land."

With wide, searching eyes, Perpetua now closely followed her mother's every word.

"I know of a few New Englanders there," Clarissa went on. "Laura Ripley, Harriet Pease and their families. Conditions are primitive, they say, and they are forever writing to those at home, appealing for things like sewing needles and spinning wheels. Some islands are like distant planets, totally barren, whilst others have volcanoes."

"Volcanoes! Like Pompeii!"

"Hush, child, no. God willing, there will never be another Pompeii as long as we live. These volcanoes have long been quiet. There is one which they call in their outlandish language, Haleakala, 'The House in the Sun.' It's ten thousand feet high and hasn't erupted in many years. No one expects it will again. All around the harbor of Lahaina, where the Captain tells me we will anchor, there is tropical jungle with wild animals. I must impress upon you not to wander far! And there are other reasons as well." Clarissa studied her daughter, her eyes pleading for her to understand a mother's concern. And there was a grim warning in her voice as she added, "This has been called the most infamous waterfront in the world."

She paused for effect.

"Why?"

"It has a sinful and evil reputation. There are bad women and bad men. There are girls who sell their bodies to drunken derelicts, to seamen who have been away from home for a long while. There are deserters and wild, loose men without fear of God— men who go to brothels, where they spend freely and take their pleasure greedily, without a thought for their wives and children at home. Now that you know a little about this, I don't want you to be too curious, for it is an evil thing they do."

Yet even as she spoke, Clarissa knew she had already given away too much, whetting the curiosity of this irrepressible girl. No doubt, Perpetua could hardly wait to go ashore, leave her mother's apron strings and wander a bit. Clarissa could almost see herself reflected in Perpetua's eyes. Yes, Clarissa thought, she must appear squeamish, too fastidious and prudish to her daughter. The time would come, inevitably, when Perpetua would have to escape from her mother, and begin to live her own life.

"Mother, if that's the place we are heading for, why do the men speak of it as 'The Gates of Heaven'? They can't wait to reach Maui. Is that all they can think of?"

"I'd rather not talk about them, Perpetua. I don't have to mix with their kind, nor do you. I can't tell you what will happen when we arrive on the island. But, for us, there will be some comforts. A few missionary women have established the kind of homes that we're used to. Some of the families have transplanted their entire homes, by sea, to Maui. You will see marble-top tables, horsehair sofas, and organs. Entire houses have been brought over by ship, board by board. New Englanders have begun over again on these islands, building homes where they can feel comfortable. While we're here, they will share with us, I am sure."

"But surely, the natives don't live in such houses," guessed Perpetua.

"I'm told the natives live outdoors or in grass huts, surrounded by flowers and palm trees. They fish and ride the surf on boards."

"And what about the young girls, the women?"

"Which women are you talking about?"

"The dusky race. I heard the men on deck speak of them. They are the young girls, my age, who swim naked to the ships and . . ." Perpetua looked away. "The men talk about them all the time."

"And I would rather not. I read something Captain Cook wrote soon after he discovered the islands. He said the people had brown skins and that their beauty was legendary! Well, maybe to him it was. I imagine some men who stayed away from decent,

New England women too long would find beauty in a black pygmy."

"They aren't cannibals, are they?"

"Who ever suggested they were?"

"Old Talbot."

"Now, let's take Old Talbot. He's a man you and I cannot trust, but whom your father does. That man is trying to poison your mind. He does this for his own purpose. Perpetua, I don't trust him. Not only my nature and intuition warn me. My nose, too, provides warning—don't trust that man!"

They both laughed.

The next time Perpetua wrote in her secret diary, she thought about all the things her mother had told her. Why did her mother, who was assuredly a sinner herself, go on so much about others sinning? Perpetua felt sure that her father and mother were fighting something within themselves they couldn't help. Was it possible to love each of them, knowing that they were far from perfect?

Perpetua glanced up at her mother, who puttered around the small cabin, a light song on her lips. Clarissa looked so pretty, so happy. How could she have an evil thought? Oh, how Perpetua loved her mother! What was difficult, she realized, was to combine this love for her mother and, yes, her father, with respect for both of them, too.

Clarissa realized that her conversation about the islands might have had a frightening effect on a young girl who was looking forward to a new life. Clarissa watched her daughter as she wrote in her diary, and saw Perpetua's hand stop in mid-stroke. The girl's blonde hair, carefully combed, looked golden even in the gloom of the cabin. Her blouse, shrunk from many washings, delineated her firm, young breasts. And her skirt hugged her body, outlining her trim legs and buttocks. Soon this girl would need proper clothes. If she were growing this fast physically, then she must be very nearly a woman. Did she think as a woman when she wrote in her diary? Or was she still a child?

Perpetua caught her mother examining her and turned away, holding her diary tightly. How confusing it still was! Her father was revered by his men for his sexual prowess. And he was bold, recalling aloud, reveling with Old Talbot over "the many fillies we've tumbled when we were young." Her own father joked about his sex as though it were public property; he was amused about "rearing a dusky race." How degrading! And how sinful—if she were to believe what she had learned in church about adultery. Yet she thought she understood something of his private agonies, too, even though she could not help but feel that her father had betrayed her mother. It was very perplexing. Both of her parents involved in some way with another. The night she had overheard the brief conversation between her mother and Everett indicated some secret affair of the heart between them. Everyone torn with guilt!

She could not make sense of any of her feelings; yet Perpetua felt as if she must have some answer, some end to the many conflicts. Maybe adults suffered as much, too. Yet, strangely, they showed so little. Why should they hide so much, unless they were afraid? Perpetua could not judge them either well or ill. She had no measure. She loved her mother despite her transgressions. And she loved her father now, at last, in a strange way, because of the problems he had to wrestle with.

Perpetua had been near fourteen years of age when they left. She would be sixteen when they anchored at Maui. Maybe, by then, all the distressing feelings she now endured would be over and she could begin to sort out her own life.

Clarissa smiled across the space between her and her daughter. She knew something bothered Perpetua, suspected in her heart what it was. The smile caught Perpetua as an expression of love, a sharing, too, of something which linked women in an understanding unknown to men.

Then, catching her daughter and holding her close, Clarissa felt tears come to her eyes. She could no longer restrain herself, nor still the tide that raced through her soul with a humming as audible as a deep-felt moan. In the arms of her daughter, she began to sob.

CHAPTER 8

Eight months later, they rounded Cape Horn. For three days and four nights, terrible storms had buffeted the ship and her passengers. But in Jared's log, there was only a brief entry:

We doubled the Cape. We will head north and make for the Grounds. All aboard are well.

The Horatio was becalmed. Perpetua stood alone by the leeward rail, looking at the sea.

"Penny for your thoughts," said Everett, stepping behind her. He looked so tall against the sky. He appeared older now, hardened by the voyage. His cheeks looked hollow; his jawline was starkly etched. Yet he still retained the courtly manner Perpetua admired, treating her as if he were paying court to a fine, grown-up lady of fashion. Shipboard life had done nothing to reshape his gracious manners.

"Old Talbot told me I would hear a sound coming over the waters," replied Perpetua. She spoke hesitantly, afraid that Everett might laugh at her fantasy. To her surprise, he had a ready explanation.

"The singing humpbacks! You will hear them indeed, but not for many miles to come. They hold to the exceptionally clear waters of Lahaina where they sing their seasonal song. 'Tis an uncanny and mysterious thing. Their powerful sounds are like songs with notes, always the same. The humpback whales can be heard beneath the water for fifteen miles. Some of their deeper notes have been heard by men one hundred miles away."

"Why do they sing, Everett?"

"No one knows. Perhaps the males sing to attract the females for mating. It is quite a sight to watch the little offspring, for the female humpback is the only whale which will tend to her young in danger. The wee ones weigh near the same as a full-grown horse, but they don't stray far from their mothers. They float along on their great fins and seem to be buoyed up by their mothers as they glide along. An offspring is always the greatest concern for a mother, be she an animal or a woman."

Everett looked at Perpetua steadily and a smile played around his lips. "But there are others, as well, that may care for the young."

Perpetua cast a cold look in response, yet her heart quivered.

"I long to be ashore," she sighed. "It seems as if there is no place aboard where I can turn. Father says we'll soon be there, another two months only. Will you be with us ashore?"

"Only when I'm wanted."

Why did she always feel as if he were laughing at her?

"You are ever welcome," she uttered impulsively. She turned away quickly to hide an uncomfortable blush. "And besides, you know so much about these islands. You must be our guide."

She felt clever for hiding her feelings so well. But, to her surprise, her offhand comments inspired an exclamation from him.

"You are fortunate! You will meet these Sandwich Island people while you are still young, while you yet have an open mind. They are so pure of heart, so truly natural in behavior. We would do well to observe them, Perpetua. They are God's own people, unembarrassed by their bodies and their desires. They are modest and unaffected, beautiful, strong in physique. What a race of humans! They live simply, without affection or hypocrisy."

Perpetua found his words unsettling, for they seemed to imply that there was something wrong with the way she had lived up to now, something amiss in the lessons she had learned from her mother and from people on the Vineyard. And his eyes gleamed as he spoke, suggesting a devil's delight in forbidden things.

He seemed to note her discomfort, for when he looked at her again, his expression and his voice softened.

"There are other things, among these natives, which we cannot envy at all . . ."

For an instant, it seemed as if he wanted to say more but stopped himself. He pulled away from the rail.

"Never mind." He smiled, his thoughts far away, then brought his attention back to her. "There will be singing whales. That much is certainly true."

Turning, he strode away along the motionless deck.

As Everett left her, Perpetua realized that he must have more knowledge of the natives than her mother possibly could have garnered through books and gossip. She turned to see her father standing near her, looking at her intently. There was something foreign in his manner. Shocked, she stared back at him without a word. It was as if they had never met. Perpetua felt strangely as though this were a confrontation between a grown woman and man, not between father and daughter.

"You seem to have weathered the voyage well, Perpetua," he began, his eyes dwelling on her body as he spoke. "Have you gained a little weight, daughter, or has your mother not seen to your attire?"

Perpetua knew that she was nearly bursting out of her clothes, that her breasts were filling out. The blouse which had been loose and comfortable at the voyage's beginning now clung tightly, sharply defining her budding nipples. Unconsciously placing her arms across her chest, she blushed at this direct comment from her father. He had not spoken to her in days. She took a firm stand with her feet apart and stared back at him, almost defiantly. It was about time he knew she was alive and that she was a woman!

Jared couldn't help himself. He hadn't really noticed before. Suddenly, one child had become a woman. How old was she? Near fifteen? Or was it sixteen? They had left harbor one year and nine months ago. Aye, she would soon be sixteen.

"Are you prepared for the Sandwich Islands, lass? Has anyone told you what it will be like there?"

As the Captain towered over her, blocking the sun, Perpetua was suddenly conscious of her father's great breadth, his height. She couldn't help but remember how he had looked on deck that morning months ago, nude, hair all over his body. She remembered the loud, coarse laughter and the reason for it. Now his shadow on her like a heavy hand brought speech to her lips.

"Yes, Father. Mother has told me." That was all she could manage. She wondered why she was so nervous, why she was beginning to tremble.

"I hope she has told you that their customs differ

a great deal from ours. Though the missionaries are doing their best to teach them that the good Lord did not put them on earth for pleasure alone, the natives are much given to sin."

The Captain felt it was his duty to warn her by expressing his disapproval of the natives. Who could say how they might look at his daughter? She looked so small, so helpless, yet she already had the body of another young woman, whose thighs and buttocks had once stirred him strongly. Was it because he thought so often of Naliki that he was reminded of her now? How he yearned for her! His sex had risen so quickly with her fluttering touch, gentle, skilled, demanding! Aye, this young woman before him might be on her way to womanhood, but she was bound by stern New England ethics which would never release her. She could never be another Naliki. She would instead become another Clarissa—cold, shunning nature's demands and never, never sinning.

"When you are ashore, Perpetua, mind you stay near your mother. Aboard this ship, I have had little time to be with you, except during meals. But when we reach Maui, I will guide you better, as a father should. I disapprove of the island ways. You must see to it that you are not misled by any of those people."

Having made his dutiful speech, Jared turned back to his command. In less than three months they would close on Maui. There were whales aplenty. Oil would make him rich. He had no more time for Perpetua. As he turned from her, he thought how her blooming womanhood was clearly evident and he felt somehow saddened that her childhood should have passed by during his absence.

* * *

Once he had left her, Perpetua stopped shaking and took a deep breath. There was something formidably masculine about the Captain, she thought. That masculinity was not unpleasant, but disquieting. She had been thoroughly conscious of his physical examination of her, and of his male approval. It was the first time such a thing had happened to her.

That evening, Clarissa, having herself made a discovery, wrote a short entry in her Journal:

> E. said he cared for me, though his words were veiled. Never have I felt such a sense of complete happiness—and safety. He spoke to me of love, I think. He could have spared his lengthy philosophy about the native ways! What has come over me?

Though Jared West had been discharging his duties to his ship and men, his duties to his wife had been ignored. Slowly he was beginning to realize this. During the long months at sea he had used her. A man totally absorbed in his own needs, he had spent hours dreaming of Naliki, spending himself on Clarissa when his lust demanded satiation. Otherwise, he had hardly observed her, save when they took meals together.

But, he had begun to be aware of Clarissa and another man of late. It occurred to Jared, as he sat before his desk, that whenever he saw Clarissa on deck, Everett Norton was somewhere about. Such encounters had to be more than coincidence. Clarissa was confined to the aft quarters, and the crew stayed forward. What reason could there be for Clarissa to speak with this man? The notion of her being unfaithful, even thinking adulterous thoughts, was inconceivable.

Or was it? Captain Jared felt his skin crawl, as

the seditious thoughts came to mind. An odd giddiness swept over him. What was it he had seen tonight?

As he had started aft, having completed the stowing of the new mizzensail, he had seen the shadow of two people who suddenly parted. Could it be?

No. He passed a hand across his brow and turned up the wick on the lamp, staring down at the journel which lay open on his desk. Two people. It was no matter for concern. A man such as Norton would never dare take liberties. He was aboard ship, and here the Captain had the power of life and death over every man.

The quill in Captain Jared's hand began to move across the page, inscribing his thoughts in the journal with firm, bold strokes . . .

Passed an uninhabited coral island today. We have set course for Maui. After fresh food, water and outfitting for bowhead, we'll depend upon the trades to carry us two hundred miles each day. I wonder who this Everett Norton is? I've seen him look at Clarissa. The other day when the wave hit her full and it made her thin dress cling to her body like skin, he stood and gaped at her. And when she washed her hair in the rainwater tub, then tossed her hair back, and the water made her breasts stand clear, he was there again. Once when she bent low over the wash, her pantaloons tight against her backside, Norton stood looking with an expression I know. His intimate ways with my daughter I have let pass.

What is he up to? He is not like the others. A learned man has no reason to be aboard a whaler where the pay is so meager. Is he here because of her? And why am I so bothered? Do I need both Clarissa and Naliki? What is the matter with me? With one, there is security, a family. With the other . . . God help me!

* * *

The next morning Jared saw Everett passing by. Now was his chance! He must speak to him. He held up his hand and motioned to the tall man.

"Stand a minute, Mr. Norton. I would speak with you."

Everett smiled and stood with feet apart. "Aye, sir. What can I do for you?"

"Just who are you, sir?"

"My name is Everett Norton, as you know from your ship's papers. I was born in the Commonwealth of Massachusetts and have been a sailor most of my life. Why do you ask, sir?"

"I know your name. I know you are from my state. Tell me—why would an educated man prefer to be but an ordinary seaman on my ship? Have you never tried for officer's papers?"

"Captain West, I have never sought rank. I sail because I love the sea. Is that all, sir?" Everett made ready to move along.

"Stand a moment longer, Mr. Norton. I hear from the men that you have traveled the world, and that you can speak foreign languages."

"Aye, sir. I've spent some days in France and the Mediterranean. But the oceans of the world are my home, sir."

"Have you ever been on Martha's Vineyard?"

"What man hasn't? Aye, I've been on the Vineyard, but 'twas long ago." Everett paused a long while. Finally, he asked, "Is that all, Captain West?"

"Hold on, Mr. Norton. I note you have a reluctance to reveal your past in any detail. Yet you spin yarns about European ports with the others, so they tell me. You give them every exotic detail. Is it that your Captain ties your tongue with a slipknot, sir?"

"What else would you know of me?"

"You strike me as strange. And your familiarity with my daughter bothers me somewhat. Your sophistication imposed upon her youthful and impressionable mind might not be of benefit to her."

Men on deck walked around the pair, giving them a wide berth, sensing a confrontation. Neither man seemed to notice the others. Everett had relaxed under Jared's hard looks and intense questioning. Now that the long-dreaded conversation had begun, Everett felt at ease. Suddenly it was Jared who found himself hard put to express his thoughts.

"I speak to her when she speaks to me, Captain. She is filled with questions, as are all youngsters. I but answer and do not embroider, nor make a net to catch the child's mind. In fact, Captain, she has captured mine. You must be proud of her."

Jared unaccountably found himself on the defensive. "That I am," he agreed slowly, staring deeply into the shaded eyes of the easy-mannered man before him. "And my wife, Mrs. West, as well. Now go about your duty, Mr. Norton. I am certain you catch my meaning. I see that they have already checked the maintop. You'd best report to Mr. Perkins, sir."

Everett looked up at the maintop; then his eyes returned to Jared.

"We should speak again, Captain. I am ready to give details should you ask." He backed away two steps and awaited dismissal.

"Shall I go to my station?"

"Aye," replied the Captain. "See to your duties, Mr. Norton."

* * *

Nine weeks later *The Horatio* entered the tropical fringes of the Sandwich Islands. At Lahaina, the ship would join the whaling fleet for the traditional stop for refitting and reprovisioning. The men would be allowed to go ashore and see the town.

Tropical palm trees, broken reeds and seaweed torn from its beds lazily washed atop the crest of the waves. Unfamiliar, brightly colored birds floated between the masts and dipped as if in salute, while screeching gulls followed the wake, eagerly seeking refuse thrown overboard.

Pausing in his duty long enough to point out familiar landmarks to Clarissa and Perpetua, Everett said, "That's Haleakala, 'House of the Sun.' It's a volcano so big across its mouth it could swallow up Martha's Vineyard and leave room for Naushon. Up there, the silverswords grow higher than sunflowers. They seed themselves in the lava and have lavender and gold blooms, reaching up, the natives say, as close as any god has ever been to the sun. Such flowers are found nowhere else in the world."

"I would like to explore Haleakala," said Perpetua. "Is there any chance the volcano will erupt?"

"No, child. Not since the 1700's has the great volcano exploded. Over there are the peaks of Molokai. South, there, you can see the slopes of Kahoolawe. When we get closer to shore, you'll be able to spy 'The Baldwin House.' It looks just like a Vineyard house with verandas on two floors. Baldwin was a missionary-doctor."

Perpetua continued to look at the sights before

her. Her mother watched as Everett began his climb up the foremast.

The Horatio was a hundred yards off shore when the first anchor slid over the side. The early morning sun sent a warm mist rising from the moist foliage along the edge of the beach. Above Clarissa and Perpetua, who stood at the rail together, was a violet-blue sky. As Clarissa looked toward the beach, she saw more than a dozen natives dash into the breaking surf. Ten more followed. Their black heads bobbed up on the near side of the rolling waves. Clarissa could see that they were girls, leaping like porpoises out of the water, displaying their naked bodies as they frolicked. As if given a signal, the group began splashing its way toward *The Horatio!*

Clarissa heard a great cry from the crew which had lined the port side, watching as she did, the oncoming girls. She looked at her daughter, who was bent forward, eyes wide open, a half-smile on her golden face.

The girls in the lead could now be seen clearly. Their unfettered bodies gleamed through the clear water as they vigorously swam their way alongside. Lines were thrown over as though the seamen had prepared in advance for the boarding, waiting for just this moment. Dozens of others streamed in a long line from the nearby island, plunging into the waves just as the nearest girls began tumbling aboard.

Clarissa heard Jared's cry of warning over the yelps of the men as they eagerly reached for the offerings. But the Captain went unheeded—unheard.

"She's mine!" cried a man in his forties, as he lifted the first girl, a tawny, full-breasted young woman, and carried her laughing to the fore hatch. Behind him came another man, younger and bare to the waist. In his arms he held a plump maiden whose

legs scissor-kicked, displaying a full thatch of black
hair between her thighs. As the men disappeared below, Clarissa saw the younger man fondling the girl's
huge breasts with his free hand.

Wild and frenzied activity exploded on deck as
the men, so long without women, cast all restraint
aside. One girl after another was tossed on her back
without preamble, each naked pair joining dozens of
other couples in a scramble of bodies on the open
deck.

Perpetua remained frozen, her two hands
clutching the rail. At her feet, nudging against her as
they moved, was a sailor and a girl. It was a young
lad from Nantucket, as nude as the young native girl
under him.

Clarissa cried out in panic. Jared's voice rose
higher. She looked at him for help, but she saw his
dark, intense eyes searching among the couples,
openly lusting. Perpetua had covered her eyes with
her hands. She tried to free herself from the legs
which were flung near her feet as the pair screamed,
reaching climax. Stepping over the pulsing bodies as
though they were flotsam from the sea, Perpetua,
flushed and trembling, found her mother's arms. She
felt the strong rise and fall of her mother's warm
bosom, the fast beat of her heart as Perpetua buried
her head against her mother's comforting breast.

Clarissa shielded her daughter's eyes as a man
with the body of a Greek god walked by, his organ
erect, the dark, beautiful body of a girl held close to
his muscular chest.

Looking away quickly to where her husband had
stood earlier, Clarissa saw Everett. Two young girls
were tearing at his pants, one with her hand caressing
his torso. The other's hand had disappeared inside his
clothing. Why hadn't he moved? Clarissa felt this was

the lower depths of Hell! As Clarissa watched, Everett quietly pushed the two girls aside, shaking his head, and stared directly at her!

He raised his hand and started to say something. But she never heard him. From behind, someone grasped her arm and she turned her head to see the wild eyes of her husband. Perpetua was firmly held in his other hand. His command to go below was directed to both of them.

Clarissa had seen the arousal in the Captain's eyes as well as in Everett's. Even she had felt wild stirrings in herself as the couples had met with wild shouts and passionate moans.

Never had she dreamed of such a bacchanal as she had witnessed on that deck. There was little her husband could have done to prevent it. It had happened too fast—the men had been too eager, their need too great. She, too, had been seduced by the hedonistic air of passion. When the Greek god from the crew had passed her, proudly displaying his condition, she had openly stared at his sex, stared at the girl's lush body so close to his.

Clarissa now let her husband direct her and her daughter to the afterdeck. Perpetua held her hand, walking stiffly, as if every muscle in her body was paralyzed.

The door slammed behind them.

The two stared at one another. Then Perpetua began to laugh. It wasn't a pleasant sound. It was more like a scream than mirth. Clarissa leaned down and held her head.

"Stop! Stop it, Perpetua! We're safe now. The Captain will send them packing."

"Oh, no," Perpetua moaned. "I never dreamed it would be like that! It was frightening!"

Then, suddenly, eyes dry, she looked up.

"Those girls!"

"Yes? Those awful creatures!"

"Mother—they were beautiful!"

* * *

Two hours later the deck had been cleared and the first watch sent ashore. It hadn't taken the men long to reach the waiting beauties on the beach. The second watch sent them off with warnings to return in four hours, no more, or they would suffer for their greediness. The longboats hurried the first watch to the island faster than a whale could have towed them.

A boat was summoned to take Clarissa and Perpetua to the wharf at Lahaina. Embarrassed by the presence of the men who settled in the boat near them, mother and daughter accepted the few bundles of clothing that were handed to them, and sat stiff and formal in the boat as it moved ashore.

Perpetua knew that she would have nightmares after what she had seen and heard. It was as if a pack of wild dogs with their bitches had been set free upon each other. The sheep and cows at home had been more gentle. Perpetua pulled her bonnet low across her eyes and concentrated on the approaching shore where she could see houses.

A buggy awaited them at the wharf. Jared helped carry their few things to it. The rest would be gathered the next day.

"I want to be certain you are happy where I am placing you. You will be guests of Jessie Percival, and she is from the Vineyard," he explained. "There are proper rooms in her house, where we all can stay for a while. After I let you off, I must go to the offices of my agents, Tobias & Smith. Later, I will come to the house."

The buggy drew up before a white, clapboard house which looked as if it might have been transplanted from the Vineyard board by board. Later, they learned this was true. There stood the familiar broad veranda. The small windows on each floor faced south, just as they would, had this been cold New England.

Awaiting Clarissa and Perpetua, greeting them with a friendly smile, was a chubby woman who, though in the autumn of her beauty, had obviously been quite striking and elegant in her day. She showed them in as if they were long-time friends rather than paying guests.

"Drat that boy from Tobias & Smith. I sent him to fetch ye, but he lingered down there, I 'magine. All these island *keiki* are *lolo*." Jessie Percival drew a circle in the air to indicate that the natives were crazy. Yet she seemed to be tolerant, amused rather than angered by their unreliable natures.

"You must be tired, ma'am," she said to Clarissa. "Come out of that sun and make yourself at home."

Clarissa felt the sincerity and warmth, and responded with a relieved smile. It was so like being down-village with an old friend. Jared began to speak, but the woman waved him in. "Now no excuses, *kapena*, don't say a word about your sudden comin'. I'm always ready for Island folks. Ye know my man, who's long gone, the old rascal. John Benson Percival came from Chilmark, too. It's a joy to have ye. How I miss the winters on the Vineyard! My John gambled away everything. If I hadn't stowed away a piece of his share each voyage, I'd not have had this place to end my days."

She walked before them, fixing her white hair which insisted on coming loose at every bob of her head. She took hold of the banister and, grunting at each step, led her new guests to the second story.

Two rooms and a bath were theirs. "Now mind ye . . . when you're all fixed, come below and share a cup of good, hot coffee with me and tell me all about yerselves."

Perpetua begged to explore the new place. This gave Jared his chance.

"First nights ashore are difficult. I have many things to do of a business nature. So, don't be alarmed if I stay aboard ship this night and maybe the next."

Clarissa nodded. She was already far off, for the familiar style of the houses stirred an unexpected longing for home. The Vineyard was flatter, with fewer hills and less foliage, and the lush palms and overgrowth all about made her feel far away from home. No matter how welcoming Mrs. Percival was, Clarissa knew she was already homesick.

Jared slowly rose to his feet and faced his wife.

"Clarissa—what you witnessed aboard *The Horatio* was not meant to occur before your eyes. I hope you can forget that it happened, Clarissa, and that you shielded Perpetua's eyes."

"There was no way I could protect her, Jared!" Clarissa scathingly retorted. "There is no way that I myself will ever forget that scene. I wish that it had never happened. I wish I could erase it from our daughter's mind. I know that the terrible memory of what we saw will live with her forever."

Jared turned quickly away. The remorse burned through his bones like searing iron, scorching him inside. But events could not be erased. Nothing could be undone that had already been done. He was falling . . . falling . . . and this island was pulling him relentlessly with its promises . . . toward its clear streams and verdant paths, toward its warm, steaming forests, toward its people . . . toward Naliki. Even now, as he turned away from his pleading wife, Jared felt the call of the girl. And he walked away—toward her—as if in a dream.

* * *

It had been four years since he'd last seen Naliki. She had been a child when he first met her, a child with the body of a young woman and ways of pleasing a man which he would never forget. The attacks on Clarissa had only intensified his lusting for Naliki, for only she could bring him to the heights which, in memory, seemed beyond reality. Taking advantage of the two nights he had created for his freedom, knowing his ship was in the capable hands of his agents and officers, he left the ship very late that night, when all hands, worn out by their excesses, were snoring in the deep sleep of men who had been satiated.

As he walked down the dirt road whose every turning he remembered perfectly, he felt the blood surge in his legs and groin. He would talk to her at first, discover whether she still wanted him. Then, never doubting that she would comply, he would have her. Ahh! There was her hut. He moved slowly in the dark, walking stealthily on the balls of his feet. Now he was not far away. A fire still glowed before her door. He reached out a hand and parted the mat.

There she lay, nude and magnificent, her *tapa* covering only her legs, the soft down between her thighs reflecting in the light from the open doorway. Though Jared had approached the hut as quietly as he could, Naliki had heard him. She stood up the moment he entered and the *tapa* dropped from her exquisite body. She looked silently at him, almost without recognition, showing nothing as her oval eyes examined him like a creature from another world. Her proud, uplifted breasts were within his reach and his eyes traveled over her, resting there as he hungered for her warmth. Her hands rose, each cupping a breast, and she covered her nipples from his sight.

It was as though he had never left the Naliki of his fantasies. Yes, those nights when he made love to Clarissa, this—this!—was the girl who had filled his mind. She was familiar to him, so familiar that it was as if he had never left her.

"It is I, Jared West," he said. "I have come back for you." He moved toward her, his hands already at his belt.

"It is too late, Jared West!" Her voice had a sharp quality he hadn't remembered. "You have waited too long." She looked at him squarely. "I am to marry an *alii*, a nobleman of my own people. I will be his bride with the full moon. I cannot be with you."

Jared gave a soft cry as if someone had dealt him a blow to the stomach. To come so far, to dream so often, only to be deprived of her—it was unendurable!

"I have waited many years for this night, my sweet Naliki. I love you. Don't you know that? I have taken my wife only to appease myself, and while I have, I have been thinking of you."

He stared down at her, and even without touching her, Jared could feel that silken skin, the touch of her hands as they passed along his stomach, downward and then . . . grasped him, holding him gently, urging him, coaxing him, making everything all right again. Why did she look at him as if at a stranger?

"My father had many daughters, Captain West."

He didn't understand her words. Staring into her

eyes, he thought he saw a slight smile, a look of so-phistication where before he had seen only innocence.

"Lai is ready. She can be yours tonight and every night. You are anxious for a young girl, are you not?" Naliki began pulling on her *tapa*. Gone forever was that beautiful body. It would never again be his. But his blood still coursed through his veins; her presence rendered him helpless. He must somehow have ap-peasement, a release from what had seemed a decade of waiting for her.

"Lai will teach you new things, Captain," she said. Jared felt like a man being carried forward in a wild, rushing river, unable to change his course, careening without direction, knowing that some shore must be reached or he would surely drown! By God, if he couldn't have her with her consent, he would take her by force! He could not endure more torment!

He reached for her quickly, and then was stilled by the look in her eyes. Her hand touched the mat which covered a door of the hut. She was poised, ready to vanish in an instant.

"I will call Lai," Naliki told him softly. "She is near."

Then Naliki was gone. Should he go or stay? Jared stood alone, feeling each moment pass. He should leave this hut, this island, forever. Yet he could not stir, not as long as there was hope. The mat moved. Two figures stood before him.

"This is Lai."

Jared did not want to look at her. But the girl stepped forward from the shadows. There, in the glow from the afternoon sun, Jared saw Naliki as she had been four years ago. The girl was lithe, with full breasts. She was slim about the waist. Her jet-black hair was flowing, glistening. Jared felt himself grow hot. It didn't seem possible! He heard the two laugh, then saw Naliki move behind Lai. Gathering her *tapa*, Naliki opened the mat and slipped away. Jared and Lai were alone.

Somewhere, not far away, a drum began to beat. The girl before him answered its sound. She began a writhing, pulsating movement, hips gyrating, breasts bouncing slightly, her hands moving the gestures of love. She reached out, suggestively fondling an imaginary male organ with long, delicate fingers. Spreading her legs wide, she pressed her hands to her thighs in jerking motions, as she slowly rocked to the beat of the drum.

In the grip of overpowering emotion, Jared felt himself so filled with lust that his legs seemed unable to support him. Though the girl before him was dancing a ritual, it delivered all the sensual meaning a man could expect in a lifetime. Now she was positioning herself before him on her hands and knees, her buttocks tantalizing him, moving up and down slowly until he could bear the delicious sight no longer.

As though knowing the moment when Jared would be ready, Lai turned quickly, stood up and pressed herself to him. Her left hand began on his coat, almost tearing the buttons in her haste. Her right hand pulled open his trousers. He helped her, frantic. Soon he stood tall, his sex fully erect before her. This wasn't Lai. This was Naliki. Her eyes were rounder, her breasts more full. But otherwise, from her long silky, black hair to her toes, she moved exactly as her sister.

Falling back upon her sister's mat, Lai lay ready for him, her legs parted, the soft down glistening, her breath coming in gasps. When she held out her arms, Jared came down on his knees between her legs. He began to thrust into her. Her long legs closed about him. He felt her legs lock. Her fingers began to knead his muscular buttocks. One hand at a time stroked from side to side, then both, ever so slowly, traced the line of his backbone.

Fully embedded in her, unable to hold back for an instant, Jared's body rocked in an orgasm so violent that he almost lost consciousness. At the instant of his first, pulsing rush toward fulfillment, he felt her soft hands gently grasp his testicles, holding them in her firm grasp until he was entirely spent. He fell limply upon her.

It was an hour later when he stood up. They had lain there, her fingernails tracing his buttocks, his muscular arms embracing her, his spine, now so sensitive, tingling in response to her touch. Jared had held her close to him, his two hands upon her back. He knew that somehow he had moved her, had made her feel his power, his energy and lust. He wondered whether she had truly gone to the heights he had reveled in or whether she had simply been trained to pretend.

As he stood, a sudden and overwhelming sense of remorse struck him a crushing blow. Why should he feel this powerful sense of guilt? Was it because of Naliki? He went back to Lai, who was now sitting. She looked up at him, expectant. They hadn't said a word.

"Lai?" he asked. "Why?"

"Why what, Captain?"

"Did you not know that I had come here for your sister?"

"You are a big man, Captain. A giant with much to please. Any young woman would wish you whether you once lay with my sister or not."

He watched as she suddenly stood up, her oval eyes half shut, her dusky skin aglow with the heat they had created. How much like Naliki she looked!

She watched him, then, as though reading his thoughts, she spoke.

"Stay the night here," she offered. "Rest here on the shore. Naliki is already asleep in my hut. We will be alone."

Without a word, Jared took Lai in his arms, felt her hair against his chest, ran his hand down her back to the curve of her buttocks. Then, he violently pressed her body to his as the lust seized him again and his organ rose against the darkness of her thighs.

They sank slowly to the ground. She began to caress him, running light fingers across his chest, finding the tangle of his pubic hair. He waited languorously, until he felt his organ come into her grasp. Delicately held, Jared felt himself awaken fully as her nails dug into his chest. Her voice began a pleading song.

Spreading her legs, with her smooth, soft belly flattened beneath him, Jared moved slowly into her. Her fragrant hair, her words of entreaty, precipitated them both toward climax. At the very moment when he felt himself beginning to rise to the trembling point of perfect satisfaction, he felt the inner caress begin!

Oh, how he had longed for this! He lay still, allowing her inner sex to act like a thousand fingers, her body to surround and engulf him, to use him as she wished. He felt her legs release him, then move until they had grasped him above the shoulders, allowing him deep penetration. The inner caress continued, demanding, asking. With a loud moan he plunged into her in a final series of thrusts. His cry, "Naliki!" hung in the air. A series of convulsions began, the heat flowing through him, into the rippling sex which still sent impulsive waves of delight to the tip of his organ.

The mat to the rear of the hut opened slightly, Naliki took one quick look, then withdrew. There was a half-smile of satisfaction on her lips. She turned toward Lai's hut, where she would pass the night alone.

* * *

It was early morning of the second day when Jared staggered back through the jungle. Only one thought occupied his mind: to reach Jessie Percival's big, white house, the house that was so like a Vineyard mansion. Clarissa would be there.

The ancient guilt consumed him. Adultery! It was a terrible sin. But his mind confused him with other feelings more strange—remorse! Not for adultery, nor for the betrayal of his wife and daughter's trust. No, it was remorse for another act, that of so easily being turned from Naliki to her sister, Lai. Was he a man who could be driven by carnal desires alone, a man who, like a rudderless vessel, could be drawn by any trivial wind or tide to any female harbor?

He moved blindly, shielding neither his face nor body from the barbed foliage.

"You lecher!" he cried out. "Weakling! What kind of man are you?"

His mind was still fogged by insatiable appetite; his wanton use of Lai burned like fire in his head. And behind that semiconscious state lay another thought, even more overwhelming than the first. Naliki could no longer be his! He had openly accepted a substitute, offered so lightly, and now he alone had sinned terribly. First against Clarissa, then against Naliki, and finally—worse than the other crimes—he had sinned against his own manhood, spirit and soul! A giant vine brushed against his cheek, tearing at the skin. A gnarled stump loomed up from the ground as blood poured down to his lips. He pitched forward into a tangle of foliage, so thick that for a moment his body was completely hidden. As he fell, his head struck a sharp rock hidden in the foliage. Blood poured from the gash in his forehead.

In pain, his leg twisted beneath him. Jared began to struggle to his feet, hands at his eyes to wipe away the stream of blood.

A fallen giant in the gloom of the forest, Jared swore at the pain that clutched at him. He felt for the knife which he always carried at his belt and thrashed wildly, frantically trying to cut himself free. The knife seemed to have a will of its own. The gleaming blade at once threatened and appealed to him, as though he should somehow maim himself, destroy his flesh. His was the flesh that had driven so willfully into the yielding body of Lai: it did not deserve life. He raised his hand. The blade was sharp. His body had betrayed his will. The betrayer must be severed from the man of God. Jared must be free at last!

Bleeding profusely, dazed by the torment that racked every movement, Jared was unaware of the figures approaching through the jungle. His blade aimed directly at his groin.

Arms surrounded his waist. He heard someone shout. He turned, but was held so tightly he could not see who held him. He felt himself lifted, saw the knife being taken from his slippery palm. He closed his eyes, hoping that the Lord had answered his prayer for death.

* * *

Slowly, he returned to consciousness. Bandages had been placed on his cuts. He was lying on a wide bed with Clarissa bending over him.

"You have been hurt. Lie still, Jared. Lie still."

"I can never rest," he managed, filled with contrition. "I must confess. I have committed a horrible crime."

She soothed him as best she could, speaking softly and lovingly, but he raised himself trembling, his face damp with perspiration. Her sweet face hovered above him. Oh, God, let it never change. Let her always remain as beautiful as she was now, in her kindness.

He told her. While he spoke, he saw her nod, as though somehow she had already known his terrible secret. When he had finished, he closed his eyes, knowing, without asking, that Clarissa understood his anguish. Then, with her gentle help, he lay down again. He felt expiated in some way. But his helplessness was something new. Absolution, punishment or purgatory—whatever lay before him was not of his doing, was beyond his masculine control.

Hours later, he opened his eyes but couldn't see. Stirring at last, he understood the quietness that had come over him while he slept. His head was between Clarissa's breasts, as soft and comforting as a mother's. He wanted to hide, to stay there away from the world. Her soft palm was slowly caressing his forehead while she hummed to herself as though he were a broken, distraught infant cradled in her arms. He hoped no one could see him in this condition, least of all any man. He tried to drive away the image of his humiliation. Failing, he drew a deep, sobbing breath, all pretense gone—discovered, disgraced, degraded. Clarissa's palm moved gently across his head and down his cheek to his beard;

then, in the soft darkness, she touched his lips with her fingertips, a touch of understanding and perhaps of forgiveness. He heard, as if in a dream underwater, her quiet singing: "Baby's boat's a silver moon . . ." a child's lullaby. He nestled closer to her, felt her body warm against his.

He struggled to free himself, to stop her and to still the self-pity he felt.

"No, Jared. Lie quiet! Sleep. You will be better tomorrow."

He pressed his tired eyes against the firm flesh and buried his head again, closing out the world. Yes, this was the way. She was the woman he loved. He had offended her beyond forgiveness, and yet she alone brought his suffering to an end. He would drift off . . . to sleep, perhaps never again to awaken to horrible reality. Clarissa would be there tomorrow, forgiving him.

Her arms pulled him to her closely as he slept. She cried softly, careful not to waken him.

* * *

Three weeks had gone by and Jared West's wounds had healed. It was to be his last day in Jessie's house. Clarissa put down her mending when Jared began to speak.

"The wages of sin are death," he began somberly. "I have sinned against you, against God and myself. Now I must go. The voyage may take three months."

Clarissa had heard similar speeches from him for the past fortnight, ever since he had risen suddenly one morning and begun packing his footlocker. He had moved about listlessly, without his usual force, no longer seeming to be the master of himself. From that first day, she had wondered whether he would be capable of taking on his new command.

"I know," she nodded. "I know. But, now, you must put all that out of your head. Time will pass and we will be together. I am only worried about your strength."

"I have been busy on *The Horatio*. I will be all right. It is my mind which sickens me, not my body."

"Live with your Bible near you, Captain. The Good Word will heal your mind."

"I will depart with my head high, Clarissa, if you will go to the wharf with me."

"We will both go with you, of course, Captain. We love you." Clarissa had returned to addressing him as "Captain," feeling the word would, in itself, give him greater confidence. As she took his hand, there was a knock at the door.

"We are here! Your footlocker, Captain." It was the voice of Old Talbot.

Jared turned once more to Clarissa and his eyes seemed lit with a strange, protracted fire.

"I am not taking Everett Norton with me. He has asked for leave from his contract. He speaks of settling here. I hope that he will look in on you and Perpetua and see that you want for nothing during my absence."

Clarissa knew that Everett would remain on the island. But she had kept the knowledge to herself.

"I may see him now and then. My thoughts will be with you." Clarissa lifted her face and Jared kissed her lips.

"Farewell, Clarissa."

They stood looking at one another for a last time.

"How long this time, Captain?" she managed at last.

"With good luck and a 'greasy ship,' I should be

back in these Roads—with the red pennant flying—
within three months. There is money in the bank. I
have left a letter to be opened later by Tobias & Smith
regarding my share of the voyage. You'll be ready to
go home with me?"

"Aye, Captain, I will."

They walked out hand in hand. Jared called Perpetua to join them.

Their parting took place on the wharf, as Jared
awaited the men in a whaleboat to draw near the
wharf. He strode to the longboat, head held high,
black beard jutting out, his hair blowing in the morning breeze. Clarissa saw him square his shoulders. So
it was not just her imagination: something in the
Captain had, indeed, been weakened, that he should
have to brace himself this way for meeting his men
again. It seemed to her as if this moment would never
end.

From the beach that lay to the west, Clarissa
heard the sounds of drums and the singing of the natives enjoying an island ceremony. It was in sharp
contrast to the heavy atmosphere surrounding the
thoughts of Clarissa and the Captain.

"The girl Naliki is being married," an old woman
from Edgartown whispered in her ear. Clarissa
shrugged.

Then she saw a huge, gaily-bedecked canoe
being pushed from the shore and in it, with flags flying, the silhouette of the bride with a tall man beside
her, his headdress rising three feet in a rainbow of
colors.

To Clarissa this pagan ceremony seemed sacrile-
gious. A prayer began in her head: "Trust in the Lord
with all thy heart . . ."

Suddenly, Jared came back toward her and she,
as if a dam had burst within, rushed forward, crying,

"Jared!" They reached out to one another—the tall, dark man and the small, blonde woman. They held each other close for a moment until, finally, Jared tore himself away from her. Stepping into the boat, he turned to Clarissa for the last time.

"We are made of rock. No storm shall harm you, Clarissa."

And as he spoke, there was an unaccustomed softness in his voice, a softness which she had never heard before. With tears standing in his eyes, he turned away and gave the order to his men to row.

He sat in the stern, a lonely but proud figure, the men gazing past him as they rowed, answering to his commands but oblivious to his physical presence. He once again seemed the master of his ship and his fate.

Before the boat had gone twenty feet from the wharf, the Captain stood up and looked back. There, beside Clarissa, was Perpetua, his only gift to her. She seemed a small thing to leave as comfort. He knew that, with her new maturity, she would be seeking experiences beyond those that a mother could give her.

At that moment, the ceremonial canoe in which sat Naliki and Kahana, bride and groom, swept toward the wharf. The canoe drew to a halt. Out of it stepped a six-foot, brown-skinned chief. He wore a cape of yellow and red feathers, a red *tapa*. Atop his head was the traditional helmet adorned with a crest of white feathers which began at the nape of his neck and became a crown upon his brow. After him, with great daintiness, stepped Naliki. She walked, as if foreordained, to where Clarissa and Perpetua stood. Reaching them, Naliki looked in the direction of Jared's longboat, now slowly moving toward *The Horatio*.

Jared and Naliki were thirty feet away from one another. Naliki's eyes fixed on the Captain's as he stood astride the stern of the longboat. Then he slowly looked away.

As his boat neared the ship, Jared watched the lithe and beautiful figure of Naliki. Once she had been his. His, alone! And now . . .

What wretched hand of fate, what devil of coincidence, had sent her to that wharf at this moment to torment him? For it was a final torture, a kiss for the damned. He could not take his eyes off her body, could not stop himself from feeding on that final vision.

Yet she distracted him. And that distraction, alone, saved him from a greater torment which he would otherwise have been forced to endure in the months ahead. With his eyes fixed on Naliki and his thoughts drifting in a maelstrom of their own designing, he did not see the man's figure coming down the hill to stand at the wharf, taking a position near his wife and only child. Nor did he see the sudden smile that replaced the grim and sorrowful look on Clarissa's face, when she turned to speak to Everett Norton.

Once aboard ship, Jared did not look back. And so he did not see Norton offer an arm to Clarissa and guide her up the hill.

No, when Captain West turned for a last look at the island, the wharf was empty and the lagoon seemed to be held in the spell of some otherworldly, timeless enchantment. It drew him with every breeze, every fragrance, every ripple of its azure waters. And yet it seemed, inexplicably, a place to which he would never be allowed to return.

CHAPTER 9

The next day on Maui began with a cloudless sky. Hand in hand, Clarissa and Perpetua walked to town, passing an abundance of plantain, banana and breadfruit trees. There were coconut palms gracefully leaning across the roads. The track they followed wandered effortlessly into the hills and valleys, cutting its way through thick, colorful undergrowth, up the mountain passes. Clusters of lauhala trees shadowed the hot, sandy roads. Soon the pair had passed the few shops, the docks and the row of offices that lined the shore. A break in the foliage and bushes gave Perpetua a view of the open sea. Ahead of her she could see the line of surf curling languidly, washing the distant shore.

"Let's walk on the beach!" cried Perpetua, darting ahead.

"Wait! Wait for me!" cried her mother, gathering up her skirts and clutching her parasol.

But Perpetua was already far away. Turning a corner which hid her from view, she paused to glance back at her mother, then raced ahead spiritedly.

"Mothers don't like to explore," she murmured to herself. "I'll find her again on the road or go home by myself."

Free from the house, from the sadness of her father's departure, Perpetua tossed her hat on a bush, reminding herself to recover it on her way back. She loosened her blonde hair so that it hung behind her, and ran farther along the edge of the line of bushes to escape her mother's eye.

Suddenly, she came upon a group of young men and women playing some game on the broad beach ahead. Perpetua drew back into the bushes. Not one of the players wore clothes, not even a *tapa* cloth. And the "game" which she had thought they were playing was a serious matter of run and catch. Without a doubt, that tall, beautifully built young man with the dark skin not only wished to catch the supple girl with the long, black hair, but to have sex with her as well.

The girl fell down laughing on the warm sand as the young man tumbled on top of her. She hadn't tripped! It had just been her way of bringing the chase to an end. Less than fifty feet away, slightly hidden by the dense leaves of the bushes, Perpetua could clearly see her playmate's erect organ. The girl feigned astonishment at seeing his readiness and she laughed shrilly. But the girl's laughter was cut off sharply as the two joined. Perpetua looked away, embarrassed.

Another couple came near her and lay close together on the sand. They apparently did not care whether she saw them or not.

Their carefree smiles, their beautiful, liquid speech, so melodious, told her that they, too, were lovers. The young man began running his hands about the young girl's firm breasts, pinching her nipples gently as she gave short cries and entangled her legs in his.

Then Perpetua saw Clarissa struggling across the

heavy sand, coming her way. How could she escape without being seen?

The water lay ahead. Perpetua saw girls dashing toward the waves, screaming with delight as the young men followed.

Dropping her shoes beside her, Perpetua stood up and ran as fast as she could for the sea.

Having spent many hours at the great South Beach on Martha's Vineyard, Perpetua knew in advance the danger of an undertow. She knew the sand beneath her feet could give way suddenly, the crashing waves could tumble her down. She had no fear here. Flying by the naked bodies of young men and women who stared as she raced past them, she reached the water, diving just under the crest of the surf.

She would join them, be one with their freedom, share in their careless, indolent life. Why not? She was a young woman now. Their joy hypnotized her.

The wave rose behind her and she was free of it. Ahead, another rose, but her dress dragged at her legs. She couldn't kick. She began to feel some panic. She took a deep breath, ready to lower herself as the wave struck.

Two strong arms wrapped themselves about her and she felt the smooth, wet skin of a man against her. His face was dark and handsome. They went below together, down and down under the third wave. It was gigantic, a wave that seemingly drove on forever, dragging them down. Her lungs stretched, aching, causing her agony. She slowly let a little air out at a time, her eyes open and smarting from the salt water, seeing nothing but foam, feeling the strong muscles of the man who held her. He began to kick out his feet, carrying her up with him, searching for air.

Coughing and spluttering, Perpetua found the surface. As her head broke water, she gasped for air. The man was now holding her about the chest, beating the water with one hand, carrying her forward. His hand grasped her breast. She tried to help herself, but her skirt was now wrapped entirely about her long legs. They were swept along by the incoming surf. An approaching wave crested just above them. Perpetua took a quick, deep breath and sank into the arms that held her. They coasted for eternities, water roaring all around them. Then, the release. The long, smooth ride atop the wave to shore. It was wonderful!

She staggered. Her feet touched swirling sand. The young man stood next to her, dark-skinned, his eyes flashing happily, black hair wet and sticking close to his well-shaped head. He must be about her age. That he wore no clothes now seemed almost normal. She kept her eyes on his, not daring to look at the body of the man who had held her so closely only moments before.

Speaking in his beautiful, unintelligible language, he held her hand, shook himself like a dog and walked with her to the dry sand.

There stood Clarissa, feet planted firmly, a frown on her face and eyes filled with tears.

"Perpetua!" was all that she said.

"Mother," Perpetua exclaimed breathlessly, "this man has just saved my life!"

But her mother refused to spare a single glance for the young man. "Just look at you! You are a disgrace!"

Perpetua looked at herself, saw that her dress was clinging to her body. Where the wet cloth clung, her breasts and nipples could be clearly seen. Months ago, she might have been mortified by this explosure.

It was like being naked in front of a man. Now, she didn't care.

"Well, I'd have been a lot safer without this dress. Do you realize I almost drowned out there!"

With a toss of her hair and a wave to the man who had now returned to his friends, Perpetua slowly followed her mother. Clarissa kept silent and Perpetua knew this was her mother's way of disapproving. How could her mother be expected to understand the joy and freedom that Perpetua had felt?

• • •

For the next three days Perpetua was confined to quarters. But Everett visited her mother each day. Perpetua heard them talking. And she heard her mother agree when Everett offered to take her on an exploration of the island.

Clarissa was finding everywhere the terribly disturbing evidence of nudity. She was unable to accept it.

Smiling, Everett tried to reason with her. "You have to realize that the missionaries are doing their best. You see women with robes wound around them, men wearing Yankee clothing and children parading to Sunday school, as well as those who haven't accepted 'the word.' Give them a chance. Forgive your daughter's impetuosity. She has to grow up sometime. Think how she felt when that naked boy seized her and carried her ashore."

Clarissa found a tremulous smile. "I know how she felt. That's what bothers me!"

Later, Perpetua was again allowed freedom to take walks, to explore. But she was warned to stay away from the beach.

Perpetua passed her seventeenth birthday in

school. Her class was a mixture of Hawaiian and
Chinese girls and boys and a few Americans. Most of
her classmates were younger, with the exception of
Michael, the son of their missionary teacher. Michael
was dark-complexioned. His large, restless eyes darted
this way and that, searchingly, as if he was never satisfied with his surroundings. He had a wild shock of
black hair and his dirty clothes always seemed in
disarray.

Most of the class shunned this arrogant boy,
which made him all the more appealing to Perpetua.
She admired his athletic ability and his sophisticated
manner. Because he was the son of the solemn man
who stood before them each day, Michael felt su-
perior, a part of the authority which ruled the natives.
His manner was bold and rebellious. Nearly his age,
as tall as he, Perpetua was seated next to him in the
classroom. Michael whispered to her every thought
which came into his head, though his father constantly reprimanded him. Perpetua seemed to him the
perfect confidante. He expected her to understand his
boredom with school. He took for granted that she
would laugh at his sarcastic comments about the dull
life he led. Everyone expected him to be grateful for
this privileged existence on a South Sea island. Grateful? The son of a missionary teacher? Impossible!

One day, Michael and Perpetua left school together, the bright student and the "black sheep," a
strange pair as they walked toward the houses on the
hill. Inquisitive, Perpetua asked him what he wanted
to be in the future.

"Will you be a missionary, like your father?"

Michael frowned. "Not likely, thank you! As soon
as I have my majority, I'll be off from here, believe
me! And I'll never come back. I'll be taking the first

ship for America and I intend to enjoy every day from that moment on."

What a tremendous boast! Perpetua thought. Michael, too, wanted to break away. How delicious, she thought, to be his confidante. She urged him on. "And how will you enjoy yourself while you're here?"

Flattered by her attention, Michael continued his boasting. "I'll spend every night with a different woman." He grinned, delighted to hear the little gasp of shock that escaped her.

Perpetua stole a glance at him. His chest was stuck out proudly. He was pleased with himself for his boldness.

"Will they be *haoles* or *kanakas?*" she asked coolly. She was pleased to see that her reply deflated him somewhat. She was not, after all, that innocent!

"*Haoles*, of course," he declared impatiently. "Have you not seen how mixed blood turns them into such luscious beauties?" Michael began to take longer strides. Perpetua had to hurry to keep up with him. She frowned, trying to understand his need to show off this way.

The frank conversation confused her but delighted her, too. She felt a little sad that she wasn't of mixed blood, as desirable to him as the island's luscious beauties.

"If you were a man," he observed disdainfully, "you'd understand what I mean." He stopped and examined her figure with measuring eyes for the first time. Then he shrugged his shoulders, seized her hand and asked, "How old are you, Perpetua?"

"Seventeen. Why?"

"Well, you're old enough. On Maui, you'd be considered too old for marriage. Did you know that? Don't you see the young Hawaiian girls here who constantly run away from school when a ship arrives?

Last week, three of them, all younger than you, ran to
the window, saw a new arrival and cried 'Many
sailors! Come right away here!' Then they ran into
the road. My father ran after them. 'Stop them!' he
cried. Do you know that they went to that ship and
climbed aboard? They were nude. You know why
they went aboard?"

"Yes," replied Perpetua. And yet she felt greatly
awed by the way he spoke of these things. Weren't
they all supposed to keep silent, turn their eyes away,
pretend that such things never happened?

"Those three, none over thirteen years of age,
were already with the men, enjoying themselves. I
ran there, too, for I love to see my father frustrated. A
sailor laughed at him, saying, 'How can you stop the
call of nature?' Later, when the girls were through,
they ran home naked through the streets. Those are
the girls who hide behind the teachings of my missionary father." Michael paused. "I have had many
such girls, Perpetua. Even the older and more mature
ones in the brothels."

"Look!" he exclaimed suddenly. A great carriage
was slowly approaching them. Michael never took his
eyes off it as he spoke to Perpetua, his voice soften-
ing. "If you were me, would you not want that one?"

As Perpetua looked where Michael pointed, she
was struck by the beauty of the woman in the carriage. Atop her proud head the woman wore a tor-
toise-shell comb in the middle of her black hair. Her
dress was of white stiff brocade, trimmed in Belgian
lace. She wore many jade rings on her fingers. Jade
bracelets jingled from her arms and wrists. She was
tall. Her shoulders were bare and as she leaned forward to look at the pair in the road, her movement
revealed full breasts which were displayed by the
opening in her low-cut gown. Her dark eyes flashed

quickly as she saw Michael. Her hand was raised only a moment. Then she was gone.

"Who was she?" Perpetua asked, breathlessly.

"Tso-Tsin, the most famous and expensive harlot on the island. I have had her twice."

Perpetua looked at Michael. He was still watching the back of the lady as if he were in a trance. "There is no question she is the most beautiful creature on earth. You cannot understand such sensations—to hold such a woman!"

"You scare me, Michael! I must hurry home."

"Wait! Did you not see how she looked at me?"

"Other women look at you, too." She took a step toward her house.

He turned to her. "Why do you say that?"

"You have a rebellious nature, Michael. That attracts women!" she replied teasingly.

Laughing at herself, she began to walk away. But he suddenly seized her, spinning her about with a strength that surprised her. He placed a kiss upon her mouth before she could pull away.

"Now you can say you were kissed by Michael, who knows much about women. I know, too, that you wanted me to do that." Grinning, he looked like nothing so much as a naughty boy as he ran in the opposite direction. A small dust cloud followed in his wake.

Perpetua didn't wipe away the kiss; nor could she forget the feeling. Three days later she still tasted his salty tongue and remembered the surge of blood, the embarrassment, the way her body had pressed toward him, responding completely to his touch. She was ashamed of herself, but eager. For that moment she had experienced danger. She had been alive.

She reached her porch to find her mother standing next to Everett. In recent weeks, he had come calling regularly. Clarissa's hair was blowing freely in the slight breeze; the custom here, she said, made it unnecessary for her to fix her hair in a knot atop her head every day. Perpetua had also noticed the easy sway of her mother's hips, now unconfined by a hot corset.

Standing still, so she would not interrupt this private conversation, Perpetua saw Everett quickly take her mother in his arms and kiss her. Unaware of the girl who was watching, Everett moved his hands to cup Clarissa's buttocks, a lover holding his loved one closely, without self-consciousness or hesitation.

A low cry came from the porch. The lovers parted quickly. There were words exchanged in soft voices, too muted for Perpetua to hear. Then Everett turned and walked quickly away. Perpetua smiled, sharing the feelings of her mother.

Suddenly the thought of her father came to mind. Her jaw clenched. She closed her eyes. Where was he? What would become of them while he was gone? This was another world indeed—a world without reason.

* * *

"Take the helm, Mr. Barker. I'll be going below. Lower sails and seek an opening through the floes. Mind you, take soundings." Then, to the shocked surprise of the first mate and gathered crew, Jared spun about, walked the length of the deck and stepped out of sight through the doorway aft.

"He's stood a lot. It'll pass," allowed Old Talbot to Jeremy. "As ye said, it's enough to break any man's back and heart. But what do we do should he stay below?"

"He's given his ship to the first mate. Accordin' to

the laws of the sea, he has abrogated his command until he takes it back. God help us. We will have to wait and pray."

A thoroughly trained seaman, Barker felt little fear. He had been on many a sea filled with ice. The ship would make her slow way until the helmsman found a break through the ice pack. At this time of the year the ice should not yet have built up sufficiently to block passage.

The Horatio made her way due north. Two days passed. Progress had ceased. Before her stretched a mighty sea of ice.

Barker knocked twice on the Captain's door. There was no answer, though Barker thought he heard the Captain speaking to someone. The first mate drew closer, listening carefully. There was a faint moan within. Then silence.

That night *The Horatio* set out sea anchors and put up extra lights. Her men stayed on deck. The sailors went aloft in the chill air, struggling with frozen canvas, taking watches as they came. In the morning, the new watch awoke to find the ship being carried against the pull of the anchors and wind . . . drawn as if into a vortex. The ice began to crunch against the hull. The cold mist gathered around them, thickening into a heavy, wet fog.

"We are becalmed!" the first mate shouted, banging again on West's door. "Held in a fist of ice, Captain. It stretches miles in every direction."

Silence greeted his words. It was as if Jared West had resigned his post for good. Barker went back on deck. There was no retreat, no advance. He must at all costs maintain the ship upright until the ice broke. Yet the first mate knew the dangers.

Bearing up against the great weight of submerged ice, clutched in the grip of shelving as solid and impenetrable as granite, the immovable ship could be crushed like an egg by the ice which surrounded it. And the Captain said nothing!

Making his way toward the galley ladder, Barker felt a shudder pass through the ship. Suddenly *The Horatio* shot up, like a kite caught in an updraft. With one mighty heave, the combination of current and ice lifted her churning hull into the air. She heeled over ominously, her rudder crushed against a fast-moving section of ice. The timbers shrieked and rumbled like some living animal torn asunder.

Rushing on deck, the first mate tore aside shredded canvas and tangled gear. There were shouts and cries for help coming from the ice flats where men had spilled out, tossed overboard from the jolting ship. Barker walked to the balwarks and stood for a moment, one foot implanted against an iron cleat. The men who had remained below yelled that the ship was floundering. Water was pouring in.

"Sailor! Go below! Rouse Captain West!" Barker shouted to one of the men. "If he will not respond, break down the door! Get him up here!"

* * *

It was dark below. Jared sat directly beneath the lamp which veered at a forty-five degree angle over his book. He read from the Bible, his fist clenched against his sweating forehead. It was icy cold in the cabin and the wind howled, blasting against the frozen portholes.

"Thou art filled with shame . . . Woe to him who looks on their nakedness and tastes the draught of sinfulness."

"That is I!" he cried aloud, striking his forehead.

"I have taken Naliki and have looked upon her nakedness while drunk with lust. I am doomed!"

He remembered the sight of Naliki with her mate. He cried out again. "But she is a whore! 'Thou hast played the whore because thou wast insatiable.'" His finger found the passage in Ezekiel. He squinted in the light and read.

Again, he turned upon himself. "No, forgive me, Naliki! I loved you too much. I loved Clarissa, too, yet I put her to shame. As in the Proverbs . . . 'I will laugh at your calamity. I will mock when your fear comes.'"

Then, again, an agony of self-pity made his body tremble. "Where is the Lord now when I need Him the most?"

He buried his head in his arms and, when he closed his eyes, it seemed to him that he walked on the ice, far from his ship. Steam rose around him and the whiteness was blinding. He looked ahead and saw nothing but a blanket of white moving toward him, passing through him and going away. Behind him was the same. The great cry of the voice above him, "Awake O north wind and come. Open to me, my beloved. Thy two breasts are my only comfort."

"Yea," Jared thought, "I shall lie between her breasts and keep warm. And she shall open to me and I shall be enveloped by her." And in the snow and ice, covered by the white blanket which came to him and passed through him, Jared dreamed that he lay down, that he was covered. And then, as if caught in a spell of prophecy, he saw his own body lying in the snow, covered and still.

The ship rose on its beam ends. Jared, shaken from his dream of the frozen wastes, was thrown against the ship's side. The sudden motion, accompanied by the pounding at the door, brought him to his senses.

"Captain!" Old Talbot shouted. "We must abandon ship! 'Tis too late to save her. The floe is upending us. We will be stove in!"

A red hue came before Jared's eyes. There was a boiling within him which would not be stilled. It began in his stomach, his groin, then went up to his chest and filled his head. With all his will he fought against the sudden violence that racked him. The battle was fierce. "I will not give in. I am strong. It is I at the helm, not the Devil I will lead my men!"

Then came a hissing, insidious inner voice.

"You are a man driven by great passions. You are overwhelmed by lust for women. You have a great weakness; you are never satisfied."

"I can be," he cried back, making a final effort at self-control. "I shall awake in His likeness. Then I shall be satisfied!"

And before the demon could harass him again, he rushed from the crooked doorway. Raising the latch he hurled back the door and looked into the frostbitten face of Old Talbot. Behind Talbot stood the other sailors, each one of their faces registering anguished helplessness. There stood Kanai, a young native sailor recruited from Maui. To Jared, the handsome native seemed to change in the white mist, undergoing a transformation before the Captain's very eyes. As Jared stared, transfixed, the face became softer. The black hair lengthened. The eyes became larger, deeper, assuming extraordinary beauty. Naliki! Her breasts were bare, she was nude and her hand was stretched forth. She wanted him! She had come back!

Then the vision was gone. Jared saw the crew around him, staring. The mist cleared. And Naliki became Kanai, the man, once again.

Old Talbot spoke in an urgent voice: "Come, Captain. We must leave the ship!" The men behind him were murmuring, fearing for their lives, anxious to escape the doomed vessel. Jared nodded and made his way among them. Seizing the handrail, he led them, captain once again, up the ladder to the sloping deck. Yes, by God, by all the Heavens, the days and nights of Beelzebub were over. The demon had vanished in the cold, icy air. He was their captain and, like his ancestors who had come to New England from Great Britain, he would lead them to safety with all the strength of the old Captain West. The devil take the Clarissas and the Nalikis!

"We must abandon ship!" he ordered. The men were ready, and they quickly lowered the boats in the cold, icy wind. The longboats were filled to the gunwales with food and belongings. With a last look behind, the six whaleboats pulled away from *The Horatio*, leaving her wealth of oil, her familiar but crippled hull to the mercy of the arctic sea and ice.

A narrow channel of clear water lay in the wake of the ship. Their only escape lay in the direction from which they had come, where the ice was already closing in from every side. For hundreds of miles in each direction there was only ice and more ice. The once slim thread of water, already glazing over, was their only hope.

* * *

For three long weeks, they rowed, then pushed, then carried their longboats. First, in wild currents which swept between the ice packs, then overland atop the ice when the streams closed in, and finally, when all hope for passage on sea was lost, the men lifted their boats and their few provisions and carried them on their backs. Had it not been for Jared West, they would not have survived the trek. One hundred miles southward, fought mile by mile, step by step, the men made their way across the stark and frozen wasteland.

"Warm to the task, men! By God, we'll live and no man will be the worse for it. Soon we'll sight another ship. There are dozens about us!" The Captain's voice strengthened them though he lurched in front of his crew like a great, ragged, frozen scarecrow. When it seemed impossible to go one step farther, he ordered a fire to be built out of wood they had saved from the wreckage. With the tarpaulin stretched for cover, they huddled close to each other beside the longboats, sharing in the flames' meager warmth.

The night they ran out of hardtack; Jared told his men, "Stay ye here. I'll take my gun. I'll bring back food."

Old Talbot rose stiffly, his clothes and muffler caked with ice. His weatherbeaten face was red and cracked, his nose chalked white with frostbite. The puffed-out lips jutted over his ice-covered beard. "And I with ye." But even as he spoke, his legs failed him. He sank back, exhausted.

Kanai, the native from Maui, sitting near Old Talbot, took the cover from himself and placed it over the old man.

"Nay!" Jared shouted above the noise of the wind. "I am in command. We'll have no mutiny among ye. I will go. Here, Old Talbot, is my grandfather's timepiece. When, by this watch, I have been gone three days, you shall report to the first mate. Should I not return, my child, Perpetua, shall have the watch. You, Mr. Barker, will assume command. It will be your responsibility to see that his watch is safely delivered. And mind ye . . ."

"Aye, what's that?" asked Barker, blinking. His lashes were stippled with ice, for the steam of his voice froze upon the hair of his face.

"I'll abide no cannibalism aboard *The Horatio* or here. Is that clear, sir?"

"Who would eat the flesh of man?" came the horrified question.

"I met a Maine man once. I asked him if he remembered my grandfather . . ." Jared stopped, his eyes wide and glittering at the near confession of a horror. "No, men!" his voice rose against the shriek of the wind. "Ye shall do no such thing." With that he lifted the edge of the tarpaulin, bowed his head against the force of the wind and plowed into the dimness. In an instant he was gone, enveloped in a curtain of deep fog.

Alone at last in the dismal fog, Jared thought he saw the shrouds of a ship, by his estimation about a half mile away. Squinting against the drifting snow, hugging his rifle to his chest, Jared hunched his shoulders against the force of the wind. Feeling boundless gratitude, enormous relief, he trudged, undaunted, step by step toward the ghostlike ship.

* * *

Five days later, men fleeing from the stricken ship *Monomoy* came upon the survivors of *The Horatio*. Kanai had died the night after Jared's departure and his frozen body lay just outside the tarpaulin enclosure, tilted on its side in the attitude of a sleeper.

The men still awaited Jared's return, knowing nothing of time. The hands of the watch were frozen.

Yet the men still waited. It seemed as if they could not stir as long as their Captain was away, searching food on the frozen, desolate wastes.

The first mate looked up at his rescuers, his eyes glazed with hunger and cold.

"Before ye lie fifty miles of unbroken ice," he explained. "Ye'll be best under this tarpaulin with us."

The seamen from the *Monomoy* looked at one another, not believing that this man would write the death warrant for an entire crew. But there was another voice to be heard among the crew.

"We'll maybe go with ye, if ye'll just tell us what day it is!" shouted Talbot over the wind. "We have our orders, and we cannot leave him afore the three days have passed."

So the crew from the *Monomoy* told him—made *The Horatio*'s crew understand that not three days, but five, had passed since their Captain had left them to go hunting. And only then, at last, could the remnants of *The Horatio*'s crew be induced to rise weakly to their feet and begin the tortuous journey across the ice.

* * *

Years later, the men of Nantucket and Martha's Vineyard still spun long yarns about the great ice floe that trapped seven whaling ships and sent hundreds of sailors to icy graves. Neither the men of the *Monomoy* nor the crew of *The Horatio* were alone on that vast, white expanse. As they traveled, laboring over the ice with their few belongings and their dwindling supplies of pemmican, they were joined by survivors of those other, lost ships. At last, the weakened men could no longer carry the heavy longboats over the frozen miles, and the thin passageways of water dwindled away to nothing as the winter storms settled in. In a last, desperate move—knowing they might well be destroying their final means of escape—the men hacked their boats into pieces, using the curved planks to make sledges that they could drag across the ice.

And when, at last, they came to the edge of the ice, they felt as though their death warrants had been signed and sealed at their own hands. Only a small bay of water separated them from solid land, the tip of Point Barrow, Alaska. As if to mock their arrival at the edge of the floe and remind them of the distance that lay between them and safety, the fog cleared. The sky brightened. And they could see land. Land, at last! But it lay just beyond reach. Not more than ten miles from that easternmost point of the ice floe, beckoning them like a mirage, lay the edge of the continent. But their sledges could not help them cross that expanse of water. Their boats had been destroyed. They had but few provisions and long days to wait until that terrible gap should be bridged by the ever-moving packs of ice.

So the sailors settled down and improvised shelters. And, as the island whalers came to this part of their story, their voices grew hushed out of reverence for those who had died at the pitiful village that became known in their tales as Jared's Hope. For, as the survivors' food supplies dwindled, and the winds howled around their makeshift lean-tos, as their fingers froze and as men died, the only thing that sustained them was hope that their Captain would return, bringing rescue. They knew there was land within reach. They knew that, finally, the great gap of water would have to freeze over. And when it did—after weeks of waiting—there were still a few men who could stumble to their feet, bow their heads into the wind, and make their way across the thickening, treacherous floes toward Point Barrow.

One of the men, an old mariner as cranky as he

was indestructible, was a whaler named Talbot. Another spouted legal terms and his name was Jeremy. And there was a third, Jethro, who had told preposterous tales of the warm whores of Maui. These, and a first mate named Barker, were the sole survivors of *The Horatio*. And one of them carried an old timepiece with frozen hands, entrusted to him by Captain Jared West.

There was not a single clockmaker in all the Vineyard, nor even in Portsmouth or Boston, who could ever get that watch to run again. Though many tried to repair it, the hands never moved beyond that moment when the Captain left it behind and plunged into the blind fog of the arctic wastes to find food for his crew. Or so vouchsafed the whalers of the islands, speaking many years later, spinning their reverent tales of the doomed voyage of *The Horatio*.

CHAPTER 10

The night *The Horatio* was abandoned in the Arctic, another, more fortunate whaler arrived in Maui. Too late to make the northern voyage that year, the whaling ship had traveled to the new Japans seeking straggling whales that had strayed south from the migration.

On the last leg of its journey toward Maui, the whaling men spotted the hull of a half-sunken ceremonial canoe ten miles off shore. The flags and native accouterments which they later pulled from the sea gave proof of the canoe's purpose. Though her Captain ordered a longboat lowered and ordered his men to search the waters, no bodies were found. At least, that is what he officially reported. Yet, from the logbooks of his own and other ships could be discerned the actual events that had taken place.

* * *

. . . The happy group of Polynesians set out from the island with the married couple aboard when night fell. Kahana sat in the stern with Naliki. They watched the oarsmen as they paddled in unison, occasionally trailing a hand to test the direction of tide

189

and the warmth of water, using these navigational signals to ascertain their position.

A great mist settled over the craft.

The men began to chant. Naliki knew she smelled the peculiar dust of volcanic fire. A drum was uncovered and one of the men in the bridal party began a steady, rhythmic beating. The sound of the drumbeat filled the night as the sky darkened. The bridal vessel became a floating island in a moonless pool of dark water, an endless, pitch-black cave which had no horizon.

"A volcano on Maui has erupted," Kahana whispered. "The gods are angry."

Why would the gods vent their anger upon her now? Naliki wondered. Now, of all times, on her wedding voyage, returning to her husband's island?

Kahana told the paddlers to lie still and await the morning. "The tides are moving us toward our destination," he said. "Tomorrow we will be near the coast."

The *tapa* covering which Naliki and Kahana shared was little protection against the fine dust and heavy smoke engulfing the vessel. The flags, which had flown so gaily, now hung limply on their staffs. There was only the slow movement of the canoe, bobbing on the waves. Naliki felt tense and miserable, waiting for unseen things.

Without warning, an enormous high shadow came out of the darkness. The shape became the bow of a great ship, her knifelike edge looming above the frail craft. It was all over in an instant. The canoe collapsed like broken matchsticks as the ship struck. It broke in two almost immediately and the sucking, churning wake of the six thousand ton barque scattered the wedding party into the black, soundless depths of the night.

A watchman aboard the barque witnessed the collision. He called out at once, but it was several minutes before the barque managed to come about. Whirlpools were created in its wake as the great ship turned. The watchman could see little in the black, churning waters, and the cries of the survivors were lost in the sound of the waves against the ship's side.

An instant after the barque struck the wedding canoe, Naliki found herself being dragged beneath the whirling water headfirst, then sucked against the barnacled hull. She fended off with one hand, holding her breath. She had no fear of the water, having swum so often in the curling green waves of the Maui surf. But the darkness, the strange eddies and the sheer power of the destructive vessel were terrifying. Other bodies struck her as she tried to surface, kicking in a fluttering movement. Hands reached above her head, protecting her while seeking the dark surface. On Maui she was capable of swimming underwater for three to four minutes. But the fear in this place was utterly enervating. She felt as if she could not escape the water. Her lungs were bursting. Then suddenly she found air, the blessed air and the deep inhalation filled her lungs at last. That single breath was like a promise. Once again, she began to hope. She struck out valiantly. One arm, bruised by the hull of the ship, delivered a searing pain. All was darkness. Was that a piece of wood she felt? Would it hold her up? She reached out and missed. Her feet kicked and she struggled again as that scrap of salvation dipped in the wave, drifting . . . She kicked harder, her heart pounding, reaching—again her hand touched wood, her fingers closed, slipped, then clutched again. With a relief that was almost like grief, she wrapped her arms around the floating wood. It was the prow of the ceremonial canoe. A flag, torn from its once proud mast, lay half sunk, acting like a sea anchor, keeping the wooden section steady. She wrapped one leg about the wood, breathed deeply, saw the ship's lights now clearly visible. Men were standing on her decks, crowded at the bulwarks. The hull bore down upon her again. This time it would surely kill her. Her eyes closed, her legs went numb. Fright completely enveloped her. She prayed to Kane. The words of the missionaries came to mind and she asked for the help of the man Jesus, the Christ. She lost consciousness.

* * *

. . . The shocking chill of the churning black water brought Naliki back to her senses. She had lost her grip on the prow. As she opened her eyes, Naliki saw Kahana's head bobbing in the spume, almost within reach.

"Kahana!" she called out, her heart filling with relief.

He didn't answer. Why didn't he swim toward her? Why didn't he save her and take her in his arms? Two strokes brought her close and she could see that his eyes were open, pleading. Had he been hurt? She reached out for him.

"Kahana!"

The head turned in the water and fell on its side. Where the neck had been, there was only a horrid gash, with threads of tissue dragging in the water.

The severed head sank. Naliki vomited.

When she came to the surface, still retching, her arms and legs were already churning frantically, dragging her through the water, away from that horrible sight. That was not Kahana. That was only a head, a piece of wood, a chunk of stone, now plunging to the depths. . . .

Around Naliki were small pieces of the once great canoe. There were no other swimmers. They were gone—all gone. A great cry of anguish was torn from her body as she reached out, all hope gone, all reason for living swept away in the dark waters. Kahana, Kahana . . . An enormous weight came over her limbs as the enfolding darkness closed, once again, around her, penetrated only by those pleading, lifeless eyes . . .

*   *   *

Naliki had never been able to concentrate much at the missionary's school, what with the heat of the classroom and the constant, distracting laughter of children playing. But she was glad, now, that she had learned enough of the talk of the Americans to understand them. When she came to again, lying curled up on the wet deck of the mighty whaler, she understood at once what the seamen were saying.

As if from a great distance, the words seemed hushed. Finally, their volume increased as her head cleared. Then Naliki understood, and sorrowed at what she heard.

"All are lost!"

"Lost, you say?"

"Aye, we circled three times. The boats were lowered at your orders, Captain Priest. The first mate took one and we were in the other. 'Twas the first mate found the girl who lies at your feet."

Water gushed from her mouth as she vomited. She felt the warmth of a blanket that was pulled over her body. She opened her eyes to find someone looking at her closely.

"She's alive! Get some whiskey, man! Move that wretched arse of yours!"

The burning liquid touched her lips. She felt a fiery sensation in her throat that turned hotter as the liquid flowed to her stomach. She retched, gasped and spat, feeling the weakness in her legs being replaced by the sensation of returning strength.

"There. She took it! Give her some more!"

Again the fire flowed through her throat and she sat up, dizzy, fighting the dizziness. Her hands hid her face. The wet wedding finery had begun to chill her, despite the blanket that covered her.

"She's a-shakin' like a young bird. Get her below and into my bunk. Easy now, ye lout! Let an Azorian help ye, ye clumsy farmer. Are ye a Cape-Codder or some sheepherder from Katama? Blast ye!"

She felt steady hands lift her and carry her a long distance. It seemed miles, a journey through eternity, traveling down and down. Yes, she was dying. This was what her father had told her it would be like. "You will be carried on arms to your rest," he had said. "As when one is asleep, *hiamoe* will come. Then you will reach heaven. There in *lani*, you will be confronted by Kane, the great, golden god who is ours. He is not white, like a *haole*, but like us. He will protect you . . ."

Naliki opened her eyes.

There he stood! It was Kane. Golden-red, and white—not as her father had said, but a *haole*—a Caucasian. And his face, though white, was topped by a great mane of flaming hair. How wrong they had been, both parent and missionary.

"Bring her food! Quick about it! Move, ye quakin' housewife! Bring her chowder!"

He spoke like a whaler. He dressed like one. He was beautiful, handsome to the point of perfection.

His hair hung low about his long, lean neck. Tanned from forehead to waist (as she could see, for he wore no shirt), he carried himself like a white god, a king from a distant country, arrogant and proud. Yet she saw a certain disdain on his lips—as if the entire proceedings should be dealt with quickly so that he could go about his other duties.

The cabin lamp swung and his frame created a vast, swooping silhouette that lunged along the cabin wall. He leaned forward with a penetrating look, searching her eyes for intelligence. Then, as one who believes the other will understand his language if he speaks more loudly, he yelled into her ear. "I am John Priest, master of *The Deep Six!*" Then, more gently, "What in tarnation were you doing in that canoe one hundred miles at sea and in the path of our barque?"

She tried to sit up to get a better look at him, though every movement cost her effort. His red hair fell over his forehead. His clean-shaven face, handsome as any she had ever seen, was so close. His breath was clean, unlike other whalers who had come near. His hand tucked the blanket closer about her body, lingered at her hips unconsciously. Then he withdrew his hand quickly as if from a hot fire. She smiled to herself.

She managed to drink the chowder, scooping up the small, succulent pieces of fish and slices of salt pork that were sprinkled with pepper. Finally, she attempted to answer his questions in a voice that was soft and hesitant.

"My husband and I were going home to his island. That was our wedding canoe."

This Captain's voice was kind. She looked at him again, a question in her eyes.

"I'm afraid all were lost but you." He waited for tears, sudden collapse. But she showed no emotion.

Destiny had taken Kahana. Even now, Kahana was with Kane, in peace, comforted. He was not lonely, for his men would be about him. And Naliki had no reason to weep for herself, for she too would be joined with him one day.

"I will leave you now. Sleep." John Priest walked to the door but before going out, he turned and asked, "What is your name?"

But Naliki was already asleep.

* * *

Captain John Priest strode the deck between the binnacle and the mizzenmast, deep in thought. A wealthy man whose inheritance had come at an early age, he still displayed no affectation in his manner to others. By his own skill alone, the red-headed giant had won his way up the ranks, among the men who dominated the whaling industry.

The presence aboard his ship of this beautiful woman posed an immediate problem. He could drop her off at one of the numerous, small atolls that dotted this part of the Pacific and let the natives see to her welfare. Or he could keep her. His passage lay south through the icy seas of the Antarctic. Then to Martha's Vineyard. His hold was high—filled with barrels of oil. But before entering Edgartown harbor, he still had more whales to take. And no woman like this—no woman at all, in fact—would make him return homeward ahead of schedule. For there, in Edgartown, was the house he dreamed of buying.

He often saw it in his mind—white clapboard, green shutters, her Victorian silhouette telling the world from atop the slope of sand, that he, John Priest, was beholden to no man. More than five thousand dollars, left him by his dying father, rested safely in a Boston bank. But his house would be purchased with John Priest's own earnings, the profit from this very voyage.

This Polynesian from the Sandwich Islands obviously came from a high class among her people. And she must have studied with the missionaries, since she had a good knowledge of English. She was well formed and graceful. This he had seen when he took her wet wedding clothes from her and pulled the blanket up over her chill body. While he had no wish to keep her against her will, the story of the disaster need never reach land, if Captain Priest could prevent the tongues of his lads from wagging.

At that moment, his first mate approached him. Slowly, Priest turned, making a decision even as he spoke.

"I must tell you," he announced to the mate, his voice heavy with authority, "the girl wishes to stay with us. She will remain below perhaps for some time. She is very ill, Matthews. I fear for her life." The mate caught the Captain's meaning at once.

"Aye, she should remain out of sight of the men, Captain. They are already talking. They have been forced to leave many like her behind in Maui. In your care, sir, she will recover. Is it your intention to report her alive?"

"When we make port, yes. But we will abide by her wishes, for she expresses herself with ease. Do not announce her presence to any passing ship. She thinks it better that others believe she has drowned with her husband. In time, she may return to her home."

"That may be years from now, sir."

"Aye, and as the years pass, she may change her mind. At the moment, Matthews, we will do her bidding. Leave her to me."

"A Polynesian girl of such beauty in your hands,
if I may be so bold, sir, may perhaps be safer ashore!"

"I mean to bring her back, Matthews. I know
that I must."

• • •

For Naliki, the next long days flowed together
into an endless passage of time. She dreamed horrible
dreams that made the legends of her land seem but
idle tales for children. She saw herself floating, sink-
ing deeper and deeper. Deep under the sea she
dreamed she found the torn, pulpy bodies of bloated
natives—those who should have been with Kane.
Sharks were tearing at the corpses. She screamed as a
shark opened its jaws around her head. She felt a cold
cloth upon her forehead and opened her eyes to meet
the Captain's worried, compassionate look. She tried
to smile, felt the warmth of his hand upon her shoulder, then a cold liquid in her parched throat.

He told her, later, that she had not moved more
than a few steps for two weeks.

But at last the trance was broken.

It happened when the Captain was with her,
spoon-feeding her from a bowl of hot soup. The
spoon clattered to the floor as she suddenly leapt up.
Her feet touched the floor as she pushed Priest aside,
balancing there like a newborn colt. Her body was
still moist, though the fever had parched her. Her
hair, long neglected, was stringy and unkempt, yet it
gleamed in the dimly lit cabin. The reddish eyes
cleared and her lower lip trembled as she spoke.

"Please," she begged, her voice dry, "may I dress
now?"

The *tapa* cloth, the gown of her wedding trip,
had been carefully washed and made ready. But first

the Captain's shirt was draped about her, openly revealing her body, wet with perspiration.

John Priest tried to ignore the urge in his loins.

"Dry yourself, Naliki," he suggested and handed her his towel. Then he turned away, though ordinarily he would not have hesitated to stare at any native girl who stood before him. But there was something so innocent, so simple and unassuming about Naliki, that he felt he must protect her. It was a strange emotion for him. She had been unconscious of her effect upon him. He must not let her know how helpless he was before her naivete.

The girl allowed the shirt to fall to the floor. She wiped herself dry. Captain Priest turned to face the porthole, seemingly intent on a drop of water which rolled across it, urged on its way by the wind.

"I am dry."

He turned. And for the first time, he knew what it meant to feel the devastating beauty of a woman. Aye, it was more than a vision. It was a sensation of beauty that seized his whole being, that made him tremble with an emotion stronger than lust and more reverent than awe.

A smile moved across Naliki's lips. Her eyes were cast to the side as if she were looking far, far away. Naliki was the epitome of all that Captain John Priest had imagined a woman could possess, and her sweetness of character shown through. He dared not let his eyes falter, look down or respond to the fullness before him.

Thus they stood, her presence a gift in return for saving her life. It was the only gift he could accept at this moment. She could not be taken thus, Priest thought. To do so would be to crush that fragile sense of beauty that was contained neither in her lips, nor her shapeliness, nor any part of her body—the beauty that emanated from her entire presence. No, he could not take those lips and press them to his, nor could his fingers touch the smooth, brown skin that had turned warm under his care. He had to admire her— admire, and hope, perhaps forever, for the end of the terrible desire surging in him.

But his strength was nothing against Naliki's training. No *haolekane*—no white man since the first landing of Captain Cook upon her islands—had found himself able to resist what followed. Nor would Naliki have it any other way. The romantic longings of a New England captain, his hesitancies and his respect for womanhood meant nothing to her. She was well, recovered at last, and her now-strong body welcomed the red-haired white man who looked like Kane.

• • •

As *The Deep Six*, a name given facetiously to the newly built ship, slowly made her way south to the Horn, Naliki gradually began to own its Captain. The trip was uneventful. The three lookouts at the masthead reported nothing unusual. As the whaling ship sped toward the ice of Cape Horn, the seamen often wondered what their Captain did below deck. They knew that the girl was in the sickbay, abed and ill, but they also saw that he, John Priest, the boisterous, fun-loving man of earlier days, was getting paler and thinner, that his hollow blue eyes were more sunken. Though he often seemed in great need of sleep, there was a gleam of unholy joy in his eyes that none could help but notice . . .

Once John Priest descended the gangway, he found a young woman waiting to provide his body with all that was needed. Satiated beyond all hope or reason, Priest learned about the inner caress, the tender kisses that she applied upon the tip of his body at the moment of his complete satisfaction. Never had he known such erotic sensations, and she, in turn, took all that she wanted from him, crying out in joy and gratitude.

And so it was until the day the Antarctic airs hit them. Thereupon the seas became rougher, the wind stronger, penetrating their cabin and bringing a strange chill to Naliki's bones. She did not complain. Yet the Captain would find her fully clothed, wrapped in layer upon layer of sailors' cast-off clothing. She seized every blanket she could drape about her, and sometimes she already lay abed when he descended with her meals.

"Perhaps you should walk the deck with me; it is not natural to be below so long."

"There are men sleeping above, you told me."

"It is too cold for that, my mermaid. The men sleep below now. You must come on deck."

She wrapped herself carefully in two, scratchy woolen sweaters, pulling on his greatcoat, his breeches and his oilskin cap. The moment she came on deck, however, she felt as if the sharp wind choked off her breath. She had a fit of coughing. The Captain took her below immediately. One man aloft saw her figure, and told the others the next day that she seemed quite ill. And besides that, he declared, her fine, young figure was gone. According to the sailor, she was now naught but a potato sack—"lumpy as any barmaid left to herself at beer."

Tragedy unfolded as they sped south around the Cape and followed the trade winds northward toward home. As each latitude passed, Naliki became worse. First, there was fever, then the chill followed, alleviated only slightly by the draught of soup or rum that the Captain brought her. Then, more coughing fits, with a residue of blood. Certain that the girl must be dying of pneumonia, Captain Priest prayed for the first time in his life. He swore wildly at the selfishness that had prompted him to keep her aboard, instead of leaving her on some sunlit isle where she belonged. He still thought of her as a tender, tropical plant, so beautiful to behold, so delicate in nature, and so tragically unprotected against this destroying climate. And he had done this to her!

When they reached Edgartown—an uneventful trip to judge from the official record in the logbooks—*The Deep Six* carried an almost lifeless Naliki in her hull, and a desperate master at her wheel.

There, high on the clay cliff, the highest on the barren, sandy isle, stood the white house John Priest had wished to own. With one dash of his pen, he bought it. Tenderly, he lifted Naliki into the carriage that would transport her to her new home.

The trees planted about the Captain's home provided Naliki with shade. The sand brought a reflection of the sun she had missed. The exotic flower whom John Priest loved began to raise her head, to smile again.

Men admired, women censured. The tongues about the island were wagging.

"She is a Polynesian!"

"A rare beauty—but, a native from the Pacific?"

"What would his dear mother have said?"

A Polynesian was an unsuitable wife for such a man, they declared. It was apparent, they gossiped, that he had been seduced.

"No wonder," reported John Priest's housekeeper, Mrs. Hiram Osborn, when she went into town. "The master departed for the sea after the death of his dear mother. And there he spent his days. He knew few local girls and now it is too late!"

Naliki heard none of the gossip. She only knew that she had begun to love the Captain who saved her life.

Only one thing broke their harmony and that was Naliki's withdrawal from her past. John Priest knew nothing, just that she came from Maui, in the Sandwich Islands. If pressed with questions, she would begin to cry. Whatever the memory, whatever the events which had preceded her rescue, Naliki's island existence was obviously a part of her life which she would hide from him forever.

One Sunday, after the regular service in the Congregational Church, John Priest and Naliki stood before the minister and became husband and wife. The event was duly recorded, as were all such matters, in the local newspaper. But it might just have been nothing more than the anchoring of a merchantman in the harbor, or a day's catch of fish, for all that it meant to the island. To the grim-faced islanders, such a marriage was beneath contempt. They had better things to do than to bring the outlandish "Mrs. Priest" into their circle.

On the whole, Naliki's life was an easy one, with Mrs. Osborn caring for the house, and hired hands tending the garden. The table was always filled with fresh food and the fine stable boasted the best of the island's horses for her husband's long rides. Mrs. Priest sat in the sun, protected from the southwest wind by a low screen of scrub hemlock. She did not wish to remember the past. She did not wish to tell her husband of things that had gone before.

Returning from his ride along the sandy stretches of the island, John Priest would sit down beside her, his bright hair shining against his forehead, the crop still held in his hand.

"What do you want, Naliki? What would entertain you?"

Her response was a smile.

"I want nothing," she would reply. And then, looking into the questioning blue eyes, she would add gently, as though to reassure him, "Naliki's life began when she awakened on the deck of *The Deep Six*. Before that, my Captain, I lived in another world. Now I am Mrs. Priest. That is enough."

CHAPTER 11

Eighteen months had passed since *The Horatio* had been lost. Old Talbot had often talked of his mission—to tell Clarissa West, with his own lips, how her husband had braved the arctic wastes and died a proud man's death. And the man who had to listen to the old man most frequently was none other than *The Horatio*'s one-time lawyer, Jeremy.

"I wouldn't want anyone else to tell her," Old Talbot confided to Jeremy, "for the final days and re-birth of Jared West at the last was biblical. And I must tell her, like one of the prophets, and yet I must be mindful of 'er feelings. To come upon 'er sudden and say, 'Woman, yer man is dead!' is a terrible thing to do. No, I have in mind to honor him in the tellin'. But I must bear witness and no one else, for only I know the way it was."

Both had returned to the whaling life, and by choice, their first voyage took them to Maui. The island looked the same, yet there was something gayer and more pleasing about Mrs. Percival's house, a difference the seamen noted at once as they approached. Dresses hung in the sun as though beckoning them. There were underthings, dainty petticoats and bright, red and blue, polka-dot skirts. The bright clothing swayed and flapped, skirts and underclothing became entangled. Nothing in the demeanor of the house and yard seemed solemn, proper or appropriately staid.

Old Talbot looked up toward a second-story window and saw the bare figure of a young girl go quickly past. Underthings hanging in the yard! Open windows while someone undressed! Such goings-on would be frowned upon in the home of a New Englander!

Motioning Jeremy to stand by, Old Talbot carefully mounted the few steps and walked to the door. It was open! Unheard of!

"Ahoy, there!" he cried.

No answer. There was a kind of buoyancy about the place, with the wind flapping the clothes about, gay laughter echoing through the breezy, open hallway. The sailor called again.

"Mrs. West, it is I, Old Talbot!"

From the dark of the sitting room, he saw a figure approaching—the figure of a woman whose hips undulated gracefully as she walked. She stood illuminated by the light of a window, her mouth open in surprise. Could this be Clarissa? Her body was wrapped in a *tapa* drawn so tightly that her shapely breasts and full hips were clearly outlined. Her face was tanned, her shoulders uncovered to reveal the straight, long neck, the rise and fall of her bosom. Suddenly, she cried out.

"Is that you, Old Talbot?"

She rushed forward. The old sailor caught a breath of perfume. Or was it the exotic flower she had pinned to her blonde hair that lent its fragrance to the air? Old Talbot felt embarrassed, as though he had accidentally disturbed someone he didn't know.

Stammering, holding himself stiff, he pulled away. She was weeping. Why did women have to cry? He grunted, looking at the floor. But she had stepped back and suddenly he realized she was smiling. Her dainty hands brushed at her eyes.

"Where is he? Tell me, Old Talbot, where is the Captain?"

Old Talbot hadn't meant it to be this way. He had hoped for a cup of coffee, for a moment for reflection to rehearse, once again, the speech he'd prepared for many months.

"I have news of him. Please, Mrs. West, fetch your daughter and I will speak." He turned and gestured to Jeremy. Sight of him brought fright to Clarissa's eyes. She cried out.

"What has happened? Why are you two here without Jared?"

At the sound of Clarissa's cry, a young woman quickly appeared. It was the very woman he had seen at the window above, and Old Talbot realized with a shock that this must be Perpetua. Seeing him, hearing her mother's anguished cry, Perpetua said, "Come, Mother. I will call Everett."

The group assembled. Looking hard at his one-time seamate, Old Talbot said, "Things have changed here, I can see. Maui agrees with all of you. You look well and happy. You, Brother Norton, have a bit of grey at your temples or perhaps your hair has been bleached by the sun."

"Please," implored Clarissa, her hand firmly grasped by Everett's, "let me know about the Captain."

Perpetua stood behind, with her hands on her mother's shoulders.

"He led us like Moses," began the old man, his face twitching, his eyes rheumy, nose mottled from frostbite. "He turned to the Bible like a man knowin' that only the Good Word would save him from doom.

During the last few days, I saw him give everything in order to save those about him. A man may be well judged by his last deeds. And Jared West was a man of such depths, of such strength that when he reached the bottom of his strength, he was still nearer the top than most of us. His resentment was gone, his hatred had cooled, and there was naught of self-pity to be found in 'im. His last night among us, he took off in search of food. All alone, he went out into that weather of the polar north as if he were our destiny. I have said many things, now and again, of Captain Jared West. But I say now, never have I seen such courage in a man. He will long be spoken of—at least as long as I live."

"And I," added Jeremy. "He was like a saint to the last, Mrs. West. To his daughter we bring his last belonging, all that remains of him. Old man, give her the gold watch."

"It won't work," Old Talbot pointed out. "It stopped when the Captain went out into that howling blizzard after meat. But here it is.

"And he said to me, liftin' the flap of our tent, 'Wait three days and if'n I don't return, go on. Give this to Perpetua when I am dead, for time is hers, not mine.'"

Perpetua took the watch and examined it lovingly, this only relic of her father. Clarissa sat staring at the men, not seeing them, her eyes brimming with tears.

"How did he die?" Everett asked.

"We were frozen in. We had no food or wood. He went for them by himself in a blizzard. He never came back. The ship is lost. We came from Seattle to tell you, lest you hear it from others."

"How did you survive?"

"Aye, that's another story!"

"You are good men," Everett remarked. "We shall have a service for him. What can we do for you two?"

"Give me a cup of coffee, and send me on my way," declared Old Talbot. "Both Jeremy and I must be getting our gear together. There is a ship looking for good hands like us even now in this very harbor."

Instead of coffee, Miss Jessie brought the two men a finger of whiskey each. When they had downed that, more was quickly brought. Old Talbot warmed to his story, as was his wont when drinking, and told them details about the ragged march that horrified his listeners.

At last, Clarissa realized that the truth of his stories was being slowly and cheerfully buried under a wealth of free elaboration, and she felt the time had come to dismiss him.

"I shall always love you, old man, for coming this distance to tell me about the Captain," she thanked Talbot. "I have not always known whether you had his best interests at heart."

"Nor I," added Perpetua. "You used to scare me on purpose, didn't you, Mr. Talbot?" He lowered his head in acknowledgment of her words, but a smile quickly replaced her disapproving expression. "Now, I thank you for bringing me his watch."

Old Talbot stood up and looked directly at Clarissa. Hobbling gingerly across the scattered rugs, careful not to mar the floor with the blunt end of his wooden leg, he came close to the Captain's wife and kissed her soundly on the cheek. "There! My promise is kept."

With that and a grumble, Old Talbot swung about and headed toward the door. Jeremy who, up until then, had said little, pronounced, "So be it." Then, dipping his head quickly in farewell, he followed the other man outside.

"See to it that they are driven to the docks, Everett," called Clarissa. And, hugging Perpetua about the waist, her mother led her upstairs.

• • •

It was three days later when Everett first broached the subject of marriage.

"There is a single matter which stands in our way, Clarissa." Everett frowned slightly.

"So, you don't want me?"

He laughed. "No, it isn't that. I am not like a woman! *Varium et mutabile semper femina.*"

"Stop showing off. What does that mean?"

"Woman is ever a changeful and capricious thing." He held up his hand. "No! I don't wish to argue the ways of woman or man. What I am worried about is only the problem which besets every woman whose husband is lost at sea. It's the matter of remarriage and inheritance. According to lawyers hereabouts, you should go into court and have your marriage dissolved. Or you should obtain a divorce."

"Merciful father—why? Jared's dead, isn't he?"

"No one actually saw him die, or found his body. Supposing, just supposing, he isn't dead. Then you'd be guilty of bigamy."

"Everett!" Clarissa's voice was hushed and intense. "Why should there be such laws? You and I know that Jared will never return, as Old Talbot and Jeremy have testified. What, then? Is this any different than a man who falls overboard or is killed by the fluke of a whale? Why should anyone speak of bigamy? Surely, such a word is the greatest sign of disrespect for the dead." Clarissa stood at the window and looked out, struggling to hide her emotions. Yet Everett noted the trembling in her voice. Suddenly she turned and, as she did so, brushed her hair away from her forehead as if clearing her mind. "So be it. I shall see that the marriage is dissolved. I see that for you and for Perpetua, I must. We'd be living beneath that cloud otherwise. And if he ever does come back . . ."

"Yes?" Everett went to her and held her for a moment anxiously.

"Well, we'll face that if it ever happens." She started to cry softly. He held her closely.

"What is it?"

"I regret . . . nothing, Everett," she began, her voice breaking with emotion. "And yet, I feel as if I had dishonored him in some way. He was so proud, Everett. So . . . proud."

But she could not go on.

* * *

The matter of divorce was arranged upon their arrival in the United States. "It will be done discreetly," Everett assured her, "as soon as you resume residence in Martha's Vineyard."

For Perpetua, the voyage was tiresome. All the adventures and new revelations of the outward-bound journey seemed to be lacking in the return.

The ship in which they sailed had provided two cabins for the trio. Everett's was alongside that of the women. As far as Perpetua was concerned, all her mother and Everett did was to gaze into each other's moonstruck eyes like two young lovers. Perpetua wasn't sure whether their behavior embarrassed her or gave her a share of happiness.

Now a young lady, instructed by her mother to behave as one, Perpetua had to restrain herself from going forward to speak to the crew as she had done

before. After months of "absolute nothing," having
read fourteen books and written one letter to be sent
off to Mrs. Percival, Perpetua was overjoyed to arrive
at Edgartown. She was worn out with boredom and
eager to stand once again on firm land.

The small wharf was busy with fishermen as Perpetua led the parade of men carrying her baggage,
with Everett and Clarissa lagging behind.

Even the solid ground felt as though it were
pitching with a ship's motion. Holding onto a nearby
barrel for support, Perpetua raised her head and
found herself gazing into the face of the most handsome, dashing, romantic figure of a man she had seen
for years.

He was actually laughing at her dizziness! Black
hair flying like a spirited horse's mane, heavy eyebrows lowered in a squint over daring eyes, the
young man didn't offer to help her, just stood with
hands on hips and roared.

Perpetua felt the baggage carriers behind shov-
ing against her leg and heard her mother cry, "Perpetua, are you all right?"

Of course she was all right. She straightened up,
took a firmer hold on her carpetbag and started to
walk directly toward the man who hadn't moved, but
stood there insolently blocking her way.

"So you are Perpetual" he said, and suddenly she
recognized his voice. It was still the warm, comforting
tone that she recognized from years before. So this
was her childhood friend, Timothy Vincentl Yet, there
was a great change in his appearance, Perpetua realized as she stared at him. He had filled out, and his
man's chest now seemed to be as broad as her father's. His clothes were clean and neat, made of the
finest cloth, and his wide belt held a pistol of curious
design, alongside a curved knife from the Orient. But

it was his bold, carefree expression which attracted her most. Now his arms swung toward her and in a flash she was in them! She felt smothered against the hardness of his chest.

"Welcome, Perpetual" she heard him murmur in her ear. She felt that his emotional greeting, so different from the taciturn welcome most islanders gave, was somehow almost pagan. She could feel every inch of his hard body, his pressure against her. Then Timothy released her, as suddenly as he had taken her in his arms. And she realized that, for that moment, she had been totally at his mercy, willing to give up any choice of her own. But the sudden release reminded her: she felt pushed away, neglected. Her breasts hurt from the strength of his embrace. She was visibly upset. At eighteen, a young lady should be able to control herself, particularly after being as widely traveled as she, as accustomed to the open, happy show of emotions that the Polynesians exhibited. Yet this sudden, single contact, this display of strength from the island man, had left her weakened.

"Who is that?" she heard from behind. "Hurry along, Perpetua, you are holding us up."

"It's me, Timothy Vincent! From Chilmark, Mrs. West!" the young man called out, bowing low. His manner was quite elegant, Perpetua thought to herself as she stepped aside to adjust her clothing. "I have just arrived from Paris, London and the Baltic." He laughed. "And your ship, I hear tell, comes in from the Sandwich Islands. Edgartown has truly become a crossroads of the world."

"That it is!" laughed Perpetua. "And if you please, Timothy, tell us at what distant corner you picked up that pretty speech!" At the moment, Timothy seemed not to have heard her, yet he stared at her possessively, smiling broadly, displaying an expanse of beautiful, even teeth. Then he took her hand, with all the delicacy and courtliness of a nobleman, and placed his lips upon her knuckles. When he came to his full height again, he seemed quite tall and formidable. He began to converse pleasantly with her mother and Everett, casting an occasional sideways glance at Perpetua.

Perpetua listened avidly. Timothy claimed he had imported rich silks from France, along with gold and silver services for the New England market. It all seemed highly improbable. Yet he pointed out to Everett that the huge crates on the dock—bearing his name!—were laden with goods fit for a prince. Impossible! Not this son of a poor fisherman from Chilmark. Not the boy who had tumbled roughly with her many years ago, who had comforted her from time to time when she was a child crying over her bruises.

Then Perpetua recalled her first grown-up emotions, when Timothy had crushed her beneath him to prove his strength. She recalled, out of a past that seemed very dim, her early childish thoughts of sex. How infantile! Pulling herself up, looking at Timothy with all the art she could muster, Perpetua pursed her full lips provocatively.

"As soon as we settle here in Edgartown, do call on us," she invited coolly.

"I'll do that, little Perpetua! But now, your mother's calling. The men are already at your carriage."

With that, he turned and strode toward the wharf, signaling several stevedores to follow him. They obeyed instantly.

'Little' Perpetua? She stamped her foot in annoyance.

"How grown up you have become," Everett

teased as they got in the carriage. "I can see you won that young man."

"Don't be silly. He still calls me 'Little' Perpetua, Everett. He is just an old friend." But Everett only smiled.

As Everett looked about the town for suitable quarters for Clarissa and her daughter, Perpetua thought a great deal about Timothy Vincent. But she didn't see him in town that day, nor the next. She and her mother settled in a small hotel until a better place could be found and there were so many small chores, Perpetua scarcely had time to think of her childhood friend.

The quarters were on the second floor and each woman had her own room and bath. They unpacked. And they bought many items—small luxuries which had been denied them on Maui. Everett took a place at a nearby pension. Everything had to be unpacked, sorted and arranged. In the general confusion Perpetua almost forgot her meeting with Timothy. Her work about the inn piled up. She arranged reunions with her former schoolmates.

Clarissa's life assumed the shape of a comfortable ritual. It was her habit in the late afternoon to take a warm bath, luxuriating in the tepid, fresh water which she had been unable to get on shipboard.

She customarily expected Everett at about five, but one night he was later than usual. Perpetua was visiting in Holmes Hole with a friend. Clarissa was alone. She enjoyed the feeling, the solitary moments. A woman needed time for herself, she felt.

After washing her hair, Clarissa stood before the full-length mirror in her dressing gown. She began brushing, a full one-hundred strokes with a strong bristle brush. The blonde strands glistened with flecks of red and gold. The robe parted and the sight of her own naked body shocked Clarissa momentarily. Before her she saw a tall, well-built, mature woman who yet had the touch of a child about her. Narrow shoulders, soft round breasts tipped with pink nipples and a slim waistline emphasized her youthful appearance. Good health and good food nurtured her youthfulness. Her stomach was flat. The roundness of her moon-shaped buttocks was that of an athletic girl. Her thighs seemed fuller, but her long legs, delicate ankles and milk-white skin denied her age.

Clarissa had never really looked at herself as a man might. The sight struck her, arousing her own senses with an admiration that was almost lascivious. It was the first time she realized the desirability of her own body.

Though she had observed many Maui women in the nude, they seemed quite different from her. Their stature and their athletic, outdoor habits disguised their maturity. She had no other means of comparison.

Yes, she was pleased with herself and with the beautiful form she saw reflected in the mirror. Abstinence during the years away from Jared had killed many of her natural feelings. Yet some still lingered. Clarissa was not a virgin, nor was she completely unmindful of the charms of men.

The door opened slowly, and Everett caught her double image, the woman who stood with her back toward him and the beautiful, feminine form reflected in the mirror. His voice was soft, but his words unhesitating: "The most wonderful sight a man could imagine! Titian in his glory never caught such tones, nor did Reubens ever picture a woman so lovely!"

She caught her breath and turned swiftly, clutching her robe about her. It was too soon. Having felt the need for intimacy, she still could not admit a

total commitment to this man. Jared's treatment of
her, his liaison with the Polynesian girl and the ridi-
cule this had brought her, had scarcely been softened
by his death. In her mind, she was still the rejected
woman whose promiscuous husband's life was known
to all. His bravery and eventual remorse, so faithfully
reported by his shipmates, was but a footnote to his
tragic life.

Her need to have another man was powerful.
That need far outweighed her anxiety of being rejected again. She had held off expertly, unable to enter a
sexual relationship with Everett, yet knowing such a
relationship was inevitable. Now he stood behind her.
His remarks were pleasing. His words were not an advance. He meant nothing but a compliment. He had
no intention of attacking her.

When she hid herself from him, though, he took
one step closer. "Don't! Clarissa, please. God's
greatest work of art is the beauty of a woman such as
you."

Embarrassment was followed by pleasure. Her
face flushed and she held the robe closer about her
breasts. "I expected you later . . . ," she began, not
knowing what she was saying or why. The moment of
decision had come. She felt only a great lassitude, as if
all strength of purpose had left her. Everett moved
against her. His eyes looked into hers, speaking his
thoughts with absolute, unambiguous clarity. Her
hands fell away.

With a quick movement his lips were on hers,
pressing. Probing, his tongue touched hers, savoring
her taste. Nothing had ever been like this. She became rigid, but the restraint left her body as she was
overwhelmed by a strange exhilaration. A sensation of
absolute bliss swept over her as Everett lifted her and
lightly placed her upon the bed. His eyes were loving

as he looked down upon her, unloosening his belt. She sighed and looked up at him, unable to resist, not wishing to protest in any way.

She surrendered herself to his arms, his moving hands. She clutched his body, holding him close to her as if she could not get enough of his splendid strength. It was as though some marvelous demon had possessed them. Held back for years, the dam within her broke and she writhed, gasped, feeling every nerve as he explored her, his hands moving across her thighs, his fingers touching her intimately. His lips parted when he poised over her. She touched his firm shoulders—so strong! His head bent over her. And she spread her legs for him as he moved gently in her, slowly. With all the need she felt, begging for his response, she arched her body against his. This was the man she had somehow always loved, who had loved her and had returned to love her forever. All of her ardor poured forth. She felt all of him, every fiber and sinew, as if his body were part of hers. He moved inside her and she felt the pulse of first response in her loins. Her lower body grew tense. Her buttocks tightened as she began thrusting convulsively. She reached a point of no return. The excitement carried her higher and suddenly she was no longer waiting, but reaching, begging, crying out with her whole being. Her cry was answered by Everett's. The sheer bliss of release, abandonment and fulfillment flooded through her. Everett had taken complete possession of her. He was hers, she his. It was over, done, more happiness than she could bear in a single moment.

Then came the remorse, the rush of fear. She had offended God. She shook her head, struggling to obliviate the echoes of childhood teachings, the voices in her head. Yet she could not banish the cautions.

She had lain like an animal beneath a man to whom she was not married! Perspiration grew on her brow. Her heart beat wildly, burdened with dread. She felt Everett move next to her. His breathing was quiet. His eyes stared up at the beamed ceiling. She wondered what he was thinking. Had she lost his respect? Her dread began to dissolve, was replaced by languid satisfaction. Despite her abandon, she had responded. The seed of desire, the possibilities of pleasure were as yet fully alive in her.

The panic, the self-reproach, then the reasoning, all seemed inevitable. But somehow, the obligations of her conscience were no longer important. Her future with Everett seemed destined.

Clarissa leaned over and kissed her lover full on the mouth. Her lover! The forbidden word thrilled her. He was now only half awake, but she whispered she had not had enough of him yet. Her hands moved across his body, encouraging him. He smiled.

"Insatiable witch! You will never be satisfied, my love." He took her in his arms.

A week later she was called to New Bedford to hear Jared West's will read in the court. Clarissa and Perpetua were the Captain's legal heirs. The courts had determined that Jared West, by the laws of the Commonwealth of Massachusetts, in the eyes of God and Man, was legally deceased.

"May God rest his soul," concluded the judge.

The reading of the will was complete.

CHAPTER 12

To Naliki, the church seemed to be the center of all information on Martha's Vineyard. There were bazaars and teas for the benefit of orphans; for widows whose husbands had been lost at sea; and for fallen women who, these people seemed to believe, could be reclaimed through prayer and good works. Naliki often wondered what that phrase meant—"fallen women."

As the daughter of a rich trader in the Sandwich Islands, Naliki was accepted among her own kind as an *alii*. Certainly, her marriage to an *alii* who shipped goods around the world had made her a noblewoman on her own island. But here in her new home on Martha's Vineyard, she was not regarded with the same esteem. When she walked down Main Street, on her way from her husband's great home on the cliffs overlooking the harbor, the women remained aloof and men shunned her. If she turned quickly, she would catch them grinning among themselves.

Naliki was proud of her husband, proud of their close relationship, the way he needed her and spoiled her. She strongly wished to repay his kindness by making herself well-liked in town. When the annual bazaar was announced, she decided to offer the church something she would cook, her own secret recipe.

Imagine, she thought, how excited her husband would be when, among the usual cakes and cookies, overgrown fruit and handsewn clothing, her pot of steaming, succulent pig and clams, with a mixture of cut greens (she hoped she could find them here) received first prize. Then she would be accepted, and he would be proud of her.

When her dish was nearly done, however, a small committee of women arrived unexpectedly at her door.

Naliki had asked the maid to step aside in order that she herself, mistress of the house, could meet them. She thought they were some welcoming group come to visit. Such Christian welcomes, she had heard, were customary in New England.

"What is that terrible odor?" demanded a gaunt woman with wrinkled face who peered at Naliki.

The heavy-set woman behind nudged her companion.

"Say it, Mathilda. Get it said and let's be off."

Naliki smiled. "Won't you come in?" she managed, in her best English. Wouldn't Captain Priest be happy that a group had finally come calling!

"No, thank you," replied the woman with the lined face. She cleared her throat before she continued. "We just want you to know that before you can enter anything in our church bazaar, you must be an accepted member of the church body! We've heard talk of your buying makin's from the grocer for some outlandish, heathen mess. But it wouldn't behoove you to waste your man's goods needlessly. You should know why we have come today, Mrs. Priest, and be good enough to advise your husband." With that, the woman named Mathilda turned, fluffed her shawl about her scrawny shoulders and shoved past the four other women. Down the walk they went, each yapping away at the others, obviously pleased, from the tone of their voices, with having put Naliki in her place.

"What strange people!" Naliki thought. And in fact, what a strange island. She began to cough. Her loyal maid, catching the end of the conversation, came to her. "Mistress Priest, you are coughing again! Best go upstairs and rest. Drat those women. They are such poor prisoners in their own world." Then, perhaps realizing she might be hurting her lovely mistress, Miss Peabody went upstairs to turn down the bed.

The cough continued that night and for two more days. John Priest was troubled by the sound of his wife's ceaseless discomfort. And he knew there were many other problems facing Naliki in Edgartown.

When her health seemed improved, Priest found time to take her in his carriage to explore the rest of the island. They passed white clapboard houses with little white board fences, small back gardens and tiny stoops. When they reached the farms, Priest pulled up the carriage so Naliki might see the cattle, sheep and horses. Though charming, the homes and beasts, with the surrounding fields, looked foreign to her. She missed the lush undergrowth, the tall palms and the heavy, exotic smell of the perfumed flowers. Here on the Vineyard, everything seemed bare and drab. Even the white clouds far above seemed to race frantically to escape from the land below.

Her islands were heaven as compared with these. Here, barren cliffs with heavy stones met her on every hand. Small, stagnant lagoons seemed humid, without life. The gulls were smaller, the ducks warier.

Everything about this island seemed as austere and rigid to her as the women callers with their vile message of hate. The whole day long, as she and Captain Priest rode about in the carriage, she couldn't wait until John brought her home.

She ran quickly upstairs. There, in her own dressing room, she lay down and stared out of the window. By now the sky had become overcast. A heavy black cloud moved over the house, hung brooding. The rain began and Naliki rushed to close the windows. One never closed windows in Polynesia! If this were summer, what would winter be like? She shuddered and crawled into bed. There she lay waiting the call for supper. She knew what the meal would be: fish chowder and greens. When the food finally was brought to her, it was overcooked and tasteless, and she toyed with it listlessly while her good husband viewed her with alarmed concern.

That night, she felt she must unburden herself of all she had kept private within her. While John sat holding her hand, she told him of her son.

"I don't know where he is now or what happened to him after the canoe took my husband. He was sent ahead of us to his island—to be there when we arrived. John," she requested, her eyes filling with tears, "some day I want to go there and find him. He must be a fine young boy by now. It was three and a half years ago that I left him. Will you take me there in your ship some day—just for awhile—to see him again?"

"Yes, I will, dear Naliki. But tell me, who was his father?"

"It is a secret which is known only to my father—and to me, John. I will share it with you. But please—" Her eyes sought his. "It may be difficult. You must try to understand our ways. What happened was only the custom. It was not my wish, nor could I deny my father's wishes."

Then Naliki told John Priest of the man who had been chosen by her father to teach her how to please men. She told how that man had been with her three nights and how his being with her had been to prove that she could bear a child. "Is it a matter which bothers you, my proud husband?"

He was silent. Then he replied, "I was not so naïve to think you were born with that knowledge of men you possess. I had heard about the training of women to pleasure men, but I thought those customs faded long ago. Now I realize that the traditions of your ancestors have not died."

"Are you not pleased that we keep them, my husband?" she pleaded, holding out her arms.

In answer he quickly slipped into her bed and pulled her close.

"I have heard of a young girl who has just come home to Edgartown," he said gently to the woman in his arms. "Her name, I believe, is Perpetua. Tomorrow, I will see if she will agree to be with you during the day. It will be a comfort to have someone your own age here while you recover."

Naliki hardly heard what he was saying, for his arms had enfolded her and she was pressed close to his bare chest.

"You mean there is actually a *kanaka* on our island?" was Perpetua's cry. She couldn't believe her ears. Yet it was Everett who had delivered the good news—and she had to believe him. He told her it would be an opportunity for her to make use of the next three months. She had graduated in the top of her class and no longer had need of schooling.

"You excelled in English. You have a choice now,

my grown-up girl of eighteen. You can either join the older folks in social activities, or go back and teach the younger ones at school. Or you can teach English this summer to a young woman your age."

"Tell me about her!"

"There is a notice posted in the general store, signed by a man by the name of Priest," began Everett. "His family is much respected, so I would not hesitate to send you to him. He seeks a 'companion-teacher of the language' for his young bride of Polynesia. While I know little of the man personally, I have heard much of his revered father and of the big house in which the family lives."

"I have heard of Mrs. Priest," said Clarissa. She spoke carefully, for what she had heard might just have been gossip and vicious rumors. In fact, Clarissa had heard it said that "Mrs. Priest" was very beautiful, but outlandish. Though the Polynesian woman dressed in the height of Parisian fashion and was the darling of her handsome husband, none of the older women approved of her. Yet Clarissa had heard no other reason for their discontent save that she was "one of those Polynesians." And to Clarissa, who had known them so well, such a description was more praise than censure.

"Mother," declared Perpetua, "I want to do something with my life! Surely, now is the time—now that my studies are finished. Let me go see this *kanaka*! I know a few words in her language. I can make myself understood. Let me—oh, please do!"

She could not tell her mother that ever since being handed her diploma, Perpetua had felt depressed. Yet the excitement at this new prospect echoed in her voice.

Life held more than just books! Taught by a girl who was only one year older, Perpetua had thought long and hard about being in her teacher's place. Unsophisticated, quite ugly and yet capable in her ability to make children understand the three "R's," Abigail Smith had projected no image that would attract Perpetua to teaching. Without a doubt, Perpetua decided, cruelly, Abigail Smith would end up an old maid with a barren womb, teaching her pupils as if she could pretend they were her own children.

The very idea of talking with a girl her own age from the Sandwich Islands was thrilling. On this cold island, so different from Maui, they would be able to compare feelings, to share their memories and nostalgia as well as those strange, womanly impressions which Perpetua felt so strongly within her. Neither her mother nor Everett had spent much time with her lately, so absorbed were they in their new marriage. And now, quite by accident, there was a chance of friendship. It was a chance she meant to take!

It was soon clear that Perpetua would have her way.

Arrangements were made between Priest and Clarissa. They decided that Perpetua would visit Naliki every morning at ten and would stay with her until four. She would receive ten dollars a week—a large sum by any standards! During her time with Mrs. Priest, Perpetua would instruct her in English and would teach the Polynesian woman how she must act in her new society. And John Priest hoped that Perpetua would gradually introduce Naliki to her own friends and make her feel comfortable with them.

On the designated morning, Perpetua waited hesitantly in the hallway of the great mansion. But all her fear and insecurity vanished as soon as Mrs. Priest approached. Behind the Polynesian girl, heavy curtains shrouded the sky. Oil paintings hung along the wall, each bearing the visage of some Priest ancestor. But Naliki's very presence banished these ponderous reminders of Yankee tradition. Her hands hung along her tight skirt. Her silk blouse was bordered with lace and the delicate handwork covered her bosom and neck. But the woman's face was what Perpetua found most attractive of all. A broad smile lit her features. Her oval eyes held warmth and a sweet, almost child-like expression played around her lips even though she was trying to keep a more sober and fitting expression. It was obvious to Perpetua that Mrs. Priest was nervously anxious for them to get along.

"This is Mistress Priest," introduced the maid, and walked away. It was not impatience that made her turn away, however, but the necessity of concealing an almost insolent smile of satisfaction. It would do her mistress good to have a friend her own age. She liked this Miss West at first sight. She was not only obviously well-born, but there was spirit in her which would match that of her mistress.

"Welcome."

Naliki's voice trembled. She moved back to make way for the tall, very beautiful *hoaloi* before her. Immediately, Naliki caught the spirited look that irradiated Perpetua's features. Naliki understood this was an adventure to Miss West. That was good. It meant their meetings would be new and exciting to both of them.

Perpetua followed Naliki, noticing the same swaying of hip, the same undulation in her walk which was natural to the natives of the Sandwich Islands. Her head was held high, allowing her black hair to fall straight along her proud neck. And the hair had not been coiffed in deference to New England custom, but hung long, flowing down between her shoulder blades to her waist. Turning quickly,

Naliki asked, "Coffee?" Then she laughed in a way that was so infectious that Perpetua joined her immediately.

"You have learned fast, Mrs. Priest."

"Ah, my name is Naliki. Everyone lives on coffee here, true?"

"It is our way of breaking the first barriers between strangers. You're right. Coffee is the first offering to a new friend. I don't know why, but it is mandatory."

"That word, 'madit-ary.' What does that mean?"

"Man-da-tory," repeated Perpetua. "It means something we are obliged to do. Do you understand?" She smiled at Naliki. They would get along well. There was no overweening ego in this woman.

"Obliged? That means 'forced'; like dressing in clothes all day long! Eh?"

They sat at the coffee served on silver by the maid.

"Clothes all day long?" Perpetua repeated. "I hate them, too!"

Naliki brushed a palm along her bosom. "It is so still, so confining. I am used to wearing nothing above my waist. Now, I dress as John obliges me to. See? There I used your word!"

"Not my word, yours! And I am obliged to wear clothes here, too. In fact, Naliki, we are actually forced to wear them." They both laughed, sneaking shy looks at one another as they shared their amusement. "You speak well. Why do you think you need to know more?"

"It is the Captain. He really was seeking a woman my age, someone who could be a comrade or friend. Which is the word?"

"Companion. So, I was elected," Perpetua mused. "What did he say about me?"

"That you were attractive. And then he said, 'Naliki, no one is as beautiful as you.'"

"He must love you a great deal. Where did you come from?"

"In your visit to the Islands, did you ever hear of the smaller island of Maui?"

"It was there my father, master of *The Horatio*, landed. I lived on your island for eighteen months!"

The fact was too much for Naliki to comprehend at first. They stared at one another. Then Naliki asked, "What was your father's name, Perpetua?"

"Captain Jared West."

As Perpetua watched Naliki, the woman seemed to shrink a little. Then she gathered herself, holding her head proudly—so very, very beautiful in her exotic way.

Naliki's hand went to her throat. She began to cough and her complexion grew suddenly pallid. Her other hand shook as she tried to place the coffee cup on the mahogany stand near her chair.

Trying to stand up, still coughing violently, Naliki began to sway. Perpetua caught her and held her. Then her hands held Naliki gently until the tremors had ceased.

The coughing fit summoned Sara Peabody with a bottle of red medicine. In a short while, under Sara's ministrations, Naliki was able to compose herself.

To Perpetua she said, "Please, I am sorry. I cannot stop once I begin." Her voice was still shaky, her hands trembling. Perpetua felt she should excuse herself for the morning.

"Don't go, please. We will have more talk."

Despite Naliki's politeness and obvious courtesy, Perpetua knew that some emotion had triggered the coughing spell. It was as though a shade had been rolled up, a moment of revelation had swept up the

island girl in feelings as overwhelming as the tremors
which shook her body.

"Your father. Where is he now?" asked Naliki politely, as though to continue the conversation pre-
cisely where they had left off.

"He died in the Arctic. His ship was frozen in the
ice last year when much of the whaling fleet was
sunk. He was among those who perished."

"I am sorry to hear that, my new friend."

Naliki seemed more at ease now. Straightening
her back, she suddenly stood up.

"Come! Come with me, Perpetua! I want to show
you my clothes. Please tell me if the Captain has
picked the correct ones for your island."

"Oh, Naliki. You mustn't move."

"Of course I must," was the bright response. "I
am all right now. That Sara Peabody watches over
me too well. Come." She led Perpetua to the second
floor, into her spacious bedroom overlooking the harbor. Then, without hesitation, she walked to a huge
wardrobe and flung open the doors.

"I'll try one on first, then you!"

Almost tearing off her clothing, the Polynesian
soon stood before the row of petticoats which filled
one entire section. Perpetua could not help but admire the lush figure before her, the ease with which
she moved, the subtlety of her graceful arms as she
selected a stiff white undergarment and slipped it
over her naked legs and pulled the ruffled edge above
her waist. Bare from the waist, she spun around like a
child. "Look at this thing! It pricks me like a sea ur-
chin!"

Her voice mixed amusement and frustration, but
the sight of Naliki's perturbed expression almost made
Perpetua burst out laughing. Only the thought that

she might hurt her newfound companion's feelings could stifle the laughter that came to Perpetua's lips.

"Here, try this next," Perpetua urged, delighted by the natural actions of her companion, who was so innocent of any impropriety of her nudity. How like all the young women of Maui she was, so uninhibited, so free! Perpetua envied her.

While Naliki pulled on a heavy brocade, Perpetua tried on other clothing. The high wardrobe was jammed with gorgeous Paris dresses. The two were giggling. Pulling dresses on and off, discarding whatever was too ridiculous or uncomfortable, soon they stood completely naked, free from the tiresome pulling of dresses about their breasts, hips and shoulders.

To Perpetua, it almost seemed she was delighting in that orgy she still dreamed of. Then her mood changed. She became practical. Not one of the dresses—and there must have been two dozen in the wardrobe—was appropriate for the Vineyard. For New York and Boston, even New Bedford, yes. But not for here. Too ornate, too much decolletage. Too many ribbons and frills. And the lace! How expensive, and in what detail! These were more like costumes than regular clothing.

"My husband would think you have a nice figure," she heard Naliki say innocently, for Perpetua had tried yet another dress, and was now staring at herself in the mirror. "Your skin is so white."

Perpetua looked at herself. The outdoor activity on Maui, the swimming and running on her own island had kept her flesh firm. Her breasts had been pushed up beyond their normal fullness with the gown gathered flatteringly beneath them, enhancing her shape and giving her the look of a woman. The corset added to the illusion that she was very well endowed. She had quickly caught her hair in a pin while trying on the dresses and by piling her long blonde hair on high, she permitted her small, delicate ears to be shown. This, with the tender curve of her neck, made her look vulnerable.

"Naliki, this is all wrong!" Perpetua frowned at her image. "These dresses are for a grand occasion like a ball, not a dull social at the church. No one on the Vineyard owns clothes like this!" Suddenly, Perpetua began to tear at the dress, loosening buttons so quickly that she ripped the delicate material in her impatience and anger to have done with the costume. What was wrong with her? She was supposed to teach this woman about their island.

Standing nude before her friend, as unashamed as before, Perpetua said, "Now you see me. *This* is Perpetua West!"

The door behind her opened. She heard a male voice. "I came home early. I couldn't wait to see how you were . . ." Then the voice stopped abruptly and she saw the figure of a man reflected in the mirror before her.

"Ah, John. Come in. This is Perpetua." Naliki showed no fright, no feeling of embarrassment for Perpetua.

"Later," she heard the man say. Then the door was shut quickly.

"See, Naliki? See? If I was on Maui, would your husband think me unusual? I am supposed to teach you our ways. I would rather know yours."

"I see nothing bad or sinful in the beauty of a woman's body, Perpetua. The bodies of woman and of man are to be enjoyed while we are young. And we are still youthful—are we not?" Naliki's eyes, so questioning, held the sadness of close memories, rarely disclosed. "One eats when hungry, so my family ate until we were full. We did not worry about food, for it was there. We swam and fished when we wished to do so. There are days for swimming in the warm sea and other days for lying naked in the sun. The sea is filled with fish. There will always be more. And so it is with our bodies. When the feeling comes over a woman to enjoy her body, she does as she would when she fishes and eats. She knows there will be no end to it, that she will feel that way again and again, and that the joys will be continuous. Did I speak English well? Do you understand?"

Perpetua laughed. "I like your philosophy." She stopped. "I mean your customs and ideas," she explained. "I would like to know all that you know." While talking she drew on her own dress and stood before Naliki. They both heard a horse leaving the yard. Looking out, Naliki laughed, "It is my husband! He cannot face you just yet! How many times has he seen me as you were? How many times has he had a woman? I couldn't count them. And yet, he is so much like his own kind when here. The men seem ashamed of their feelings. What is the word, Perpetua?"

"Hypocrisy. That is the word. They think one thing and pretend another." Perpetua hesitated a moment, then blurted out, "Are you happy with your husband, Naliki?"

"Oh, yes. So very happy. He is with me every night. And I have taught him many things. We share everything. He is so strong and fierce when he takes me. I have never felt so wanted by a man."

Naliki began to talk very fast. It was as though she had been keeping thoughts of her life and John Priest to herself, when all the time she wished to share these thoughts with another woman. She told Perpetua of her rescue, of the long days on the ship, headed for some destination, she knew not where. Naliki recounted how he had come to her on deck and how, each night ever since, they had made love. She gave details which Perpetua couldn't believe. Imagine such heights of pleasure!

As Naliki described it to Perpetua, it sounded as if this exotic island child had complete freedom of expression in the act of sex. How could she ever manage "the inner caress" herself, Perpetua wondered. How could she master the touch that drove men into ecstasy? And what were the perfumes and oils which Naliki described—those special fragrances which a woman must know about, those subtle odors which aroused men to the heights of passion? These were the secrets Perpetua yearned to know, and all that Naliki told her was only a temptation to learn more of such intimacies.

"My new friend," Naliki said gently with a smile, "I see your eyes are wide, but your mind is still confused. I have asked you to teach me. But I see there are things I can teach you as well!"

Perpetua smiled, feeling her face grow hot. The blush at her neck spread all over. "Yes, Naliki, you have opened my eyes and my head. Now tell me, how can I learn these things?"

"You must have a teacher. I will ask my husband!" Naliki meant it. She was excited at the thought. She ran over to Perpetua and sat before her with her dress billowing out and her eyes flashing.

"Yes, I am sure he will agree. Allow me, Perpetua. Let my husband be your teacher."

Perpetua shook her head, smiling at the mere idea. It was preposterous, of course, but she wasn't shocked. Perpetua accepted the idea in the spirit with which the offer was made—out of generosity and friendship. Perpetua shook her head again, just as the clock struck the hour. "It is two already and we haven't eaten a thing," Perpetua noted lightly. "Come, let me teach you how to make a real deep-dish apple pie. Have you any apples?"

It was late in the afternoon when Perpetua finally left Naliki. Going home, Perpetua felt as though she had taken a cold bath followed by a brisk rubdown, the kind she had been forced to take aboard *The Horatio*. Her head was reeling. Her skin tingled. Her uninhibited thoughts and Naliki's offer of her husband hadn't seemed real. She knew she would be asked all about Naliki by her mother. She would paint quite a different picture than the one she had seen!

After Perpetua had left, Naliki took the pie they had baked and placed it on the window of the kitchen "to cool slowly," just as her friend had told her to do. It smelled delicious.

Then Naliki went over her first day with Perpetua. That she, Naliki, of all women, should be teaching the daughter of Captain Jared West about making love, about building desire in a man! It was the strangest thing that had ever happened! Yet, maybe Kane had willed it. Tomorrow, she would go with Perpetua and buy a few things more appropriate for her home. Then, after trying on the new clothes, she would talk again about the most important thing in the world, the art of making love.

As the friendship grew, Perpetua felt more and more out of place in Edgartown. Naliki always had such vitality. Yet she seemed to suffer greatly from her persistent cough and Perpetua wondered how long the Polynesian woman could endure the damp, chill climate. Perpetua knew that Naliki suffered, too, from lack of activity and the stultifying social atmosphere. On Martha's Vineyard the only thrill seemed to come from making money and more money. Everett had opened a land office. He was helping Clarissa prepare the sale of the old West farm up-island, which was now too distant for them to travel to each day. Barring an occasional, chance meeting with Captain John Priest, Perpetua spent most of her full days alone with Naliki. She and the Polynesian girl had become inseparable. They laughed behind their hands at what they knew to be the local gossip about them in the village, mocking the conversations they had overheard when they made their forays into Edgartown.

"Ever since the day my husband saw you in front of the mirror, he has admired you," Naliki confided. "He says he had heard of your father, the Captain, a man, he said, of firm religious feelings. And my husband professes a great admiration for your mother. He thought your mother and father had a true love affair." Perpetua did not comment on Naliki's words. Instead, she quickly changed the subject.

"Your English is improving. Now what can I teach you in return for your friendship to me?"

"Teach me how to walk in a room and how to curtsy. I would like to know, too, the proper way to address people when I meet them."

"Oh, there are so many trite phrases in our language! But you have to say them nonetheless," Perpetua complained. "My mother is different," she added suddenly. "You will not have to curtsy to her, nor say, 'How do you do?' She has asked to meet you."

"Oh—I would like to meet her!" exclaimed Naliki. When the two women met, Clarissa was immediately struck by Naliki's presence. It was something she couldn't define. Clarissa was certain that this young and most attractive woman was hiding something. The Polynesian seemed to know some secret which involved her, as well. Clarissa had poured tea. She let her daughter prattle on about how wonderful Naliki was. Clarissa learned that Captain Priest was then building another vessel. And she learned what Perpetua had taught Naliki, how the two young women spent their days. But occasionally, in the ebb and flow of conversation, she caught Mrs. Priest staring at her openly, looking her over appraisingly.

When Perpetua began retelling the marriage ceremony, recounting how the canoe had taken Naliki to sea one day, Perpetua noticed her mother's eyes. They were tightly shut. When Clarissa opened them again, she looked directly at Naliki.

"We were there that day!"

"How could we have been?" began Perpetua. Then her hand flew to her mouth. "I remember! I remember the procession and the flags and the man with the headdress and . . . you!"

The three women were on their feet, exclaiming to one another, excited and pleased.

Naliki said shyly, "And I remember a boat leaving the wharf as our canoe passed, and a man in the boat being taken to his ship."

"Father!" cried Perpetua. "That was my father, Jared West."

"Jared," repeated Naliki. "What a strange name." Then, having learned some discretion, she fell silent.

When Naliki left she was coughing continuously. Perpetua noticed that her mother refrained from mentioning the visit afterward. Instead, Clarissa told her daughter that she and Everett would be going on the next day to Holmes Hole for settlement of the sale of their Chilmark farm. "You must be with us. Be ready at eight. We must drive to Holmes Hole to meet with the lawyer, Ed Daggett. Then we will meet the Fullertons, who are buying the place."

CHAPTER 13

The day of the sale, Ed Daggett's office was crowded. To his left, under the painting of his grandfather the judge, sat Clarissa West Norton with her daughter. Seated in the chair opposite the young attorney was Everett and the papers he had been examining were laid before him on the desk. His nod indicated that the papers were accurate and the deed for sale was in order. The buyers of the property, the Fullertons, sat in straight-backed chairs. Asked to wait patiently, they heard the reading of the official document by Everett.

After the seller had been legally identified, Ed Daggett slammed the law book closed, carefully smoothed the pages of the document before him and called for the tall, blond six-footer who sat against the wall to identify himself.

Rising, the man placed a hand upon the shoulder of the tiny old woman next to him, and spoke. "I am Joshua Slocum Fullerton, late of Taunton, in the Commonwealth of Massachusetts. I was born in that township twenty-eight years ago this July. This lady next to me . . ." He stopped, looking down at her white head and narrow shoulders, ". . . is my beloved mother, who bears the maiden name of Ross. She is a

member of the Ross family of Virginia, sir. I have the
deed of sale for our farm in Taunton and certain papers regarding my late father's will. Is that sufficient?"

Perpetua moved slightly toward the man, unaware that she did so. To her, this tall blond man
named Fullerton was indeed very interesting. She
liked his capable-looking hands, his gentle manner.
To her astonishment, she was relieved that Fullerton
had no wife.

"Have you read this deed of title, sir?" Ed Daggett asked of the Taunton man. Fullerton nodded. "I
have, sir. And it seems in order, though I be no lawyer."

His mother moved quickly beside him, seized the
papers from her son's grasp and tired to read them.
Perpetua thought the woman seemed rather domi-
neering in the way that she snatched the papers without words, as though she considered her son an idiot.

Fullerton slowly took the papers from his
mother's hands, "Without your glasses, Mother?" She
grimaced and let them go. "So—I'm forced to trust
your judgment!" she snapped. Then the old woman
closed her eyes. The entire procedure obviously was
of no further interest to her.

"My mother read the first draft, sir . . . unfortu-
nately, her glasses fell and broke on our way up-island. However, we succeeded in completing a final
survey of the property," he added, in explanation.

"Then you both approve? I must have affirmation, for the deed is in both your names. Is this how
you wished it?" They nodded their approval.

"All right!" Daggett said. "Now if you will just
sign where your names appear, the deed will be ex-
ecuted." No one smiled as the papers were handed
over. From the expressions of the participants, it appeared no one was happy with the sale. Perpetua

sighed as quietly as she could. This was taking forever! But Joshua Fullerton, ten years her senior, was a man who held her with a kind of fascination that was part curiosity and part a kind of rapture. Such nice manners. Look at the gentlemanly way he pardoned himself as he passed before her mother!

The three signed, each using the quill and inkstand upon Daggett's desk, each stepping away and watching with a kind of reverence as Daggett sprinkled sand upon the ink scrawls.

"I have prepared a bank draft . . ." The tall blond man reached in his waistcoat, bringing forth a piece of paper.

"The bank draft is for Mrs. Norton. And the legal fee . . ." Daggett looked expectantly at Everett, who silently handed him a sealed envelope.

"The sale is hereby complete."

Fullerton stepped forward, giving the bank draft to Clarissa. She carefully placed it in her purse. "Now," asked Everett, "when do you intend to move here permanently?" With the formalities complete, there was an audible tone of relief in his voice.

"In less than a year. I should have enough of a home built so that mother and I may move· in for good. We intend to keep cattle, horses and chickens. We'll do a little farming for our own purposes and use the ten acres of field for corn. The pond I intend to leave as is. I believe there is a spring beneath it, since the water is always fresh."

"Oh, yes," nodded Clarissa. "There's a spring there. It is a dear pond, so tranquil and lovely. I hope you will delight in looking at it. I used to sit on the veranda and watch by the hour." She laughed. "The wife of a Captain has time for such things!"

"Will you have many horses?" interrupted Perpetua, anxious to find out more about this man. It was almost as if he were moving into her own home, all the places she had known so well.

"Six of 'em," he replied. "Thinking there'd be no delay in our final purchase, I have brought them this trip, for your barn is fit for the livestock already."

With a bow to Clarissa that included her pretty daughter, Fullerton added, "It would give me great pleasure if you, Mrs. Norton, as well as your husband and daughter, would consider the farm a place you can visit often when I am done. It is a true homestead. The mere passage of a plot or parcel of land has not changed the feelings you still have for the land, I'm sure. I would like any of you to visit me and my mother any time you wish. You would be especially welcome to go riding, as the horses are well-bred and saddle-trained, fit for either a man or lady's use."

His kind invitation accepted, Fullerton left the lawyer's office, carefully helping his mother as she made her way down the steps to their horse cart. Alongside the tall, blond man, she appeared shrunken, diminutive and feeble.

On the way home, Perpetua chattered away in excitement. "Mother, just imagine! Thoroughbreds! Please, may I accept his offer?" Her expression was imploring.

From her seat in the front of the buggy, her mother turned and smiled at Perpetua. But she cautioned her daughter, "You must await a real invitation, dear. Perhaps he was just being kind. If his invitation was sincere, he will repeat it."

"A good man," grunted Everett, more to himself than the others.

"Strange, he is unmarried." Perpetua's words were almost lost amidst the noise of the buggy wheels on the cobblestone street. But her mother overheard.

Upon arriving at Naliki's the next day, Perpetua immediately described Mr. Fullerton in detail. As she spoke, she saw a stern look of disapproval pass over her friend's face.

"He is not for Perpetua," she decided firmly. Then, guided solely by intuition, Naliki steered the conversation a different way. "Tell me more about Timothy Vincent."

"What's wrong with Joshua?" Perpetua demanded. Unmarried, good-looking, he seemed so much more powerful than Timothy, her childhood friend. And in Joshua's expression Perpetua had fathomed unmistakable desire.

"You like his horse, not him. And he has an old mother. He will take care of her as long as she demands his attention."

"He is much older than I," Perpetua conceded. "But certainly he is not decrepit!" The mere idea made her smile.

"How old is Timothy?" Naliki interrupted insistently.

Perpetua looked away so that her friend could not see how the mention of his name affected her.

"Two or three years older than I," Perpetua replied. Once that had seemed like many years' difference, but now the few years seemed inconsequential. "It is true, Naliki, he has no one to care for. His mother died years ago. And he is rich! But why would I wait for him? I never see him!"

"I am not saying you must, my friend. Only that you must not think just of one man, but of all those who will court you. Am I not teaching you the ways to a man's heart?"

"Oh, yes. That's easy to say! But there are so few men I could wish to spend my life with, among all these simple farmers here! I feel wasted here, Naliki. You are the only one who understands me!"

Perpetua stopped suddenly, silencing her impetuous outburst. The woman seated next to her began to cough. The cough racked her whole frame. Naliki retched, quickly covering her mouth with a handkerchief to hide the blood-specked sputum. As Perpetua rushed to her side, Captain Priest appeared in the doorway. Without a word, he picked up Naliki in his arms and carried her quickly upstairs to bed. Perpetua waited until he returned before taking her leave. Before she could depart, Captain Priest took Perpetua's hand and looked deep into her eyes.

"Perpetua, you have made Naliki happy. She and I are very grateful. She rests now. I must get her to a doctor. Go on, now, and I will summon you for more lessons when she is amply recovered."

CHAPTER 14

Few doctors had set up practice on the islands.
Families on Martha's Vineyard might send a second
son to the mainland to learn medicine, law, pharma-
ceuticals or accounting. But few returned and those
who did were relatively young and inexperienced.
None were as practiced as Dr. Mathias Mayhew. He
had come from the mainland many years previously,
of his own free will. His practice occupied a store-
front on the main street of Holmes Hole.

With a store of pills for every ailment, plus
bottles labeled in Latin in fine penmanship, he dis-
tributed cures, brought island infants to birth and
quieted mothers' fears over fevers and coughs. In his
later years, he realized that he was a pacifier of ap-
prehension as well as a medical professional. He became known as "a good man," and patients came from
the islands to see him, as much for consolation and
reassurance as for their troubled bodies.

So it was to Dr. Mayhew that Captain John
Priest took Naliki when her cough persisted.

On their first visit, the quiet, intelligent Polynesian beauty immediately impressed Mayhew. He
took Naliki's hand and kissed it in an enthusiastic
demonstration of his inbred courtliness. The gesture

was managed with an amusing flourish and a final tap
upon his own ample belly. Looking at her exquisite
hand and its tapering fingers, Mayhew sighed. He let
her hand drop with apparent reluctance. Naliki
smiled at him, though she wondered about the gesture, not realizing that he meant only to acknowledge
her as a lady.

Taking his place alongside his wife, John Priest
asked if they might be seated. He adjusted his tall
frame to the stiff wicker chair and began at once to
describe his wife's symptoms to the doctor.

At that moment Naliki coughed, quickly covering
her mouth with a dainty lace handkerchief.

Doctors were men of magic to her. She had
longed to meet such a healer and had great expecta-
tions for the help he might bring her. Yet this man
looked as did so many others—indulgent and red-
faced, he sized her up appreciatively, like a sailor
who had been too long at sea. Of late she had been
feeling somewhat better. Occasionally she experienced spells of high exhilaration when she felt completely healthy. But inevitably the racking cough
resumed. Each time, she spat blood. Though the sun
had warmed her in that protected patch of garden
John had prepared for her, the warmth never lasted.
Always, the spasms recurred. They frightened her beyond description. She needed help, and she prayed
this man would help her.

"It won't hurt you, my dear," Mayhew soothed,
taking his stethoscope from a hook on the wall. As she
watched his movements, Mayhew gently placed the
end of the instrument against her chest, inserted two
plugs into his ears, asked her to breathe deeply. She
obeyed.

"I can't hear a thing. You'll have to disrobe."

John explained. "He is listening inside you,

Naliki. But your clothes are in the way. Please take off your blouse. I'll be right here."

Later she recalled every detail, for there were hours and hours when she was left alone to remember.

Naliki had immediately taken off her upper clothing. Startled, Dr. Mayhew stared at the woman who stood so unashamedly before him. With her head cocked to one side, as if asking his appraisal, she made ready for "the white god" to proceed with his magic in the only way she knew how. Her hands cupped her breasts. She slowly turned front to back. Her exquisitely molded buttocks quivered before him.

Wiping perspiration from his wrinkled brow, the good doctor took the cold stethoscope in his hands to warm it. Then, as if approaching a bird about to take flight, he gently placed it upon the warm skin of her chest and listened intently through the ear pieces while he told her to breathe deeply.

"Take another deep breath," he requested. The doctor then asked her to turn about. Beneath the scrutiny of his owlish gaze, her sensuous buttocks shivered as the stethoscope began its travel across her shapely shoulder blades. Then the stethoscope re-examined her chest. The fingers holding the bulb lingered on her skin at the slope of her breasts. Apparently satisfied, Mayhew put the device down and looked at the ceiling as if recovering from great emotion. Almost regretfully, he asked her to get dressed. She left the room to do so.

Seating himself, Mayhew took four red pills from a glass jar and gave them to Captain Priest. "One every morning," he ordered. "Bring her back in four days. I'll need to watch her . . . very carefully. Very closely."

After negotiating terms, the Captain left with his

young wife on his arm. When they were gone, Dr.
Mayhew removed a book from his case and began to
read up on the symptoms of consumption.

The second visit was a copy of the first. The doctor struggled for words, his mouth dry. At last he
found the question. "The blood in your sputum?" he
asked. "Does it appear often when you cough?" He
looked up.

She nodded. "Always."

"You may dress."

While Naliki moved to his dressing room, Dr.
Mayhew called in the Captain from the outer lobby,
where Priest waited anxiously. Meanwhile, in the hot,
stuffy dressing room, three ladies of the island—
starched in manner and dress—looked up and down
with disdain, like buzzards regarding a bird of paradise.

"It's consumption," the doctor told Priest. "She's
in serious condition. Whatever made you think she
could live through these winters, these foggy, wet
days and nights? She's a hothouse flower, rooted in
the Pacific climate. You can never transplant such a
woman to a climate such as ours. It will never do."
Dr. Mayhew shook his head emphatically, "No,
never."

John Priest lowered his head. Long before Mayhew spoke, Priest had feared such a verdict.

"It is obvious that she has had lesions of the
lungs," Mayhew continued. "Such lesions may have
been arrested, but I suspect not. If they've become
calcified, she will recover in time. But it's a great
risk." Mayhew leaned forward and lowered his voice.
"My advice is, take her back to where you found her,
Captain. I cannot predict that she will recover, but
I'm certain her best chance is in the climate from
which she came. Warm her body in the hot sun.

Bring back the heat to that body. I hate to deliver this prescription, but I have to. My conscience as a doctor will not permit me to remain silent."

Captain Priest found his voice. "Consumption! But she was so healthy. Had I left her there," he mused, "she would live to eighty years or more. The Polynesians, Doctor, they are distinguished by their glowing health. She could be a queen, my Nalikil"

"Who can say what harms our climate might do their race," observed the doctor. "And then there is the change of food. She was no doubt used to fish and fruit. Perhaps, too, these people take sustenance from the sun. What do you know of her past?"

When Captain Priest hesitated, Mayhew went on.

"In any case, sir, you have a duty, if you truly care for her."

Again Priest waited.

"You must take her away from the climate in which we prosper. You also have a duty to the community. Consumption is contagious. It can be transmitted by breathing the same air as the infected person. I must watch her and examine her. If it seems permanent, I will have to report her case to the authorities. Then you and she and everyone exposed will be put in quarantine. In God's name, man . . . take her from our island and back to her own!"

"How long does she . . ."

Mayhew began shaking his head.

"I mean," asked Priest, "are you certain she has it?"

The doctor nodded.

"There is another thing, Dr. Mayhew." Priest was uneasy. How could he bring up such a subject and not seem unmanly, for it had to do with secrets between husbands and wives.

Mayhew was used to the questions of a hesitant father-to-be, and he realized how such a taciturn man as John Priest might be reluctant to speak, despite the strong emotions that were hidden within him. "Go ahead," Mayhew urged, leaning back in his squeaking chair. A benevolent smile spread across his broad face. He acted as though nothing anyone said to him could possibly surprise him. Hadn't he diagnosed venereal disease, snake bite and overdosing of pills! Into this office he'd welcomed the opium eater, the whiskey drinker, the impotent men, the homosexual. Ah, yes, Mayhew thought, he had seen the worst of men's afflictions and heard them all. It was difficult for the doctor to conceal a smile as he waited for the tall, haughty captain to confide in him.

"It's like this," Priest began, standing feet spread as if to steady a rocking deck. "Why can't she conceive a child with me?"

Easy, thought Mayhew. Why did men think themselves so constantly virile, so masterful that they felt compelled to control nature's course?

"Captain Priest, this woman should not, under any circumstances, be burdened with a child. Once she has recovered completely, perhaps she will be strong enough to bear. I must ask you—has she ever had a child?"

Captain Priest lowered his eyes as he replied.

"She told me she had a child once. I do not know its father. The child was left behind on an island in the Pacific and she will not speak of it, yet I have found her weeping at times. I have not pressed the question."

Then, with eyes still lowered, John Priest told the doctor how he had rescued Naliki.

"So she was a bride snatched from the sea?"

"Married that very day."

"What did I tell you? Those native girls! They begin as children."

"She is quite broken, depressed—even . . . hysterical at times, whenever she thinks of her boy. But now, Dr. Mayhew, now that I intend to take her back, we will visit Maui and find that child. I must hurry, you say?"

"One cannot always tell."

"Are we speaking of days, weeks or a year?"

Mayhew shrugged his shoulders.

"Do I have time to finish the building of my ships? I intended to start a fleet of whalers under my name."

Dr. Mayhew put a hand on the disturbed man's shoulder. His eyes closed. He spoke in a whisper.

"She's but a native Polynesian. She will never be happy here. Our island women don't even accept those from the mainland, John—how could they accept this strange girl? She's better off away. She is better off on her own island—even without you."

Priest thrust the offensive hand from his shoulder. His eyes grew fiery at Mayhew's well-meaning, but cold suggestion.

"Never! The Vineyard will accept my wife as she is. And me, too."

"Be that as it may," Mayhew ended the conversation. "I have other patients with more understanding of their island than you. But mind, she's near death here."

Captain Priest walked to the anteroom without a backward look. But his hand shook as he opened the door and he had to pause for a moment to calm himself. When he entered the waiting room, he appeared composed. He smiled as he offered his arm to Naliki.

She rose quickly, glad to escape the hostile atmosphere of the doctor's waiting room. As the couple

walked out into the street, stepping gingerly around
mud and horse droppings, Naliki hugged the strong
arm of her husband. He looked down at her, forcing a
smile.

The parting was very difficult for Perpetua and
Naliki.

At first, Perpetua could not believe that Naliki
was going away forever. After a private conversation
with Captain Priest, however, she began to understand the seriousness of Naliki's illness. And she also
realized that his move from the Vineyard was almost
an act of desperation on the part of John Priest.
Despite the Captain's haste to carry out Mayhew's orders and return Naliki to a familiar climate, there was
little hope for her survival.

Naliki showed little emotion as she quietly
handed her friend all the clothes she would not need
on shipboard. "Take them all, Perpetua. I won't need
them on Maui." And then she exclaimed quite suddenly: "Oh, just think, Perpetua! Soon I will see the
waves of Maui! I'll be able to enjoy the sun all day
long and I will have my Captain. I will send you a
message from there, I promise."

"And you will be happy, too, Naliki. I just know
it! But, oh, how I will miss you!"

They kissed quickly, for neither wished to cry.
Then, without a backward glance, Perpetua walked
out of the house she had learned to love. Now she
must face the Vineyard's ungiving, insular life alone.
When she had walked beyond sight of the house, she
began to cry uncontrollably.

The Deep Six sailed from Edgartown harbor in
August, 1856. Captain Priest stood aft, surveying the
platform which would house Naliki. The ship's car-

penter had devised a private sun room for her, an in-
tricately designed haven surrounded by four wooden
side pieces and sailcloth, where Naliki could enjoy
the full rays of the sun without being visible to any
sailor on deck. Only those who might be in the top-
masts would be able to see the Captain's wife while
she enjoyed the fresh sea air and sunlight.

The master let his crew know that he owed no
agent a penny on this voyage; that it was fully fi-
nanced by himself and that the crew would get their
shares from him in cash, for he meant to undertake a
fast voyage to the South Pacific. And he promised, in
case the ship did not return, all seamen were released
to join another crew for return passage. Captain
Priest was aware the voyage would cost him much,
for he vowed he'd not stop until his ship reached the
Sandwich Islands.

As *The Deep Six* moved farther southward,
Naliki spent many hours on her private sun deck. The
sailors lounged about aimlessly and many wondered
why this whaler had been made into a passenger ship.
And they did not hesitate to peer down from the top-
masts to catch a glimpse of the Captain's beautiful
young wife. Thinner, larger of eye than before, yet
with the same breathtaking beauty, she lay, her amber skin and jet-black hair contrasted, like in a portrait of an Oriental princess being carried by her
royal master to some exotic destination.

The nights were star-filled. The vessel, like a
stately carriage, glided across the southern sea.

Naliki's excursions on deck beyond the confines
of her sun room were rare. But when she appeared,
the men gathered to admire their master's woman. A
young man from Gloucester, Robert Tompkins, spent
more than his share of time watching her from the
topmast, a fact noted by the older seamen. Yet even

the veterans permitted themselves a moan of lust as they admired the graceful proportions of their master's rare tidbit.

Walking to the sunlit retreat from her cabin, Naliki customarily wore a rose-red *tapa*, her long, silken hair reflecting the sun. The men sighed as she passed by and disappeared behind the sheltering wood and canvas.

"I've sailed with a master's wife before," allowed one chap with a lantern jaw and bony cheeks. His red eyes devoured Naliki's movements. "Never have I seen a woman like that," he confessed to the others. "She makes my old bones weak. My head swims in yearnin' for the touch of that smooth skin. What I would give for the chance to grasp those animal thighs of her'n!"

"Old age is always awake, for it has been longer linked with life," said another sailor, considerably older than the lantern-jawed youngster. "Life has sure passed ye by if ye've never laid your staff into one like that. They abound in the Sandwich Islands. But she's one who makes the million seem tame, don't she now?"

"Who is she?" asked the younger sailor, turning his head to the crowd about him.

"His wife, you lout!" answered a Vineyarder who had shipped out as a harpooner. "They lived in a great white house above the harbor. She's sick with some rare disease, I've heard. They never mingled with folks. She comes from the South Pacific, as ye can see, a Polynesian plucked from some jungle island to meet his fancy. And now he aims to transplant her before she dies of the cold."

"Well, he better hurry," responded a serious-looking man. His bushy eyebrows scarcely shielded the look of worry in his black eyes. Dressed in a severe,

long coat with high collar turned up against the fresh
wind, the man seemed more selectman than sailor.
"From the looks of her, the roots were torn too violent
. . . she'll never make it."

At that moment, a cry came from aloft. "Blows!"

The sound of the man in the crow's nest brought
Priest on deck in a single bound. "We're passing her
by, man! Come off of there!"

"Blows!" the man shouted again, unable to control his excitement as he pointed from one spout to
another. . . . "Thar' and thar'. Must be ten o'them,
Captain!"

"Down ye come, man. We're not taking a whale
lest we run her down!" All hands stood at the ship's
side, their eyes hungry for the kill. "I'll pay you share
for share as if we'd taken tons of oil, like I promised
you. But I won't stop this ship. Keep her full and by;
we're holding this wind while she's strong." With that
John Priest turned from the men, parted the canvas
side flaps and joined Naliki in her retreat.

"It's the Cap'n's prerogative," shrugged the lantern-jawed man bitterly. " 'Tis happier work between
those legs than tryin' out for the next day and night."
Then he shrugged again. "But it's share for share he's
promised us, and so what matter? I reckon that first
one was worth a fortune and all the rest of 'em together makes me a rich man."

"Yep," replied the Nantucket lad, watching the
whales sporting away. "You'll land home with fifty
dollars this trip."

The man aloft now began his descent. As he
came lower, his position on the yardarm permitted
him a breathtaking view of the naked Naliki lying
spread-eagled upon her mat in the sun on the deck
below him. With his back to the seaman, Priest was
gently massaging her legs with oil.

"Up there?" cautiously called the lad from Nantucket. "Now what are ye starin' at—as if we didn't know full well, ye Peepin' Tom."

"Such a sight it is," admired the seaman as he climbed down from the shrouds. "She's bein' warmed for the consumption of her and oiled like a tender piece of meat for a man's satisfaction. It's too much for me, mates. If'n I look on that sight ag'in, I'll fall for sure."

The men crowded around him.

Enjoying his sudden popularity, the lookout cleared his throat, spat to leeward and settled back against a stay.

"Get on with it. What did you see?" the men cried.

"Well, it appears she lies there nude as she can be and that's mighty becomin', ye might say . . . and, well, she combed her hair . . . and then he bestrode her."

"Bestrode her?" demanded the Nantucket harpooner. "What in blazes did he do?"

"Like a bloody horse, he got into the saddle, ye might say, easin' in all comfy and that's when . . ."

"That's when what?" they asked in unison.

"When the Captain looked up and saw me . . . so I scrambled down."

"How in blazes could he see ye, man? Ef'n he was head down, bestride her as ye put it?" inquired one scurvy-yellow sailor, scratching his ears and squinting.

"He warn't head down."

"He warn't?"

"No, he was on his back, ye might say."

"Then she was ridin' him, ye lout. Not him her."

"He eased it in, none the less, then over they went, her on top, to his joy no doubt. That's when he spotted me comin' down. Not a flicker of his eye told, yet I knew he saw me, for he grabbed her about the bottom and squeezed hard, callin' out to her so that she stopped."

"Stopped what?" the scurvy one asked, though he knew well enough.

"Postin'. Yes, that's what she was doin'. Like she was ridin' a horse, him bein' the saddle . . . if you understand my meanin'." He winked.

"That's all?"

"Except she had another coughin' fit, like we hear her havin' . . ."

The Deep Six and its inquisitive crew rounded the Horn on a strong, following wind, with not a single barrel of whale oil in the hold. Her Captain tended to his wife, and she to him, above and below deck, as all the sailors noted. Yet her manner seemed more languid every day.

The ship reached the Fernandez Islands without incident. But the Captain was uneasy and restless. John Priest looked out of the sea-encrusted porthole and wondered about a future he could not control. This was a new situation to him, for he had always planned for attack or retreat. But the condition of Naliki was so serious that he felt shaken. Should she live—and he prayed that would be so—he would be leaving her in Maui. In that case, he would stay with her to set up a house and staff of servants. He planned to make Maui his home, but to keep *The Deep Six* in harbor, taking the ship on frequent forays for the whales of the Western seas. Using Lahaina as his main base, Priest would continue to deal with his present agents. If he could produce his oil there and keep Naliki on her own soil, John Priest could forge a new life for them. Should Fate decree Naliki's passing, Captain Priest would instantly turn his ship into a killer vessel, for he had the crew to do it, though they had been told no whales would be taken on the voyage. Priest was ready, in a practical sense, for any eventuality. But his emotions were not.

Naliki seemed to weaken with every league traveled. As the ship's bell tolled each quarter hour and Priest's men lolled about on the sunny deck, she lay in a deep sleep before him, her slight body bare in the heat of the cabin, her hair entangled like so much seaweed, a pattern of perspiration glistening about her oval face. Of late, her appetite had waned and she showed no desire to eat the tempting dishes the cook struggled to prepare. Her cough had increased and her body was constantly hot.

Kneeling in unaccustomed prayer, Priest spoke to whomever would listen. "This flower must live. The air is hot and clear, the way easy from here on. My God, if You are listening, though my sins may stand between me and You, save this child for better days. Make her well, I pray. I love her, Lord. Like the Centurion in the Bible, I will do what I am told. Guide me in my thinking, Oh Lord. Bless this child, I pray . . . make her well."

She had not moved. Her breathing was gentle and unsteady, for she seemed to be struggling inwardly for each painful breath. John Priest leaned down, placed his mouth next to her ear and whispered to her, "I am here with you. My strength is your strength. Your destiny is mine."

Slowly her eyes fluttered open. Her pupils widened as she struggled to focus on his kind face. John Priest pressed her hand and forced himself to smile. "Naliki?" he whispered. "Can you hear me?" Her smile told him she could. Her eyes closed for a moment as she tried to draw strength, then she reached out for him, her arm limp, her hand pleading. The Captain took her wet palm and held it, supporting her elbow. How weak she had become!

"John," she whispered hoarsely. "Why am I so weak? What is it? John . . . am I going to die?"

"No, Naliki," he replied. His voice was husky and he grasped her hand tightly, "You are not going to die. But you must try to eat. Please try—for me. You must eat to give you strength."

Again there was the sad smile and she closed her eyes. She had heard the catch in his voice, seen his unhappiness. He could not hide the fear of losing her. She wanted to please him—to eat, to regain her health and free him from this worry. Yet she seemed to have no strength.

With his free hand, Priest poured cool water from a pitcher and held the liquid to her parched lips, pressing the edge of the pewter cup to her mouth. She turned her head away. She could not bear the effort it took to swallow.

Then suddenly, she shot straight up. Her naked, perspiration-drenched body was pressed to his. The cup rattled to the deck. Her eyes opened wide in her sunken cheeks. She felt about blindly for her husband, clutching with her hand. John Priest placed his arms about her. He kissed her upon the lips as she struggled to speak. Her lips felt hot and dry. And then he just held her tightly, struggling to buoy her fading life with the strength of his arms. "Go to my island, John," she murmured. "Whether I go with you in body or not, I will . . . in spirit. I came from there and there I must return. Find my little boy. Care for him. Tell him of his mother . . ."

John Priest felt his heart clench. All his strength and wealth were useless. He was helpless at that moment when he was needed most.

"Naliki, I love you. You will live! I know it."

But the words meant nothing. All their meaning was in the arms that held her, as the man struggled to cling to her and save her.

"I love you, my *halokane*, my Kane." He listened, holding her, not bearing to look in her eyes. He heard the faint words, "My dear John," then, suddenly, her arms fell away from him. She collapsed on the bunk, hemorrhaging from the mouth. The trembling ended, her face assumed an expression of repose and finally she lay still. John Priest bowed his head. A deep and penetrating exhaustion seeped through his bones.

The Deep Six anchored, that morning, near an island off the west coast of South America. When John Priest came on deck, the breeze had died. Sails were furled and the men stood waiting. A Boston man approached the Captain.

Seeing the man approach, John Priest waited aft. He must contain himself, show no emotion. It would not be becoming in a Yankee master. He squared his shoulders and waited.

"Your orders, Cap'n?"

Priest hesitated, doubting his own ability to command. Yet the man awaited orders. He could not divest himself of this final responsibility.

"Take the body ashore," he directed. He could not return her to the sea from which he had rescued her. "Up sail to make the cove to the south. We'll drop lead all the way and call the soundings loud and clear. This island is on no chart of mine and has no name. We shall call it Naliki." The captain turned, addressing the men who stood aft in a silent circle.

His voice had gathered strength. "Up sail to land her, mate. My wife will have a proper burial, but mind you, we'll sail out with the noon tide, for we have much to do. This funeral voyage will be turned into a 'greasy' one. We'll be sailing home with casks full, or I'll know the reason why!"

The tall, tanned figure of John Priest led the procession, a ragtag group of men dressed in the most somber gear they could muster on short notice. Behind the captain walked the lean and dignified man the crew had come to call "The Reverend," a sailor who had once preached in Boston. In his hand was a large, worn black Bible. Behind him strode the mates, in sequence of rank, each with head bare. Among them was borne the casket which had been fashioned only that day by the ship's carpenter. The wood sides of Naliki's sun room made up the planks of the coffin and her body was shrouded in the canvas.

On top of a small, sandy rise, in a grove of trees protected from the wind by hillocks and stones, John Priest had ordered Naliki's grave to be dug.

As the procession neared the spot where sandy soil was piled in mounds around a steep-sided hole, Priest nodded to the mates, and they gently placed Naliki's coffin in the ground. A gull swooped low. In the trees that surrounded this gathering of men, a sudden wind stirred the leaves. Then the freshening wind died as quickly as it had come.

"The Reverend" stepped forward and read: "He that heareth my word, and believeth in Him that sent me, hath everlasting life and shall not come into condemnation; he that believeth, though he perish, may pass from death into life."

"She believed in love . . . ," John Priest spoke aloud, ". . . and knew not our God. Yet love is heaven and heaven is love, so she'll abide there without a question, Reverend. And I thank you for your reading."

"I come to that, Captain Priest," replied the man, deftly turning his page.

" 'He that loveth not, knoweth not God; for God is love.' "

He looked at the coffin, then down to his book.

" 'Be thou faithful unto death—and I will give thee a crown of life.' " Then, apparently inspired to boldness by his own duties as preacher, the sailor raised his right hand over the grave, "Naliki, let this be consecrated ground in your name," he intoned, "and this island be known hereafter as 'Naliki,' for we who knew you will ne'er forget you. Amen."

"Amen!" echoed the voices of the other men.

A spade was handed forward from the first mate to Captain Priest. The Captain leaned forward and the spade bit into the soft, sandy loam.

As the Captain carefully dropped the sail upon the coffin, "The Reverend" pronounced, " 'Unto the pure, all things are pure.' "

Priest handed the spade to the first mate and turned aside with a hand covering his face.

At noon, *The Deep Six* pulled up anchor and sailed from the island cove. Her Captain remained below.

Evening fell on a solemn ship. At nightfall, the Captain strode forward, dressed in his finest, head held high, his eyes taking in the men and ship in one sweep. Instinctively his men gathered about him, for they knew he would speak.

"We've come too far to waste this voyage. It's time we went about our business. This, friends, is *The Deep Six*. May I introduce her to you anew? She's a ship built to kill whales and to make money for her crew, officers and owners. Well, that is what we are about to do. You, Matthews, a Nantucketer, are you?

I hear you can cast an iron as well as any Vineyard Gay Header or Azorian. Is that true, now?"

"Aye!" shouted the lad. "That I can, if I but have the target!"

"And you, Perkins, chief mate? Have you seen a whale spout blood this trip?"

"Nay! That I haven't. But I await the chance!"

"And all you men from the Azores and Portugal, I've heard you boast of breaking your backs at the oars. Will you be as good as your boasts when we sight a school and you're tossed overboard to meet them?"

An enthusiastic shout of affirmation was the crew's reply.

"Well, from this day forward, that is our duty. Now hear this! By all that's mighty you'll earn your keep, take home an earned share from the sea. We'll make this a 'greasy voyage,' by God, or I'll know the reason why. Enough of standing around. The time has come. We'll scour the fathoms below us from the Archer Grounds to the Bering Sea, from Japan to Greenland if need be, but I'll not bring you home 'til we can't get another barrelful on her. What do you say to that?"

Without waiting for a reply, the Captain shouted the course to his chief. Then he turned on his heel and went below.

But in the privacy of his cabin, with the charts spread before him, John Priest first laid a course for Maui. He was intent on finding Naliki's child. It was unnecessary for the crew to know his intentions. Between *The Deep Six* and that island, his path would cross many a school of whales. His casks would be full this trip.

A shout came from the foretop.

"Blows!" John Priest raised his head and pushed

his charts away. The chase, at last. He lunged for the galley ladder and made the deck in two bounds. "Where away?" he yelled, looking aloft.

"Off the port beam! Lord, it's a whole school o' them! Thar! 'N' thar!" The man's arm pointed like a pennant.

That single hand, raised as a beacon day after day, was to point John Priest's vessel on the most successful voyage ever recorded in the history of American whaling. But for the Captain, that voyage out, there was only one search—for a single, young boy on the dot of an island lost somewhere in the vastness of the South Pacific.

CHAPTER 15

The Annual Picnic was held on South Beach that summer. It was a Sunday in July during a hot spell that had lasted for two weeks. The village fathers were in attendance, as were many youngsters who enjoyed the cold surf. It fell to young women like Perpetua to watch over the frolicking children as they jumped in and out of the water.

The wide sand offered room for games. No one was to be let out of sight, the minister told Perpetua, and the most lively ones were to be watched with special care. "I know what comes into little heads," said the minister. "This is your charge, Mistress West. Mind you, watch with care."

After two hours of exhausting observation in the hot sun, Perpetua decided to name a few assistants so that she could have a respite. Leaving her parasol and the large beach baskets behind her, she wandered slowly up toward Squibnocket and the cliffs. The low flight of white gulls, the intense heat and the touch of the warm sand on her bare feet soon made her long to lie down. Pulling her skirt high about her so that the sun could bake her legs, she threw an arm across her eyes and dozed off, luxuriating in summer's warmth while, inevitably, her dreamlike memories brought back languid days in the sun of Maui.

Suddenly a shadow passed across her eyes. She moved her arms and she had the strong impression of a man standing there, looking down at her. It seemed to Perpetua that the man's eyes were, at that moment, not on her face, but on the long, bare legs. Obviously he admired her, and she was certain she saw him smile.

Without a word, he came over and sat next to her. "Washed up from the sea?" His voice was deep and resonant. She sat up and quickly covered herself. "You have the most beautiful and shapely legs I have ever seen," he continued insolently. "Here, let me touch to see if you are real." His hand reached out toward her thigh.

Eyes flashing at the bold man with the bright blue eyes and dark brown hair, she pushed her skirts down farther and slapped him away.

"How dare you!" she began, then began to laugh. He seemed so astounded that he looked a little ridiculous, unlike the threatening male he had seemed at first.

"My name is Edward. What's yours?" he stammered. Obviously her laughter had not been expected.

"I am Perpetua West." Standing up to brush off the sand, she felt his left hand stroking her dress as though to help her.

She did nothing to stop him. Who was this Edward, and where had he come from? She liked everything about him, even his way of assuming she was his to be taken. His were not the ways of an islander. Maybe he would understand her, appreciate how much she disliked the confines of her life on the Vineyard.

Having gently helped brush away the loose

grains of sand from her skirt, the man stood silently, appreciatively looking her over.

"Now what?" she asked.

"Now, you and I . . ." he said, "well, since I have come upon a mermaid, a Lorelei, I will ask her to be mine." With that he pulled her to him, taking her the way a pirate might seize a woman he had captured.

Forgetting where she was—forgetting everything but the man who held her—Perpetua reacted spontaneously. While the man held her tightly and gently moved her hand around toward his, she recalled what Naliki had told her and she moved her hand down between his legs. The touch shocked him. He pulled away with a cry. "Who are you?" he demanded, his eyes wide and hungering, with a kind of madness in his expression.

"I am washed up from the sea, Edward. Your Lorelei led me here for you. Don't you want me?" Perpetua could not help but mock this suddenly prudish young man. He pulled away quickly, shaking his head.

Perpetua watched him go, running along the beach, his feet biting into the sand, his back stiff in the distance. She laughed, then stopped herself, sorry for her haughty forwardness. She had, after all, enjoyed the pleasure of his touch.

It was three days later before Perpetua summoned the courage to question her mother about the man.

"Edward Luce?" her mother asked. "That must be Leander Luce's son. His mother's dead. He went to school off-island, but now Edward works at the bank. His father is a director. He thinks the boy's a little wild and wants him settled down—married. But it's my opinion there's no real harm in the young man."

Clarissa looked thoughtfully at her daughter, then laughed. "Come, time to fix dinner."

Three days later, Edward and Perpetua met again. This time he politely asked Perpetua if she could attend an "island sail" to Chappaquiddick. "There will be ten small catboats. Would you come with me? The cook will take care of food and water. It would give me great pleasure."

Seeing the humbled look upon his face, she smiled and answered yes. She felt confident, almost exuberant with good spirits.

Other than Perpetua, none of the ten young people who left the harbor that day noted the dark sky to the north that foretold squalls. But Perpetua, mindful of the gathering weather, wore a bathing dress under her light skirt and blouse. The wind died soon after they pushed off from shore and the sails hardly fluttered as the tiny fleet drifted toward the "separate island," as it was known. There, the young people expected to picnic on the expanses of flat beach, surrounded by low hummocks of beach grass. They planned to gather driftwood, make a fire for baking the clams they gathered and share their food with one another.

When the fleet reached the outer harbor, Perpetua's premonition of a storm was confirmed. The wind hit Edward's ten-foot boat broadside, sending water over her clothing.

Edward thrust the tiller to port, bringing the small cat into the wind. With sails flapping, fending off the other boats that came too close, Perpetua disrobed and stood in her black swimming dress. Shouting directions, finally taking the tiller forcefully from a muddled Edward, she let the wind carry them to the nearest spit of land. Behind them, they saw the boats turning, scudding toward the mainland in hasty retreat from the passing squall.

A half hour later, the squall was gone. The clouds broke and the sun shone. Yet it appeared that none of the others would attempt to make the island. While Edward stayed behind to make the craft ship-shape, Perpetua wandered off alone, heading toward the sand dunes, wondering about the men she knew.

Joshua Fullerton was all horses and farm. He never spoke of anything else. And his mother dominated him. What a waste! Timothy Vincent hadn't come near her in recent months. Though he had interested her for a while, he now bored her to death. And Edward? Pretending to be so much a man of the world, he wilted when the prize was offered. Even now, he was fumbling helplessly and unintelligently with the simple things of a boat. Merciful father! A man who couldn't make a ship do what he wanted could hardly take her!

She walked on. Soon she came to a rise followed by a deep hollow in the hot sand. Heavenly! She was out of sight of the boat and an engrossed Edward. This haven was hers alone.

She disrobed completely. At last! She let her hands run over her skin, down her hips and thighs. What a sensuous feeling to be nude again in the hot sun!

It was like Maui.

She cast her head from side to side, letting her long hair unfold. Then she immersed herself in a beautiful dream . . . that a man worthy of all her hopes was making love to her exactly as Naliki had described.

It seemed that a long time passed before, far away, Perpetua heard the petulant voice of Edward. "Perpetua, where are you hiding? Oh, this *is* tiresome!

Do come out, there's a good girl . . ." Quickly, she
drew on her swimsuit and waited impatiently for Edward to appear. He came over the top of a big sand
dune, and looked down to see her lying there, her
head resting on her hands. She lay on her back, the
swimsuit covering her legs below her knees. How
beautiful she was! Edward started down, slipping and
sliding as he made his way toward her.

As Perpetua opened her eyes she saw that Edward stood there with his shadow falling across her
body, just as on the day he first saw her on South
Beach.

"You were asleep."

She sat up, frowning. "Was I? I don't remember."

All the way home, she was silent.

Had she been asleep? Was it all a dream—a fantasy? During that interval before Edward appeared,
while she lay nude on the beach, some change had
come over her body, as if there were some truth to
her dream of love.

Reaching her bedroom she found that her legs
were sore. When she shed her clothes, she saw there
was a bruise on her left thigh and she felt a stiffness
in her groin.

Whether it had been a dream or not, one thing
she knew: That moment of bliss in the warm hollow
of sand had given her intense pleasure, an emotion as
strong as any she had ever known.

The day after the sailing picnic with Edward
that ended so disappointingly, Perpetua went early to
the post office to inquire about Timothy Vincent, of
Chappaquiddick.

"Yes," old Jeremiah told her, "he stops by here on
Mondays and picks up his mail."

Perpetua handed the postmaster a letter. It was

addressed to "T. Vincent, Esq." "Please put this in his box."

"Well, if'n ye wait, he'll most likely be by. It's almost time."

Waiting outside, Perpetua took up a position near the General Store, where she could see everyone going in or out of the post office.

She didn't have long to wait. When he appeared, he was dressed in a fine blue suit. His head was high and he walked like a man in a hurry. When he came out, he was holding a package. As he started his fast walk toward her, Perpetua began to fidget. She looked down, avoiding his eyes, but he quickly spotted her.

"Well, Perpetua West, where have you been? I've missed seeing you."

Perpetua took Timothy's hand and smiled, almost afraid to look at him. He held it very tightly. His hand was strong, his muscles bulged when he grasped her fingers. Wincing, she released her fingers from his grasp.

When he spoke, Timothy's manner was strangely intense. "I had a dream about you last night. I thought I saw you during the day. It was about noon. Was that you lying in your black swimming suit in a dune out my way?"

"On Chappy? Why, yes, Timothy. Edward Luce and I were virtually shipwrecked! What a lark! I went off to sun-bathe while he made repairs."

"I see. Well, last night I dreamed about you."

"From time to time, I have dreamed of you, too," she replied. She felt somehow humiliated, utterly disconcerted by her frankness. But he didn't seem to notice her lack of composure.

"Now that we have met, will you join me?" he asked. "I'm about to have a late breakfast with my aunt. She's my only relative alive. Perhaps you remember her?"

Perpetua didn't reply. He seemed so sure of himself—and of her.

Perpetua found herself carried along almost blindly by this masterful young man as she started out to spend the morning with "Mrs. Charity," as his aging aunt was called. Having married a Portuguese with the name of de Silvia, she kept her given name for identification "with her kind."

Perpetua was dismayed to meet a hard-bitten, opinionated crone, who spoke out against everything Perpetua liked. "Mrs. Charity" didn't like young people going on beach picnics. She condemned Perpetua's friend, "that Polynesian creature," Naliki, as being "carnal-looking," declaring that the girl was given to "turning men's heads." Mrs. Charity thought Priest a fool for bringing her "on island." As she offered Perpetua a limp hand in farewell, the old woman looked the young one in the eye and said, "You are a bold one, child; mind your behavior around my nephew. He is strongly attracted to the wildness in women, which we must tame, and which I see ready to take possession of you." With that, Mrs. Charity excused herself and returned to her airless house, slamming the door behind her.

Perpetua and Timothy began seeing each another regularly, nonetheless.

They became inseparable, going together to every possible social occasion, and arranging to meet by themselves when there was no social call. Perpetua became accustomed to the feel of his arm about her waist when they were alone. She experienced the crushing kisses he pressed upon her lips when they parted.

One night, after he had taken the boat from his

great home on Chappaquiddick, Timothy Vincent was closely questioned by "Mrs. Charity."

"How old are you now, young fellow?"

"I'm twenty-three."

"And you've already made your fortune?"

"Yes, Aunt, from overseas trade. You know that well."

"How much have ye made?"

"Now, my dear aunt, you must be satisfied with knowing I am well settled."

"Well then, why don't you get married?"

"I am about to do so."

Mrs. Charity paused, pursed her lips and adjusted her wig. Then, looking down her nose at him, she roared, "Not to that Perpetua, never! That girl flaunts her body. She behaves like a heathen! I hope and pray you will never, in my presence, suggest marrying such a one, nor ask for my blessing."

Timothy Vincent stood up so suddenly his aunt started back in alarm. Clearing his throat, the young man began, "She's been courted by richer men than I. Two, in fact, are at her feet now. She seems good enough for the son of old Mr. Luce, director of our bank, and good enough for that rich farmer, Fullerton. Well, Aunt, she's not only good enough for me, but I mean to have her."

"Timothy Vincent, how dare you speak to me like that?"

Walking stiffly, bearing her weight with a cane, Charity made her way to the horsehair sofa. There she sat down, spread her skirts about her and stared up at her nephew.

With a smile of indulgence, Timothy reminded her, "When you inherited their farm in Chilmark, you never expected that one day I'd be supporting you. Dear Mrs. de Silvia, you not only went off to Boston with the money, but you managed to squander it with your departed husband. That money took you on a trip to Seattle. I remember it well. Not that I care."

"Land's sake, Timothy, you do have it wrong! Anthony de Silvia was a fine fisherman. He always wanted to move to the Far West. And when we had our chance, we fully expected to set up out there. Who knew that you'd accumulate your own fortune?"

"That fortune, I'm glad to say, gives me the right to see whomever I wish."

"I would have thought that after building that strange-looking house on Chappy, you'd settle down with a nice island girl, not a heathen like Perpetua West!"

"You are incorrigible, Aunty." Timothy approached her, stopped for a moment as if gathering strength, and did what he knew always pleased her. He planted a wet kiss on the leathery face, and, teasingly, untied the bow in her grey hair.

"Oh, stop it!" she exclaimed. "You always know how to get to me!" She pretended shock, but her quick smile told him she had given in, just a little.

"You are just like Anthony!" she went on hurriedly. "Whenever we disagreed about the smallest thing, he kissed me." With that she looked for a moment out to the little rose garden where Timothy knew she had sat with her husband during those days she so fondly remembered. She retied her bow.

When Timothy left his aunt, he headed at once for the landing. Perpetua had promised to spend the entire Sunday on "Chappy" with him. It would be the first time she had seen his grand house.

Perpetua's hand was clasped tightly in Timothy's as they came across the clearing.

"Now," he said, his breath coming fast, "dead

ahead, a little to the right, down that road, you'll see
the roof of the house."

They had taken his cutter to cross the small deep
channel between Edgartown and Chappy. As the tide
had been running at seven knots, their little sailboat
had been carried far off the point on which Timothy
had hoped to land. That had meant a long walk down
the narrow, sand road.

Very few farmers then used the fertile soil on
"the separate island," for not only was there much
more available near the roads and docks on the main
island, but crossing the channel was a time waster,
and one couldn't always count on the weather. Yet,
for some unexplained reason, Timothy had built out
there.

Perpetua saw the roof, or what he called the roof.
It looked so much like the roofs she had seen on
Maui! The house was covered by a thick thatching,
nearly six feet deep, mounted at a pitch which would
allow rain or snow to fall off easily. And beneath it, as
they came closer, she saw that it was indeed a "grand
house." The building was one story high, with a series
of dormer windows peeking out from beneath the
roof's great overhang, providing shade for those inside. A long, winding roadway ended at the doorway.
From the wide wooden doors of the side entry, a
small trail led to a number of outer buildings, each a
smaller edition of the great house. In them, Perpetua
imagined, Timothy kept his team of horses, carriages
and farm equipment. To the right, behind the house,
the field held a stand of corn covering at least twenty
acres.

The wonderful house had huge windows. Their
size was unusual in a coastal home. In that windy climate, on an island threatened often by nor'easters and
sou'westers, windows were kept small. Timothy's

great farmhouse was an exception, but still he had provided it with enormous, sturdy shutters which could be closed in case of a strong blow.

Perpetua had brought along a few possessions in a carpetbag—a change of clothes, the ugly swimming dress which dangled to her knees, and a small bottle of jasmine scent.

Timothy put the bag down just inside the door; then he proudly showed her around the house, taking obvious pride in every detail. Low beams, heavy timber struts and a huge fireplace were the main features of the parlor. Beyond were three large bedrooms, each furnished with rough-hewn beds and bureaus. The kitchen obviously belonged to a man. Perpetua was amused to see that pots and pans were in a muddle, cans filled with flour and coffee standing where Timothy had last used them.

Returning to the wide porch, overlooking a still cove to the southward, Timothy asked Perpetua to be seated.

"Right down there," he pointed, "is where I saw you on the beach. Why don't we go for a swim, then come back and take a ride? I have two saddle horses. Do you ride?"

"Yes, Timothy, I love to ride. You've heard me tell about riding with Joshua Fullerton."

Timothy came to her, helped her to her feet and stood next to her. "Do I have anything to worry about with that big farmer?" he asked quite calmly. Standing so near him, a man so big and sure of himself, asking such an innocent question, Perpetua couldn't help but tease him. "You should always worry—when it comes to me!" With that, she retrieved her bag and dashed to one of the bedrooms. Then she turned, "Is this room mine?"

"Forever, if you wish."

She went in and closed the door. When she was alone, she looked around, wondering if Timothy had chosen all the furnishings himself. The room had a marvelous atmosphere, touched by a hand that was quite original and fresh.

But there was nothing—not even the plump blue comforters on the bed or the Java batik curtains—which couldn't have been his idea, for she knew his good taste. Besides, she reasoned, much of this must have come from overseas. Then, too, old "Mrs. Charity" might have helped. How she disliked that woman! Even though she knew Timothy would not await Mrs. Charity's advice, Perpetua found it discomforting to know that the old hag didn't like her. How could she win over the old lady?

Dressed in the despised swimming costume which successfully hid everything female about her, and with a black mob cap over her blonde hair, Perpetua walked out of her bedroom.

There Timothy stood. She couldn't believe her eyes. He was nude.

"Take that wretched rig off, Perpetua! We have plenty of privacy here. There is no one around for five miles each way and with this wind, no one will sail out here."

She laughed, beginning to strip off the annoying swimsuit.

"Oh, it's much better without this horrible suit!" she exclaimed, tossing the black fabric aside.

Only when she was completely naked did she realize she had never been nude in front of a man before. She had no idea what to do next, so she simply stood and stared at him.

Miraculously, he looked exactly as she had imagined he would. He had the tapering waistline, the huge chest, the expanse of hair. And the appearance

of his sex, so fragile and innocent-looking, and yet
somehow frightening, made her look away.

Timothy laughed, "I have lured you out here, my
fair lady, knowing that sooner or later we would be
together this way!"

"I am glad!" she exclaimed with hushed excitement. "Dear Timothy—do you mean you want me?"
She stepped toward him, chilled in her nakedness, but
needing him, overjoyed by their shared isolation.

Timothy looked from her pert mouth to her half-
closed eyelids. He admired the pointing breasts, the
upturned nipples, the fullness of her figure. From the
flat stomach to the tapering, delightful curve of her
hips, she seemed made to accept him, and her long
legs were wonderfully strong. The small V of blonde
hair was so virginal, so tempting. Though a spirited,
teasing girl, Timothy knew at once she was a virgin.
Everything about her, her marvelous awkwardness,
screamed it. Yet, he knew, too, that she was a true
product of the eighteen months she had spent on
Maui. He knew she had been aboard ship when men
had indulged in orgies with native girls. No high-spir-
ited girl could avoid being aroused once she had
witnessed that!

"Come on, let's run."

His change of tune was so sudden, the shift of
tone so abrupt that she felt discarded. If he wanted
her, he wasn't showing it! She ran after him crossly.

Out in the hot sun, out there in the sand, so
much like Maui for an instant, she recalled those days
on the island, the beautiful girls and handsome, virile
young men whom she had known and run with. But
there she had no real thoughts of submission, just a
sense of wonder and freedom.

Oh, she had seen naked men before. First her father, then the men on board ship. And she had gone

on prohibited trips with some of her Polynesian girl friends. Though forbidden to swim to the whaling ships, they had nonetheless shed their clothes and gone into the surf with young men.

But never had Perpetua agreed to go inland to take part in the rituals and orgies of food, dance and sex which her friends of Maui had described to her. Now, fully aware and sexually alive, Perpetua looked at Timothy in a way she had never regarded another man before.

Attractive, virile, appealing to her in his love of the outdoors, testing life with gusto and lust, Timothy was the man she knew she must join for life. Now, standing next to her as though completely dressed, he was at ease and in no way ashamed or embarrassed about his body.

Like the other half of a pair on a barren island, Perpetua felt she was the tempting Eve while he played the strong Adam who would feed her, make her comfortable, find a way to build a nest for them and, finally, enclose her tenderly in his arms. A great warmth came over her. She touched his arm unconsciously. He placed his arm about her waist and remained looking straight ahead.

"Lord have mercy on me!" he murmured. She knew what he meant, for the attraction between them was almost unbearable.

"Before we run away forever, wherever that is to take us," she said, "tell me, am I the first?"

He looked down at her, surprised. "Perpetua, you are my first guest, the first woman to be with me here except for Mrs. Charity and the women who occasionally come to clean my house. Now, see that clump of bushes in the sand over there?"

He pointed to a spot two hundred yards away. She nodded.

"I'll beat you to it."

He made a mark in the sand. They bent down, raised their haunches and toed the mark. She laughed. He looked deadly serious. He counted to ten and they were off.

He was ahead of her immediately. She saw the muscles of his buttocks, their taut action, then their release as his feet flew. His thighs were like those of a panther and the movement of his arms was that of a fighter, hammering his way toward a goal of victory.

He reached the goal and turned, looking at her.

She was suddenly conscious of her bouncing breasts, aware of the clear view he had of her. And she was proud. Running up to him, she flung herself at him, crying, "You are fantastic! I could run faster than anyone on Maui, but you beat me by twenty yards."

He pulled her to him, whispering, "No wonder you can run. Look at those long legs."

He was warm against her and she never wanted him to let her go. She felt her breasts crush against the hardness of his chest, the tingling sensation of his curling hair upon her sensitive nipples.

Without more words they slowly walked back to his house. Perpetua felt herself dissolving with desire.

It was more than a dream. She was aware with all her senses. When Timothy lightly picked her up and carried her to the bed, she felt certain there could not be another man as strong as he. He had flat, hard muscles and his skin was warm and smooth. His arms lifted her, pressed against her back and breasts. He looked down at her and his breath warmed her face; his eyes, half-closed, were clouded and warm as though they peered through a dream of his own devising. She felt herself being lowered to the bed. She touched his face with her fingertips, shaping his chin, feeling the slight stubble, the bones which structured his strong, masculine jaw. He smiled. She closed her eyes.

She felt his hands moving over her, his exclamation when he reached the fullness of her breasts. She heard her own whimper of delight, felt the beginning of lust.

He was kissing her nipples, slowly circling them with his hot tongue. She opened her eyes and saw his black hair spread about her chest.

His head came nearer and she felt him lie next to her, take command of the soft body and press her to him. His hand explored, probing and caressing. Never had she felt such desire! His leg moved strong between her thighs. His knee came up slowly, crushing against her with a gentle impulse. Then, slowly, he moved upon her until she felt a slight convulsion, a need for more. Wrapping her long legs about his, she held him, their bodies pressed closely. She hoped he would never leave.

He caressed each breast lightly. What should she do? Everything that was happening defied her control. She could only wait and feel. This was beyond anything she had conceived, beyond all sensations Naliki had described to her. Now his lips were upon her body, slowly tracing a line downward, his tongue moistening the luxurious, hungering skin, his head moving from side to side as he whispered warm breaths across her body.

This was what she had wanted, what she had waited for so long. She had observed others and wondered what it was like. Now, she was sharing it with the man she loved, whose hands fondled her so excitingly. A great languor came over her. She felt her body turning moist, receptive. Her legs parted against her will. The deep breaths that shuddered through her were like a warm sea whose waves carried her upward to meet him.

He was on top of her! His chest was pressed against her. For a moment she couldn't breathe. Then, slowly, remembering the soft words of Naliki, she relaxed, loosening the muscles of her back and legs, feeling him, his hard body pressing against her. It seemed impossible that they could continue. She pulled away, hoping he would understand.

"It's all right, Perpetua. Don't be afraid."

"Please, Timothy . . . remember."

"Yes, I remember. You are a virgin."

He kissed her and moved more forcefully between her legs. Timothy was going to take her and she wanted to be taken. She felt the hard muscles of his shoulders, the ribbed muscles of his back, and the tight, bulging muscles of his buttocks. She trailed her fingertips down his backbone, wanting to know all of him. Then she felt his movement, like a ritual of love. He was entering. An impossible huge thing pressed against her, a living part of him that wanted to be inside of her. She felt the sudden urgency that possessed the big man on top of her. She would take him all! She would let him be there like a child in a womb. She would comfort him, care for him, once he was inside her. She was not to feel compassion, she knew, but to feel the urgency that he felt and respond with her own urgent desire. He was furiously, wildly consuming her! His lips flew over her body, his hands grasped her soft buttocks and Timothy hugged her to him. Then he was there.

She had opened up. The convulsions began. A tingling which had begun between her legs spread and grew, consuming her inwardly. His hips moved down. She arched her back and spread her legs wide.

She was back on Maui, observing the Polynesians. She was a native now! She was aware of every sense, every pulse of her own response. She responded passionately to his need.

She must give. She must accept. She heard herself cry out. There was a sharp pain followed by a slow, dull ache that spread across her open body. Then a warm, slowly widening series of pulsations began. She was in the center of a whirling ecstasy, with her unbounded lust at the center of her desire. Her hips began to undulate, then jerk and writhe, begging more for her body. Timothy moved within her. Timothy, her man! Now, she knew! Now, she felt it!

Thrusting slowly, he moved in unison with her, each savoring the other totally. She felt herself go, become abandoned, wild. The drums of Maui beat in her head. She screamed and grasped Timothy as hard as she could, creating one person, bringing him so far within her that she felt she had swallowed him. The sensations were unbelievably delicious. The response to him, buried between her thighs, sent her blood rushing, whirled her mind into a kind of dream state. Was this actually happening to her? To her body? He had found things in her she had never dreamed of.

Always, she had thought that being with a man would be sudden and quick—that, somehow, though there was pleasure in it, the act of sex held a kind of unknown, unlabeled pleasure. But never before had she felt so utterly possessed, so needed, so desired and so happy. Then, she remembered what she had been told by Naliki. Using muscles that came alive with her dawning consciousness, she began the "inner caress." She felt Timothy growing, enlarging, almost hurting her. But it didn't stop her from responding with those quivering, newly found muscles.

Heat, blood, heart, hands, legs and mouths—all were consumed in a single, fixed awareness. Perpetua was totally possessed by this huge, virile man. Slowly, as he continued his rhythm and she hers, she began to feel a swirling tingle begin in her back and hips, which grew until it had taken over her lower body. Violently, almost like an animal, she began to respond thrust for thrust, eager, lusting and finally screaming as she felt herself near death, the convulsions continuing until she couldn't bear them, until they left her spent.

As though her movements had been a signal, Timothy penetrated her body even more deeply, holding her so tightly she couldn't breathe. She felt him grow and thicken inside her and she reached down to hold him to her. And then, in a moment of stillness that was broken by his release, he flooded into her.

He sighed as she held him tightly. His body was suddenly heavy, but she wanted that. She hoped he would never leave her. She wanted to savor every feeling, to feel him there forever. She would be afraid and alone if he left! What would she do without him?

"Don't ever leave me," she whispered.

He didn't speak. He took a firmer hold on her hips, each big hand spread wide.

Long minutes passed before he rolled away. But Perpetua did not know, nor did she feel Timothy withdraw from her body. She slept. He walked quietly to the dresser, drew out a linen sheet and placed it carefully over her so as not to awaken her. How childlike and safe she looked, tucked in that way, a sleeping kitten.

When she awoke, she smelled coffee. Where was she? She stretched, felt her body. She smiled with the consciousness of complete pleasure. She was in heaven. She would never let Timothy go. She was the luckiest woman in the world. She loved Timothy—totally and forever!

Their sexual bond, as both Timothy and Perpetua understood, contained an unwritten pledge of marriage. Now that private pledge had to be accepted by others.

Perpetua hadn't wanted to leave Timothy that day. But she knew she must. But from that moment on, she lived for their wedding day, when she could live on his island and enjoy the uninhibited life they had chosen.

"No relatives out here!" Timothy had proclaimed. "No friends, just us! That's the way we must begin. Perhaps, in time, I'll be willing to share you." He winked. "But I doubt it!"

"Timothy, I could be perfectly happy with you forever. Every day, every night, three times on Sunday—we'll just enjoy each other, my love."

"Insatiable. And I love it." He had kissed her and helped her into the cutter. "Who do I ask for your hand?"

She smiled. "I suspect Mother will be glad to give her consent." Holding the mainsheet, Perpetua pulled in the line until the sail was taut, then eased it to full. The cutter got underway, slicing through the waves. Way off there was reality. Timothy steered for Edgartown.

"Shouldn't I be asking Everett?"

Perpetua had to laugh at Timothy's seriousness.

"Well, both of them, of course! But they won't argue. You're a fine man, Timothy. And you made your fortune yourself. They will admire that."

"I expect a huge dowry," he said teasingly.

"That explains it! That's why you lured me to your house and bed. You're after my money!"

"No." He grinned broadly. "I did it to disappoint Mrs. Charity. She thinks you're a wild, passionate pagan. That's what she said. And after those things you did to me, I must admit she's right."

"Be still. That comes with having a good teacher."

"I knew you had to be taught. Who was he?" Timothy glowered.

"You insult me. It was 'she,' Naliki, the wife of John Priest. I have told you about her, how I was her companion. We talked of everything—we were such friends. She had been taught on Maui."

"I traveled there myself."

"I thought so. You waited for those wild girls on your ship."

"No. But I became very much in love with the islands. I could not help watching those people and I think perhaps I absorbed their customs. When I built my house, I surely had theirs in mind."

"I knew it. Timothy, we have so much in common. We will make a fine couple."

"It is what is so different about us that attracts me to you, my passionate mate! Come here!"

She made fast the sheet, and sat near him on the thwart. For the rest of the trip, he held her closely, his hand brushing against her breast.

News of Perpetua's interest in Timothy had already spread about the island, reaching both Joshua Fullerton and Edward Luce. Fullerton, now well established as an up-island farmer, was forced to listen to his mother rail at him that he was "the luckiest man on the island not being hooked by *that* one!"

And he might almost have believed her—until the day he and Perpetua met by accident in Holmes Hole.

Clarissa was buying dresses and it was she who first caught sight of Fullerton. The man was standing at the feed counter. "Hello, there you are!" Clarissa called. "Perpetua, look who's here!" Then Clarissa moved away to leave her daughter alone with the young man who had courted her so formally.

"It's been a long time, Perpetua. I've missed you. But I think I know why." Joshua had put on weight and he looked more mature. There was a certain sadness about his eyes. Perpetua took his hand.

"Then, if you understand, please remember that I will always be grateful to you for the friendship you offered when I needed it." Perpetua smiled up at him. "Give my best to your mother," she said. Then she was gone.

Edward fared less well, if only because his own family chided him for his failure. In his own mind he was forced to recognize that he had never been a serious suitor as far as Perpetua was concerned. Yet his father bore down relentlessly, with constant complaints that Edward "had missed the one chance in life. That 'spirited' girl would have brought some *gumption* into the line," declared the elder Luce with severity.

Still smitten, Edward arranged to see Perpetua for what was to be the last time that summer.

Seated on the broad veranda of the Norton house overlooking the harbor and the rose garden, he took her unresponsive hand, looked at her with great longing and intoned, "Dear and wonderful girl, you have always been meant for me. Ever since my shadow fell across you and you awoke, I thought that Edward Luce might awaken your feelings of affection. I don't know what your heart told you at that moment, but I do know what happened to me. I fell in love. I know now that I should have asserted myself at once. And I regret . . ." He broke off, unable to couch his intentions in the formal tone he had adopted.

Perpetua felt sad. How could she comfort him without insulting him?

"I think it was my upbringing, so different from yours, that made it impossible, Edward," she replied. "I know that your family home is secure and that you can always work for your father. But for me, other things are important. I have had to find my own way, always. It is true that, at the time when I most needed it, you couldn't help me. But that is no reflection on your strength of character. I know you fell in love with me, Edward, but I couldn't fall in love with you. Not then, maybe never."

And so he left her, feeling that perhaps it hadn't been totally his fault, that she might be right. Who could handle a girl with such a free soul?

His life would be calmer and more controlled without being buffeted by the constant changes of such a woman. He could go back to his father and tend to his bank chores without seeing her and hearing her voice in his mind. The dull figures in his accounts would become interesting again and the pride in his accuracy would be gratifying again. What relief! As he waved good-bye, Edward cried out, "Ask me to your wedding, Perpetua. Count me as one of your friends, always!"

CHAPTER 16

Everett Norton had prospered. Having joined Clarissa's funds with his own, he had invested their savings in land within the boundaries of Edgartown, where property values increased constantly. Admired by the island people, who looked upon his financial expertise with approval, Everett was often asked to make profitable investments on behalf of others. His marriage to the widow of the respected Captain had brought him honors in the town, and he now was a member of the Council and an appraiser of land.

Having chosen a fine, four-story, white house on North Water Street as a new home, and having carefully placed Perpetua upon the marriage block, Everett and Clarissa were not surprised when the young woman announced her intention to marry the one-time neighbor boy from up-island. And the older heads readily approved the match. Timothy Vincent was respected for his single-handed ability to trade. Judging from the speed with which he had built his own, fine house on Chappaquiddick and his interest in town business, he was clearly a young man who could handle his own affairs.

One thing annoyed Clarissa: Mrs. Charity and her gossip about Perpetua. It didn't take long in that

community for the tale to be told and the teller of the
tale to be identified. Soon after the family arrived on
the island, Clarissa had heard Mrs. Charity's description of Perpetua:

"She's a wild one. Lived on an island with natives. One of those Sandwich Islands. Got strange
ideas. I don't like her. Better watch out." Mrs. Charity's biting words echoed through the town.

And finally, when it became clear that Perpetua
intended to marry her nephew, Mrs. Charity declared, "She has my Timothy's head now. Put a real
spell on him. Don't like it a bit. But, I'll stop that
hussy."

Unable to meet this kind of shameful talk head
on, Clarissa largely depended upon her own good
name and that of Everett to force the rumors to die
out.

But when Perpetua announced her love for Timothy and made Clarissa understand that he would soon
be asking for her hand, the mother decided to squelch
the gossip herself.

It all began when Clarissa met Mrs. Charity
briefly at a church tea and suggested they talk.

"What about?" was the sharp reply.

"About my Perpetua and Timothy Vincent."

"Well, you better forget it. I will have nothing to
say." Mrs. Charity hobbled off, clearing the way with
her cane. The other parishioners, those who had overheard her, looked at Clarissa and smiled. They understood the eccentricities of the old woman.

Undefeated, Clarissa chose a Saturday afternoon.
It was by intention, the kind of day which kept most
people at home, for the weather was hot beyond be-
lief. Clarissa knocked on Mrs. Charity's door at high
noon.

Taking her time, tapping her way to the door,

Mrs. Charity seemed to have been expecting her. "Come in, Mrs. Norton. Come in."

Behind her stood Timothy Vincent.

"The stove was backed up. Something wrong with the draft. He came and fixed it. Meet my nephew." She aimed at him with the point of her cane.

"We've met many times," replied Clarissa, smiling. "How do you do again Timothy?"

Clarissa understood perfectly, from Perpetua's ill-concealed excitement when she spoke of Timothy, and from the intimacy of the two when they were together, that their relationship had already been consummated. Yet she would not permit a loose-tongued harridan to scorch such tenderness with her harsh and biting words. Timothy seemed to sense immediately that Clarissa's was a mission of understanding, not merely a formal call.

Timothy took Clarissa's hand. "I'm glad you're here," he welcomed her. "My aunt and I have just been talking about Perpetua."

"Yes," cut in Mrs. Charity, hardly pausing to show Clarissa in. "This young man wants to marry her!"

"Aunt Charity!" barked Timothy, his eyes flashing. The reproof hung in the air. Boldly, Timothy turned to Clarissa. "She is right. Mrs. Norton, it would make me the happiest man in the world. May I have your . . ."

"Of course," replied Clarissa. "Don't go on. This is hardly a surprise in our household. You've been mooning about, eyeing one another long enough. Both Everett and I feel it's high time we blessed you both!"

Though her words were directed to Timothy, the message was for Mrs. Charity. Clarissa stood with her hands in front of her, looking down at the bent figure

of the little old lady whose eyes were now unexpectedly filling with tears. Without a second thought,
Clarissa stepped forward and took Mrs. Charity's
hand. "Don't cry, my dear Mrs. Charity. We will all
be one family now, don't you see? Nothing will be
taken from you. We all love these young people and
that will bring us closer together. Why don't you
come back with me and speak with my husband, Everett? We have plans to make for this occasion."

"One family, eh?" Mrs. Charity's tremulous voice
wavered on a note of hope. "Closer together, you say?
You, me and Timothy here?" She took Timothy's
hand, letting go of Clarissa's. Then Timothy folded
her gently in his arms and hugged her. As he stepped
away finally, Clarissa saw understanding in the man's
dark eyes.

That night, after two hours of discussing clothes,
cakes and canapes, Clarissa and Perpetua finally were
left alone to talk seriously. Everett departed
discreetly to tend to some land sale matters with Mr.
Luce at the bank.

"All right, young lady, tell me." It was Clarissa
giving Perpetua her chance.

"Oh, Mother," came the surprising response,
"wouldn't it be just wonderful if Timothy and I had a
love child."

She should have known. Perpetua certainly had
more of her father's impulsive nature than the cau-
tiousness that was Clarissa's. Yet, the older woman
had to admit she had succumbed to her instincts of
love in much the same way as Perpetua. How could
Clarissa blame the full-blooded free spirit who
danced about the room like a wanton? How grown-
up, how mature Perpetua looked, even as she spread

her arms and swept ecstatically about the sitting room, exclaiming her love for Timothy!

"I knew," she spoke out, trying to catch her daughter in midflight. The dance stopped abruptly. Perpetua turned wide-eyed.

"You did? How did you know?" demanded the girl. Then she ran to her mother and buried her head in her lap.

"Oh, Mother, I forgive you. I forgive you everything I ever held against you. I know now, you see. I understand!"

Clarissa smoothed her hair, pressed her to her bosom. "Forgive me—whatever for?"

Perpetua raised her head, looking deeply into Clarissa's eyes. "Yes, forgive you." Perpetua straightened her skirt and threw back her hair.

"On *The Horatio*, I saw you and Everett. I knew what you were doing to the Captain. You pretended to care for Father so, yet . . . Well, then when Father went away, I couldn't stand it. First, I had heard things about him on the voyage. From the men—they said he had made love to girls on every trip; that he, like they, had fathered children on the islands. When I saw some of those girls on the ship, what they did and what the men did, I was aware of exactly what Father must have done. I hated him then. And there I was, hating you both, not knowing why you and he could do such things to each other. And to me!" Perpetua began to weep. Then, quickly, she dried her eyes with the back of her hand.

"Now I know." She smiled at her mother.

"Are you sure you do?" By Clarissa's expression, Perpetua knew she had stirred memories in her mother, thoughts and words difficult to face.

"Yes." Perpetua knelt before her mother. She reached for her cupped hands. "Mother. It must have been difficult for you, and for my father, too, with his great demands. I had no right . . . If you will forgive me for my . . . for my immaturity. Please, Mother, can you?"

"Of course, my daughter." As Clarissa and Perpetua kissed, the mother's happiness was almost unbounded. It was as though, somehow, the Captain had spoken through his daughter.

Two hours later, she sat alone. Perpetua had gone to her room. The next day, Clarissa knew, would be a busy one. After returning from the bank, Everett had kissed her and said a few words before retiring to his study. Clarissa thought of Jared.

It seemed an eternity since she had last thought of him. Life had been so good, she thought, that the difficult times had become clouded. She recalled the night Jared had come home and confessed.

She could still hear his voice: "Clarissa, please find a way to forgive me. I had meant to keep my sin to myself, to endure my secret alone, if necessary, unto death. But now, after tonight, I cannot face myself. I have sinned again." Then he had told her all about a young woman, "no older than Perpetua in years," whom he had met and bought. "Her father traded her to me for gifts, and like a starved seaman, the scum from my own ships, I bought her for one night. I could not help myself. The minute the music began, the minute I saw her move, I was lost. Lost! And I must also tell you that I wanted her again. All the way back to Chilmark, even that first night, with you, I thought of her."

Clarissa had put her hand to his mouth. "Don't." Her voice had been low and hoarse with tears. But he had gone on, driven to speak, to purify himself, no matter what burden it might put on her.

"Though I truly loved you, and do now, I was so taken by her beauty and her way with me, that I had to go back. And I did! You should have stayed on the Vineyard, as I tried to convince you. But you insisted on coming. I hoped your presence would restrain my lust, but it didn't. I found her tonight. She rejected me. And, seeing me filled with lust for her, unable to satisfy myself with her, she simply handed me over to her sister, as in a brothel! Clarissa, I am a man who no longer knows himself. I have simply ceased to be the man I thought I was."

Clarissa had comforted her husband, tried to soothe him, to make him realize that she understood. And behind her understanding, a voice had whispered, "Clarissa, you are as bad as he. Everyone is the same. We are no different. Do you not feel a great physical attraction for Everett? Suppose you and Everett had the opportunity to sin? Would you be able to resist? How can you blame this man who has bared his soul to you amidst all his agony of doubt?"

Sitting there in Everett Norton's warm house, remembering so clearly, Clarissa thought to herself, "There is something lacking in you, Clarissa. If you had given Jared what that young girl gave him; if life the way we live it on this island of whaling men had provided them a better way to earn their money, and they had been home, no temptation like this would have had a chance. No! The men who stayed home would never have met the unbridled and free girls of Maui! I saw them! I saw what they did to men." And finally she contradicted her own thoughts again: "You are wrong, Clarissa. Men, long at sea, want only women—any women." And she recalled how Jared had taken her on his return from the voyage.

She stared absently out of the window. A ship was slowly entering the harbor. The red portlight

gleamed as the ship made her way past Chappaquiddick. This was her island, Clarissa felt. It was her fate
to have been born there, to have met and loved on
this island. Here, Jared had been given to her, with
all the strength of his generous love for her, and the
whaling ships had taken him away. He was dead, and
yet she felt his living strength. Now, she thought, it
was time to put him out of her thoughts.

Clarissa listened, hearing soft music. Then she
smiled. It was only Perpetua singing to herself, a song
the girl had learned on Maui.

When Perpetua had taken off her clothes that
night, she laid them carefully alongside those she
would take on her honeymoon. Gazing into the mirror, she looked at herself inquiringly, anxious to see
what he admired in her, yearning to know why he
wanted those breasts, why he would kiss her neck and
welcome her legs about him. How could she have
captured such a man! Her skin was warm to the
touch. Every fiber of her burned. Now she turned her
sleek body, glorying in the sight. Yes, she was all his.
In her was a love she could never lose, never give to
any other man. She would be Timothy's forever.

She heard her mother coming up the steps and
Perpetua felt a great compassion for Clarissa. Life
had given her mother two men. Was that possible for
Perpetua? If something happened to Timothy, could
she ever feel the same way about another man? She
tried to imagine herself letting another man have her
as had Timothy. Impossible! She put the thought out
of her mind.

CHAPTER 17

Late that night, there was a loud knock at the front door, followed by the noise of men shouting. Clarissa couldn't make out what they were saying until she heard a man yell, "Norton, come down! We are all gathering at the town wharf. There's news!"

Everett grunted and rolled over. An instant later, he was up and leaning out the window. A few words were exchanged and then he called out, "I'll be there!"

Everett and Clarissa dressed quickly and came downstairs. Surrounding the front porch was a group of excited men, all close friends of Everett's. "It's *The Deep Six*! She's back with her hold, her decks and fo'castle filled with barrels. She's the 'greasiest ship' ever made this port!"

Clarissa remembered the red light she had seen earlier that evening. It had been Captain John Priest returning, hull down with oil!

"Come along! Let us welcome her!" Everett cried as he took Clarissa's arm.

From her window, Perpetua called out, "What is it?"

"*The Deep Six* is home, with a full hold!" someone yelled. Perpetua's hands trembled as she hur-

riedly dressed. She couldn't wait to see Naliki! What
a stroke of fortune, to have her arrive now—just before the wedding! Perpetua had so much to tell her!
Naliki was the one person in the world to whom Perpetua could confide everything—everything!

Oh, the hours they would spend together. Without even bothering to completely fasten her frock,
Perpetua rushed from the house and ran at full tilt
down toward the wharf.

The Deep Six had made fast to the outward
pilings of the long wharf. Her hull was so low that
her decks were almost awash. Cries of "How many
barrels, John?", "How did ye ever make it back?" and
"Come out of your cabin, lad, we want to drink to
ye!" rang from the men on the wharf. Perpetua shoul-
dered her way through the mob to the edge of the
wharf. Men carrying lanterns formed a row to the
starboard port opening, bottles appeared. Townspeo-
ple continued to gather, crowding the street and
wharves all the way back to the general store. Now
the store was lit up, ready to do business. There was
an infectious atmosphere of merriment on all sides. A
prize whaler had returned fully laden, and from the
men's shares of good fortune would come enough
wealth to enjoy for the whole, long winter.

The seamen from *The Deep Six* were busy on
deck. Hundreds of caskets of sperm oil had been dou-
bly secured to make sure they would not tumble
loose. The barrels were as high as a man's shoulders,
each holding fifty gallons or more. Watching the
sailors at work, Everett turned to the two women who
stood near him. "The seamen don't seem as joyous as
we," he muttered. "There is a kind of pall over them.
I wonder where John Priest is?"

"And Naliki?" added Perpetua, worriedly pushing

forward. A strange feeling of dread had begun to form in the pit of her stomach.

Then he appeared. The tall, red-headed giant who had brought fame to Edgartown stood at the rail of his ship, looking from side to side almost as though he wasn't certain where he was. Then, alone, he reached the gangway and began to walk toward the shouting crowd.

"Where is she?" asked Perpetua softly. Her hand reached out, grasped Everett's arm for support. The feeling of dread refused to go away.

"I don't know. But I see Captain Priest has a small boy beside him. See how he grasps for his hand?" Perpetua cared little about the child. She felt herself being pushed forward as the men made a rush toward Priest.

Priest had reached the gangplank. There beside him was a boy of perhaps five or six. Perpetua couldn't tell the boy's precise age, for he wore bulky clothing. But his little brown face looked up suddenly as the shout went out, and he smiled at the man who held his tiny hand as Priest leaned down and said a few words to him.

By this time, Everett, Clarissa and Perpetua had reached the front of the shouting crowd and could easily be seen by the Captain. His face lit up in recognition. Then a more somber look flashed across his handsome features, a look that was weighted with pain. Boy in hand, the Captain moved down the gangway and stepped onto the noisy, crowded wharf. His eyes were on Perpetua the whole time, and in those eyes there was deep sadness, as though she reminded him of the past. When he stood in front of her at last, he lifted the hand of the boy and placed it in her own. "This is Naliki's son. Will you take care of him while I see to the unloading?"

"Where is Naliki?" Now frightened, Perpetua could not think of anything else to say. There was a lump in her throat.

"Gone, Perpetua. She is gone. We buried her on a little island in the sea off South America. She never made it home." Captain Priest turned quickly to hide the expression in his eyes, and, looking down at the little boy for a moment, he walked into the crowd. Triumphantly, the men of Edgartown lifted the Captain up on their shoulders and carried him up the brightly lit, noisy streets of the jubilant village.

"He looks just like her," observed Perpetua softly, looking down at her charge. The dark lowered lids seemed to shade his thoughts, but there was amusement, too, in his young, serious expression. How still and obedient he was! In her heart Perpetua tried to quiet the sorrow. Naliki would never be back. That realization was as sharp as a pang of loneliness. Perpetua recalled the day Naliki had left, remembered how they had held one another. And Perpetua remembered Naliki's promise to send a message. This, then, was Naliki's message: her own flesh and blood.

Squatting down, Clarissa took the little boy's free hand and spoke to him. "Don't be afraid." Then it occurred to her that perhaps this little Polynesian might not be able to communicate in English. But he looked directly at her and said, "Kaoli is not afraid. I am the son of an *alii*. Some day, I will be king."

"How perfectly dear," a voice said behind Clarissa. It was Mrs. Charity, wearing a big smile. "Who will take care of him?" she asked, looking at the crowd of women who had stopped to stare at the strange, dark boy wrapped in a huge pea jacket.

"He'll be my charge for the while, Aunt Charity," Perpetua heard herself say. "Captain Priest has asked me to look after him." Suddenly gathering the boy in her arms, she kissed him on the cheek. Without another word to Mrs. Charity, Perpetua turned and made her way up the crowded streed toward the big house.

Timothy was standing at the door when she arrived.

"You weren't supposed to see me until the wedding," Perpetua laughed. "You know the rules. We can't see one another for four days, now that the banns have been posted."

"Four days!" he laughed. "What a rule! I doubt I could live four days without seeing you!" But his laughter was stilled by the serious expression of the boy in her arms. "Is he from the ship?" asked Timothy.

"Yes, his name is Kaoli. Timothy—he is Naliki's son. Oh, Timothy!"

She could not go on. Blinded by tears, she felt the strong man lift the young boy from her arms, felt his gentle hand as he brushed the tears away from her eyes. She leaned against him, her arm surrounding him for support.

His deep voice soothed her and the strength of his arm supported her. When she looked up at last, the little boy was gazing at her with such an expression of serious distress that she could not help laughing at his demeanor. And as laughter mixed with tears, Timothy whispered, "Here come Everett and Clarissa. Take the boy or we'll be spotted and I'll be pilloried for defying the banns."

Perpetua looked up at him gratefully. Timothy lowered the boy to the ground and Perpetua took Kaoli's hand.

"Thank you, Timothy—my husband." The word

was so strange on her lips that she had to smile. He answered with a kiss and then was gone.

That night, Kaoli was bedded down on a small cot near Perpetua's bed. She didn't know whether he had ever slept in a real bed before, and she put a set of armchairs against the side of the bed to make sure he wouldn't roll out. Downstairs, her mother was still busy. It was very late. What could she be doing?

"I'm waiting for Captain Priest," Clarissa explained. "I thought he might prefer to spend this first night ashore with us, rather than return to an empty house of his own. And, of course, the boy is here."

"I hope Kaoli will stay."

Clarissa looked at her daughter closely. "You don't mean ... ?"

"If Timothy agrees and if the Captain does, too."

"But your plans! Timothy spoke of taking you to Boston and New York!"

"Well, that can wait! We need two months on Chappaquiddick to make his home into a place suitable for our kind of living. We can do that first."

"I hear it's already very comfortable. You said so yourself!"

"It is! But still, there's so much to do. I would like to put up a windbreak so we'll have a courtyard, completely protected, where we can have our South Sea garden. The only plants and flowers will be those which remind us of the Sandwich Islands. And we'll build a little pool for summer. We're planning a conservatory, too, full of windows, and Timothy wants to build a dock and a larger barn and a tool house and a place for the servants ..."

Perpetua's exuberant description was interrupted by a knock on the door. Clarissa jumped up to greet Captain Priest. Though he had been accepting the toasts of the town, the Captain was still very sober. As he came into the room, he approached Perpetua and at once took her hand.

"I am sorry I had to tell you so abruptly," he apologized. "Sometimes it is the only way."

"Of course," replied Perpetua. The expression in the Captain's eyes made her want to weep. But his voice was firm as he began to speak. Without prompting, he told everything that had occurred on that voyage. When he came to Naliki's death and his promise to find her son, there was a catch in his throat. He paused, then continued in a steadier tone. "When we arrived at the island, I went straight ashore as soon as we threw out the hook. It didn't take me long to find the boy, for his uncle was king and the islanders were willing to introduce me to him. Mind you, that little fellow will be king one day. I must take him back to the island then. I must . . ."

But Captain Priest could not go on. The shoulders shuddered and the women watched helplessly as the big man was consumed in the depths of his grief.

To her surprise, Clarissa found herself arguing on Perpetua's behalf when she talked to Captain Priest the next morning. It was perfectly sensible, said Clarissa, for the boy to be kept by Perpetua for the next two months.

"Perpetua and Timothy Vincent are to be married this Sunday," Clarissa explained. "Perpetua is anxious to care for Kaoli, and you know it will be good for the boy to have a woman's care. You know Perpetua's regard for Naliki and her affection will be felt by the child."

"It is certainly all right with me," Priest agreed. "It must be understood, I wish to take him with me when I sail again."

"Of course!" exclaimed Perpetua, who had remained silent until then. Clarissa and Priest both
laughed at the young woman's abrupt outburst.

"Who was his father?" asked Clarissa.

"Aye, there's the question. They honor his lineage
on the island. No doubt he will follow his uncle to become king of that island. However, word is that
Naliki, like all on Maui who hold to the old rituals,
was given a teacher who taught her how to please
men. She told me that herself. But she also told me
there was another man . . . a sea captain who came
and bargained for her hand with her father, the
trader. It is hard to tell by looking at the boy whether
he is the child of the teacher or the captain." Priest
cleared his throat. "No matter. He was Naliki's child,
of that there is no question. And you are right that he
needs a mother's love. If you don't mind, Perpetua, I
will visit you and get to know him so he is not afraid
when I am around, but otherwise I will not interfere."
The Captain looked at Perpetua. "I know he will not
lack love with you near him, Perpetua, for you were
his mother's dearest friend."

It was the morning of the wedding. Clarissa sat
for a moment, watching the boy play.

"Look," said Clarissa, "how black his hair and
eyes are!" She was smiling, but her heart felt icy.
Who was he, really? Could Naliki have been the girl
Jared had worshipped? Impossible! Fate would not
play such a trick on her. Yet, how much like Jared he
looked. And certain mannerisms. There was that sudden glance, cast over his shoulder from time to time,
his intense stare as he looked deeply into one's eyes.

The story Naliki had told of being pulled from
the shipwrecked canoe now recurred to Clarissa with
renewed clarity. All the puzzling pieces fit together

into a whole. Aye, look at him, so solid, so strong for his age. Well, she would never know. She didn't want to. Now the little boy was Perpetua's. Her daughter had fed him, held him in wonderment and exclaimed over him. The little boy had responded to her. In only a few days, they had already become inseparable.

Clarissa's thoughts were abruptly interrupted by Everett, who came down to the sitting room with Perpetua on his arm. "How do we look? Isn't she the most beautiful bride you have ever seen?"

Indeed she was. The wedding gown, which had been in Clarissa's family for three generations, fit her perfectly. The twenty-three inch waist suited her, with only a little help from a tightly-laced corset. And now Perpetua stood looking so proud, so beautiful.

"Take my arm, Father," she spoke to Everett. "Lead me to our carriage. Today I am getting married!"

"Father, it is, at last!" he said, holding out his right arm. "Come, daughter, to the church! Timothy Vincent won't wait forever, you know."

Perpetua thought that her mother and father must have invited the whole island! The small church was packed. Even the narrow balcony which hung over the altar was jammed. The weather had cooperated. There was sun and no wind, so the women could wear their broad-brimmed hats without fear of losing them. While the men were in black, the women had selected an assortment of colors and they formed a gay array, gathered in the pew. Bridesmaids chattered away as though the occasion was their own. After a last-minute examination of herself in the long mirror, Perpetua listened closely while the minister described the formalities of the occasion. Clarissa and Everett, the latter acting very much the part of a fond father, led Perpetua to the narthex, while she tried to still the nervousness that swept through her.

When Aunt Charity approached her, just prior to the opening hymn, Perpetua could sense her warmth. Already, the old woman had forgiven Perpetua for taking her nephew away from her.

"This day reminds me of my own wedding to Mr. de Silvia," she recalled. "I was so excited. Suddenly I was all alone, committing myself to a man forever. I would hope that you don't feel as lonely now as I did then, child."

"No, not at all." Perpetua searched for words, sensing that Mrs. Charity longed to be comforted. "I know that you will always be around, to be like another mother to me, Mrs. Charity. We will be one family, won't we?" With that, Perpetua kissed her old leathery cheek. Then she turned and stood, waiting impatiently for the signal to go into the chapel.

Later, during the reception on the Norton lawn, Perpetua felt dazed. She looked around. Everett was talking to Mr. Luce and Edward. John Priest, with long strides, walked about the garden with Kaoli's hand in his, catching up on all that had happened since *The Deep Six* sailed from Edgartown. And meanwhile, the animated gossip of Aunt Charity held in thrall a closely packed audience of elderly citizens.

There alone, watching her, was Timothy! Excusing herself from her bridesmaids who had gathered to whisper advice, Perpetua went across to him and took his hand. "Is all this too much for you?"

"All of this is worth having you." He looked around, lowered his voice and a mischievous expression appeared on his face. "When can we leave?"

"The carriage is ready. I must change and then we can be off."

"For the Lord's sake, change, then."

"Patience, my eager husband. I must say a few good-byes."

As Perpetua and Timothy spoke together, three women were watching from a short distance away.

"Look at Perpetua. The way she holds onto Timothy Vincent, you'd think he was about to fly away."

"No fear. He's been hooked and brought on deck. They say she's been a wild one, that she knows mysterious ways to hold a man."

"How's that, Grace?"

"She was taught things by that Polynesian girl, Naliki. I'm told such women know the secret rituals and rites of the 'god of fertility.' Like as not, that pagan idolater Naliki passed on a word or two of advice to her friend there."

"Nonetheless, Perpetua will hold tight to Timothy, I warrant. Look at the adoration of the lad as he circles around her. And he's canny enough to keep off the other men. He knows. Ah, he knows what he has, by God. Just look at him."

"Aye," allowed Grace, "he acts like a man who brought a virgin to the town bar!"

"Humph! Her a virgin?"

"Now, look." One of the three gossips turned their attention in another direction. "Look, there comes Captain Priest with that strange, dark boy. See how he leans over and kisses Perpetua on the mouth. What familiarity! I wonder if the three of them indulged in those rites together? Well, you never know. Perpetua and Naliki reveled in almost anything sinful, so I hear—almost anything strange had appeal for 'em. Who knows what went on?"

"You can see that John Priest, too, is bewitched by her. Now the boy is being held up to kiss her. She holds him as close as if he were one of her own. Do you see, Ruth, how that child clutches her?"

"Aye, all males seem attracted to her," replied Ruth, snickering. "Even the youngest, heathen tyke. What is it, Grace? What is it we don't understand?"

Her friend straightened her back and smoothed her bustle. "Unbridled lust, my dears. A man knows a harlot when he sees one."

The band struck up a rousing tune; a long parade of ships had begun to arrive at the town wharf, which stood a hundred yards away. Each was decorated with bunting and carried signal flags on every line and halyard.

"It is time!" Everett shouted over the band, looking to where Perpetua had suddenly disappeared to change. "Hurry all, to the boats!"

The Chappaquiddick Channel remained to be crossed, just five hundred feet of fast-moving current separated bride and groom from their island. Once across, the pair would go to Timothy's house alone.

Ten minutes later the bride and groom boarded the lead cutter. Many hands helped them up the gangway. The air was filled with cheers.

"They are so in love," Clarissa whispered to Everett. "See how they hurry."

"Aye, they can't wait. How much like her mother she sometimes is!"

Clarissa turned to Everett. "Oh, yes," she agreed, pulling his arm close to her breast. "I am still in a hurry, my true man." Her look underlined what she meant. She had never openly asked him before. He looked down at the lowered lids and the smile, seeing the rush of blood that came to her cheeks. Taking her hand without a word, he walked with her through the crowd, up the veranda steps towards the staircase. He acknowledged greetings with a nod, ignored a maid's request for directions. His eyes were on Clarissa as she walked ahead of him, her hips swaying seductively beneath the gown, her head held high. When they entered their bedroom, he closed the door behind them and bolted it. She had already begun to undress.

From their parlor, Perpetua and Timothy silently watched the people on the road.

"They are still waiting and watching," she said, impatiently. "When will they go away?"

"They will always watch, Perpetua," replied Timothy. "You are one of those women whom people observe and discuss." Perpetua remained at the window, watching until the last of the wedding guests had drifted away.

Finally only Captain Priest and the small boy remained on the road. As Perpetua watched, the boy threw back his head, took a bold stance and waved. Perpetua drew back, almost shocked. Something in the proud position of the boy's head, his pose, there on the road, stirred the memory of an older man, a man who had traveled the world, threatened her with his presence and passion, awed her with his boldness. The young boy reminded her of her own father, Captain Jared West.

She shook off the impression and turned away from the window, but there were tears in her eyes. Her father's presence and his blessing were the only elements missing in this perfect day. Then Perpetua looked at Timothy Vincent and smiled. If the Captain had been there, he would have been proud, she was sure.

She reached out and Timothy Vincent took her hand.

ROMANCE LOVERS DELIGHT

Purchase any book for $2.95 plus $1.50 shipping & handling for each book.

____ **LOVE'S SECRET JOURNEY** by Margaret Hunter. She found a man of mystery in an ancient land.

____ **DISTANT THUNDER** by Karen A. Bale. While sheltering a burning love she fights for her honor.

____ **DESTINY'S THUNDER** by Elizabeth Bright. She risks her life for her passionate captain.

____ **DIAMOND OF DESIRE** by Candice Adams. On the eve of a fateful war she meets her true love.

____ **A HERITAGE OF PASSION** by Elizabeth Bright. A wild beauty matches desires with a dangerous man.

____ **SHINING NIGHTS** by Linda Trent. A handsome stranger, mystery & intrigue at Queen's table.

____ **DESIRE'S LEGACY** by Elizabeth Bright. An unforgotten love amidst a war torn land.

____ **THE BRAVE & THE LONELY** by R. Vaughn. Five families, their loves and passion against a war.

____ **SHADOW OF LOVE** by Ivy St. David. Wealthy mine owner lost her love.

____ **A LASTING SPLENDOR** by Elizabeth Bright. Imperial Beauty struggles to forget her amorous affairs.

____ **ISLAND PROMISE** by W. Ware Lynch. Heiress escapes life of prostitution to find her island lover.

____ **A BREATH OF PARADISE** by Carol Norris. Bronzed Fiji Island lover creates turbulent sea of love.

____ **RUM COLONY** by Terry Nelson Bonner. Wild untamed woman bent on a passion for destructive love.

____ **A SOUTHERN WIND** by Gene Lancour. Secret family passions bent on destruction.

____ **CHINA CLIPPER** by John Van Zwienen. Story of sailing ships beautiful woman tantalizing love.

____ **A DESTINY OF LOVE** by Ivy St. David. A coal miners daughter's desires and romantic dreams.
